Every Little Kiss

Every Little Kiss

A SEQUOIA LAKE NOVEL

MARINA ADAIR

Montlake
Romance

Published by Montlake Romance, Seattle

www.apub.com

Amazon, the Amazon logo, and Montlake Romance are trademarks of Amazon.com, Inc., or its affiliates.

ISBN-13: 9781477848784
ISBN-10: 1477848789

Cover design by Janet Perr

Cover photography by Regina Wamba of MaeIDesign.com

Printed in the United States of America

To my dear friend and plotting partner,
Skye Jordan. You never fail to amaze me.

CHAPTER 1

After ten years of working graveyards in the ER, there wasn't much Olivia Preston couldn't handle. She was skilled, calm under pressure, and knew how to take charge in even the most life-threatening of situations. Yet, as Liv walked around to the back of her car and saw Superdog Stan crumpled near her bumper, lying in a puddle of his own stuffing, a button eye hanging on by a thread, panic bubbled up until she could barely breathe.

With her heart thundering in her chest, she scooped up the patient and raced across the parking lot, bursting through the doors of the closest shop she found open. The sun had just risen, the day had barely begun, and already she had a code red on her hands.

"I need a twelve-gauge needle, the thickest thread you have, sanitary wipes, and something to pack wounds," she called out to Mavis, who stood by the checkout counter flipping through a stack of gossip magazines.

Mavis Bates was the owner of the fastest senior scooter in town and Pins and Needles, Sequoia Lake's one-stop shop for all things quilting and crafty. When riled, she had all the softness of a knitting needle.

"The needles are on aisle five. Thread, aisle six," Mavis said without looking up from the centerfold of the magazine—clearly not catching the urgency in Liv's voice. "I've got an appliqué class starting in ten minutes, so just leave your total by the—*Oh my.*" Mavis practically purred, her eyes wide in appreciation. "I can see how Beckham was nominated the sexiest man alive, but I still think it should have gone to Channing Tatum."

"Mavis," Liv snapped, burying the panic and taking charge. Story of her ever-loving life. But for Paxton, she'd buck up and do it. Her kid wasn't going to suffer. "I need you focused."

Mavis looked up and, when she saw the patient, gasped. "Good heavens. Is that Stan?" She dropped the magazine and rushed around the counter. Her face showed all the worry and desperation that Liv knew better than to give in to. "What happened to him?"

"I don't know," Liv admitted, hating those simple words that had somehow managed to define the past two years of her life. The same words she'd recently vowed never to fall victim to again.

"I was next door at the Bear Claw Bakery having breakfast with Paxton," she said, her voice cracking on her son's name. "We'd just gotten served when he realized Stan was missing. I went out to look for him and found him in the parking lot. Lying there, crumpled next to my back bumper."

"Poor thing looks like he was run over." Mavis ran a hand over Superdog's torn ear with a seriousness that Liv felt to her core. "Does Paxton know?"

Liv's palms went sweaty at the thought of Paxton's crooked smile disappearing, the one they'd worked so hard to find—the one so much like his father's. Her heart tripped when she imagined that newfound light in his eyes going dull again.

"No," she said, breathless. "He's still in the café eating his big-boy breakfast. Smiley-face pancakes with the works to get him through his first day of summer camp. You know, a fun morning to ease him into a new routine."

"Poor thing, his morning needed to go smoothly," Mavis said quietly.

Paxton had a hard time with change, and he'd had enough heartache in his six-year-old life that he deserved some fun. They both did. It was the main reason she'd agreed to superhero summer camp. Her brave guy wasn't a social butterfly by any means, but he loved comic books—and pretending to be invincible for a few weeks wouldn't hurt.

But thinking about leaving him at that camp was nauseating. And part of her considered taking this as a sign from the universe, a good enough reason to march next door and admit to Paxton that his sidekick, Superdog, was down for the count and camp was canceled.

That was the old Liv. The tragic widow and single mother whose life had forever been changed with one wrong turn. Which was why the new and transformed Liv was stepping into the driver's seat this time.

She wouldn't let Paxton's fresh start or favorite stuffed toy be reduced to nothing but tattered roadkill. Not when she was one meeting away from securing them a safe future.

"It still can," Liv said, as if it were suddenly that simple. After a difficult two years, including a disastrous year of preschool, her family was desperate for a perfect start to what she'd hoped was going to be a perfect summer.

"There isn't a seam I can't stitch or a fabric you can't clean," Liv said, channeling her inner nurse. She'd made a career out of fixing life-threatening problems. Surely a stuffed dog wouldn't take her out at the knees. "A little extra padding and some TLC, and all will be good as new."

Maybe it was that simple, Liv thought as clumps of stuffing floated to the floor.

She knew firsthand that once broken, things could never be the same. But for Paxton, she let herself believe, because Stan wasn't just a stuffed animal—sadly, he was her son's best friend. And the last present he'd received from his dad.

"I need a needle, stat," Liv ordered, sticking out her hand as if she were in the OR, prepping a patient. Or donning her Supermom cape to save her son's world.

Mavis pulled a sewing kit out from beneath the counter. "I've got a variety of needles and thread inside here. Cotton balls are on aisle three, and I'll go find my special cleaner so we can get the dirt off him."

Liv had selected her tool and got the thread through the needle when she felt Mavis pause at the end of the counter. "You okay?"

She met the older woman's concerned gaze head-on. "I'm going to be."

"Thank God," Mavis mumbled. "This whole 'Kumbaya' moment was weighing on me. My heart can't take it."

Good thing Liv's heart was strong enough to take on the world if need be. Because thirty-seven balls of cotton, nineteen of the best vertical mattress sutures Liv had administered since nursing school, and a few silent prayers later, Superdog Stan was one knot away from resembling a toy dog instead of a dog's toy.

And Liv was one step closer to being the Supermom she knew she could be. So when Mavis approached the counter from behind, she said, "I need your finger on this spot. Push, and push hard."

When no finger appeared, Liv said, "Finger, spot, push. We're talking life or death here!"

She was about to cut Mavis a look when a hand reached around and a finger landed on the thread. Only it wasn't a pudgy, arthritis-riddled pointer. It was a strong, masculine index finger attached to a hand that looked capable enough to balance the world in its palm.

Liv turned her head to see who this hand belonged to and froze.

Her hero looked more Paul Bunyan than Superman, in a gray tee that clung to his biceps, a ball cap pulled low, and enough stubble to take that ruggedly handsome vibe he had going on to the next level.

But it was his eyes that got to her. Gunmetal gray with a hint of amusement and a spark of excitement she'd been missing as of late.

"I didn't mean to keep you waiting," he said, his voice a low thunder that shook her to the core. "I was just trying to figure out which one you meant."

"Which finger?" she asked, a little too breathy for her liking.

"No, which spot." He grinned, and *bam!*—it was powerful enough to jump-start spots she'd long thought shriveled up and dead. Spots she'd promised to Sam for eternity.

"But now that you bring it up," Mr. Bunyan said, "both are equally important. So why don't you show me exactly what you need, so I can be sure I get it right, Doctor."

Liv's belly pitched low. Just because she hadn't dated since college didn't mean she couldn't recognize flirting when she saw it. The fact that he looked like *he* could be in college was as thrilling as it was ridiculous. Reason enough to create some much-needed distance.

"I'm a nurse, and I've got it," Liv said, moving away from him— and his more-than-capable arms. Arms that had ink peeking out from beneath his sleeves and bulged when he crossed them over his chest.

His well-toned, in-the-prime-of-his-life chest.

But Mr. Bunyan didn't leave. He stared at her for a long moment, studying her as if he had something important to say. Just when Liv thought he'd turn and leave, he smiled instead. But this smile felt different. Still flirty, still wickedly tempting, but now it was softened with an emotion that sucker punched Liv every time.

Kindness.

He looked down at her scrubs, which had little pink cupcakes on them, and grinned. "Nurse Cupcake, then. And of course you've got it." He reached out and placed his finger on the knot again, with a look that meant business. "But doing it with someone else is a hell of a lot more fun."

5

Her stomach flipped, and a strange little flutter danced around in her chest. "Someone like you?"

He looked around the store. Empty, except for the bottle-red halo and bifocaled eyes peeking over the 100 percent alpaca yarn display on aisle two. "Or you can go it alone, but you look like you can use someone in your corner."

He had no idea.

Liv nodded and made a knot, having to navigate around his big hand in order to secure it in place, their fingers brushing in the process. Her eyes were firmly affixed to the task at hand, but she could feel the weight of his gaze.

She double-knotted it, just to be sure it stuck. So what if her finger accidentally grazed his again? Personal space didn't exist in the OR.

Except they weren't in the OR, and that graze hadn't been accidental. In her defense, it had been a long time since someone's personal space had interested her, and his space smelled good. Really good. Like early-morning, fresh mountain air, and rugged-man good.

He felt even better.

So with a third knot that lingered a little longer than necessary—followed by a secret little zing of excitement—she snipped the ends with a pair of scissors and stepped back.

Only her zing wasn't so secret, because the second she met his gaze, her face flooded with heat, and that smile of his quirked slightly as if he were amused or—

Oh God! He knew.

"We all good?" he asked, his finger still on Superdog Stan.

"Yes." She shoved her hands behind her back before she did something else embarrassing, like touch his arm that was right next to her. "I don't know how to thank you."

"How about over a cup of coffee?" he asked, gesturing to the door. When she didn't move, he pointed to the checkout counter. "Unless you have another patient in the waiting room."

"No." She laughed, picking up the stuffed toy. "No other patients. Just poor Stan here." Liv looked at the nubby old toy and found herself smiling. This dog had been through the wringer, and he was still holding his stuffing. "Who is a lot tougher than he looks."

"I can see that," he said, examining their handiwork. "He's in good hands."

"He's also expected next door," Mavis said, waddling down the aisle, making a shooing gesture with her hands. "In fact, so is Liv. She was headed to the Bear Claw Bakery, home of the best bottomless drip in the Sierras, fifteen years running."

"Sounds like I'd be a fool to pass that up," he said, flashing a smile that, *holy cannoli*, was wicked enough to tempt a widow right out of mourning.

Not that Liv was still mourning. She'd moved through that stage of loss. But while she'd managed to put the worst of her grief behind her, there wasn't room in her life for temptation. Or to accept a coffee date with a handsome man when her son was waiting for her next door.

That didn't mean that she couldn't take another minute or three to enjoy the incredible view or recommend a good place to get a cup of coffee.

"There's also Java House on the other side of Lake Street that has a beautiful view of the mountains," she offered. "If you wanted something more exciting than your basic drip."

"Java House?" Mavis harrumphed. "The only people who go to that overpriced stain on our town are yuppies, tourists, and idiots who don't know better." Mavis gave him a full head-to-toe perusal, taking her time and tutting when she got to his chest and those arms. "Which one are you?"

"Thankfully, none," he joked.

"Yet, I don't know you." Mavis crossed her arms and narrowed her eyes. "How's that?"

Liv seconded that question, because Sequoia Lake really knew how to put the *small* in small town. Although hundreds of thousands of weekend warriors visited their legendary slopes and fishing holes every year, less than six thousand were lucky enough to call it home.

And Liv might have been a bit insulated from the happenings in Sequoia Lake as of late, but she'd have to be living under a glacier to miss a man like him in a town so tiny.

Sequoia Lake was as known for its brawny, badass, beautiful men as it was for its gossip. And the only recent hottie sighting in the area belonged to Sequoia Lake's newest hero-for-hire who'd moved in down the street from Liv.

She couldn't be certain, since she'd been staring at his backside when he'd moved in, but she was pretty sure she was staring down the much-anticipated Officer Cub Candy—as her friends had started referring to him.

"I'm renting a place in town for the summer," he said.

Yup. "With your family?" she asked, and then realized she sounded as if she was asking if he was single, so she clarified. "I mean, your parents."

His lips twitched. "It was just me and my mom growing up, but since I'm out here on work, asking to bring my mom along would have seemed odd. Plus, she's a little busy with her own life." He feigned embarrassment. "Unless you bring your mom to work. Not that I'm judging—whatever works for you."

He was teasing her. She'd openly questioned his man-card status, and he'd turned it around on her. Funny and smart. *And young.*

Not as young as she'd originally thought, maybe midtwenties, more Man Candy than Cub Candy, but definitely in a different phase of his life than a thirty-four-year-old single mom. "You're staying at Old Man Keller's place, right?"

"Spying on me?"

"No." *Yes.*

She'd spent the better part of Nicholas Sparks and Sangria Night spying on him from her living room window. Even her besties had forgone watching Zac Efron get naked and naughty in the shower to watch Zac Efron 2.0 unpack his truck.

"There's a contest on the Hot and Ready to Trot Facebook page," Liv explained. "First person to snap a picture of your face gets a twenty-five-dollar gift card to Petal Pushers."

His eyes sparkled with interest. "I passed that yesterday. It's the lingerie shop in town."

"They also sell a variety of cute and quirky socks," Liv pointed out primly. "Ones with dogs or frogs or owls on them. I bet they even have mountain-climber ones."

He looked down at her socks, which were blue with dancing kitties on them, a gift from Paxton, and smiled. "Do they purr?"

Thankfully, a bright light filled the room, followed by the click of a camera. Mavis lowered her phone and grinned. "I bet a picture of your backside will land me the grand prize."

"What's the grand prize?" he asked, but Mavis was walking back into her office, her fingers working the keyboard as fast as her legs were pumping.

"Trust me, you don't want to know. By the way, I'm Olivia Preston." Liv stuck out her hand. It was, after all, the neighborly thing to do. "But my friends call me Liv."

She almost snorted out loud at how lame *that* sounded. Had it really been so long since she'd talked to a man that she'd forgotten how?

"It is nice to meet you, Liv. I'm Ford. Ford Jamison." He took her hands in his, and there went that annoying zing again. This time she was certain he felt it too, because his shocked gaze met hers and held. So long she lost track of time.

He just stood there, holding her hand in his, silently staring at her as if waiting. For what, she couldn't be sure. But for the first time in what felt like forever, she felt a lightness in her chest, in her feet, as if all she had to do was take a single step and she'd finally be moving forward.

"If you're renting the old Keller cabin, then that makes you my neighbor," she said. "I live right down the beach from you in the yellow-and-white one-story with the white dock off the back."

If he was surprised by the news, he didn't show it. In fact, he just released her hand and casually gestured toward the door. "Well, neighbor, how about you show me the home of the best bottomless drip in the Sierras?"

Was he asking her out on a date? God, just the word felt foreign and irresponsible and reckless—and so incredibly intoxicating she wanted to say yes. Almost said yes, but then, as if the universe was reminding her that one had to learn how to swim before diving into the deep end of the lake, her phone pinged.

"Excuse me." She fished her cell from her back pocket and read the screen. It was a text from her mother-in-law.

Pax is holding his privates. I asked if he has to use the little boys' room. His answer was silence . . .

That Carolyn believed his silence was Liv's fault was hidden between the three dots.

Paxton suffered from select mutism, a form of social anxiety that affected a child's ability to communicate when expectations become overwhelming. When Paxton felt secure and comfortable, he could out-talk an auctioneer. But the only person who saw that side of him was Liv. With a sigh that she felt all the way in her toes, Liv accepted that her time was up. Life was calling, and she needed to respond. "It's my son. I have to go."

"So do I," he said in that same easygoing tone that made her legs wobble.

But his smile dimmed at her statement, and his eyes flashed something close to regret—or maybe it was relief. The poor guy had nearly asked the town's only widowed single mom to coffee.

Either way, Liv admitted that even though it was summer and the sun was about to embark on a new cycle, the frost had only thawed enough for her to dip her toes in the lake.

CHAPTER 2

An hour later, Liv had dropped off a very tearful Paxton at camp, fielded three calls from the camp counselor saying Paxton was still standing at the edge of the park waiting for pickup, and pulled into Mercy General with twenty minutes to spare.

Paxton had taken a huge step in the right direction today, and now it was Liv's turn.

And she was ready. She had to be ready. It had taken her a full year to accept that Sam was never coming home, which was step one in *Finding Life after Death*. Step two had been terrifying, experiencing the loss and grief, which was why she'd acted on that step right away. Moving back to Sam's hometown to be around people who had known and loved him was as much for Paxton as it had been for Liv. Which got her to today.

Step three: *adjusting to the environment without the deceased.*

Liv pulled out her phone, pushed the bottom button, and said, "Siri, what is listed in 'Olivia, Take the Wheel' under step three?"

"All right. Here is what I found in your notes, Take the Wheel, for what is listed under step three," the computer-generated voice, which she'd set to sound like 007, said. "Survivor must assume some of the responsibilities and social roles formerly fulfilled by your husband. Change a tire, empty the rain gutters, tie a tie, throw a curveball, master the grill, and bring home the bacon."

Check. Check. Check. Check. Work in progress. And as soon as she had her meeting with the head of family medicine, check.

Even though it was summer, a crisp early breeze blew past, bringing with it the scent of fresh earth and rustling the pine trees. Liv looked up at the jagged Sierra Nevada, which towered high above the small town she'd only recently begun to think of as home, and guilt seared a hole in her chest.

If she could come to think of this treacherous terrain that took her husband's life as beautiful, then why did the idea of moving on feel like such a betrayal? Sam had been gone for two years, and nothing she could say or do would change that.

At least, not now.

And Liv was focusing on the now, the future. She had to if she wanted to give Paxton the kind of childhood he deserved. And he deserved so much more than a mom who worked swing shifts.

Shoulders back, Liv grabbed her job application and updated résumé off the passenger seat and headed into the hospital. If there was anything the past had taught her, it was that nobody cared about her family's future as much as she did.

It was a mantra that had seen her through some of the roughest patches, and a mantra she'd adopted long before Sam's accident. So when she reached the office of her boss's boss, unannounced, she gave a strong, confident knock.

"Olivia," Nicole said, glancing up from her desk.

Dr. Nicole Brown looked like a preschool teacher with her brightly colored glasses and pigtail, but she ran her career like a sniper. Precise and purposeful—leaving no room for surprises or error. Which had earned her the respect of her peers and the position of head of family medicine at Mercy General.

She looked at the papers in Liv's hands and lifted a brow. "Did we have an appointment?"

"No," Liv said, channeling her inner Xena, Warrior Princess, and entering the office, because while Liv's surprise appearance might not have been a smart choice, with the board picking the final team in a few weeks, it was the only option she'd had. "I had some time before my shift started, and I wanted to congratulate you on your new Mobile Medic project."

A project Liv desperately wanted to be a part of. It would get her out of the ER and into a position with stable hours and potential for career growth. It was also a project that spoke to Liv's heart.

Having a mother who'd passed from diabetes, Liv knew how important it was to get medical care to residents who had difficulty getting to the hospital, and that's what Nicole's Mobile Medic project was—a fleet of mobile clinics that would service the surrounding community.

"Thank you," Nicole said skeptically.

"I also wanted to speak with you about applying for the open RN position," Liv said.

"You know that I'm only considering senior staff for the position," Nicole said.

"I know I've only been at Mercy General for eighteen months, but I've been a practicing RN for more than ten years." Granted, eleven of those eighteen months she'd been working part-time, but she didn't need to point that out. "That's four years longer than Kevin, who is one of the board-approved options, so I wanted to come and deliver these to you personally."

Liv held out her papers, and to her utter surprise, Nicole took them. "I see you've done your homework."

It wasn't an official invitation for a meeting, but Liv knew that in order for her to take the wheel, so to speak, she first had to take a seat. Then lean in. So she did both. "They don't call me the research queen for nothing."

Nicole didn't smile, just flipped through the pages of information, spending extra time on the referrals—of which Liv had collected several. She skimmed the last page and then set the papers down.

"Last week the board approved Mobile Medic on a trial basis, and they want me to finalize my team so we can be ready to go next month," Nicole said. "However, they only funded one van so far."

"Which means you're only hiring one team," Liv guessed, thinking that she hadn't researched enough.

"You got it," Nicole said. "And while I think you'd be an asset to any team, my job is proving this is an effective solution to the problem so that they will continue to fund this project. To do that, I need to pick the right team." Nicole studied Liv for a long moment. "Do you know why Kevin is on the short list?"

Like Liv, Kevin Curtis was a registered nurse working the ER. Unlike Liv, he was Sequoia Lake royalty, his family going back five generations of Lake Sequoians, with the most recent generation being one of the largest donors to the hospital.

Not that Kevin relied on his connections—he was a great nurse. But for this project Liv was better. Sam wouldn't have backed down because he lacked a few years of experience. He'd gotten ahead in his career by being the guy who showed up at the table and turned his weakness into a strength.

"Because he wasn't afraid to apply even though he was a few years short on the required minimum?"

That earned Liv a smile. "There seems to be a lot of that going around."

"I may not have the flexibility to work as many hours as some of the other applicants, but my patient-care rate is the best in my department."

Nicole's face softened. She was a working mom too, so she understood the struggles. "Your hours wouldn't be a concern since the mobile clinic will be open in different locations around town from eight thirty until four thirty. No more on-call, but also no more overtime."

There would also be no more swing shifts or split shifts. Kindergarteners qualified for after-school care, so she could pick Paxton up after work, and they could have dinner together every night. And the weekends would be family time.

God, to have the whole weekend with her kid would be amazing. Not to mention the money. Liv knew that this promotion also came with a nice pay bump—she'd heard Kevin talking about it. There was still some of Sam's insurance money left over, but that was for Paxton's college. Anything extra, she'd have to earn.

"If you took my collective experience into consideration, I would be the most experienced nurse applying," Liv said confidently. "I've worked the ER, the OR, trauma, and family care. Which means I know how to follow directions as well as take the lead."

Nicole glanced at Liv's résumé again, then looked up over her glasses. "Working in the field is different than the hospital. We won't have files at our fingertips and the database that we do with patients here."

"I understand," Liv said, a glimmer of hope flickering in her chest.

"That means it will be imperative that every team member can summarize their patient's history in a matter of seconds. Knows who they are, what medical issues they've had in the past, and how to proceed." The doctor gave a long, thought-provoked pause. "Kevin is in the Lions Club, belongs to the Sequoia Fishermen's Association, and is in the local football hall of fame. He has that knowledge. I'm not sure you do."

"Kevin was also prom king, but that doesn't make him more qualified. And I just moved here from Sacramento two years ago," she said, because Liv had learned just how many hats she could wear since becoming a single mom. But if the deciding factor came down to birthplace, that wasn't something she could compete with.

"And in those two years you haven't ventured very far outside of work and home," Nicole said, and Liv wanted to point out that she didn't have the time to get involved with the community, but she knew that would be a lie.

Liv had been selective in whom she opened herself up to, and it didn't take a therapist to tell her why most of them hadn't known Sam well. It was hard to find closure when surrounded by people who wanted to reopen the past. It was even harder when the past had so many different perspectives.

To the town, Sam was the hometown hero who went off to save lives as one of the top thoracic surgeons. To Liv, he'd been the love of her life who'd constantly chosen his career over their family. Well, Liv was choosing her family first, and that meant getting this promotion.

"I have a stellar memory, I'm a fast learner, and I work hard for my patients," Liv assured her. "I might not know every detail of their history yet, but I will, if you give me a chance."

"You don't have to sell me on your qualifications," Nicole said with a genuine smile, and that flicker of hope caught fire. "It's clear that your patients love you, you have great instincts, and more importantly, you have a gift of putting people at ease. You seem to find common ground with every person you come across, and when we're dealing with on-edge patients, you're the kind of nurse I want in my corner, but—"

"Oh God." Liv scooted to the edge of her seat. "There's a *but*? That's like offering up a box of cupcakes, then saying they're sugar-free."

"It's not as dire as sugar-free cupcakes." Nicole laughed. "And while I know that you like your cupcakes sugarcoated, the facts not so much."

"I'd rather leave with everyone on the same page than be blindsided," Liv said, speaking from experience.

"This project's success is going to hinge on my team's ability to reach out into the community, work with different local organizations and groups, get the citizens to feel comfortable coming to us," Nicole said with an apology already in her voice. "My strength is with hospital administration and the board. They trust me and my judgments based on my reputation in medicine and what I did with the clinic in Boise.

I need a nurse who has earned the same kind of confidence within the community."

Nicole pulled out a file from her top drawer and displayed its contents on her desk. It was charts, graphs, expected patient profiles. "These are the kind of people the Mobile Medic will serve. Sure, many of the patients we're hoping to reach don't come to the hospital because they can't, but a good chunk of them simply won't." She flipped the page to a chart that showed the statistics of different outreach programs in the past. "As you can see, most of these failed. The ones that didn't had two things in common." Nicole looked up. "A fresh, new approach to draw interest from the community. And the patients had a personal connection with one or more of the staff members. I need to make sure that people feel as if they're visiting an old friend when they seek care with the mobile clinic."

"I belong to Living for Love."

"Living for Love is a bereavement group, which you joined because it allowed you to do outreach without leaving the safety of medicine," Nicole said, and Liv swallowed down the growing uncertainty.

There hadn't been a lot of room for opportunity in Liv's career. It was hard to move up the nursing ranks when Sam was transferred every few years to study under a new surgeon or learn a new procedure, but Liv had adapted. Finally, this was her big opportunity, her time, but in order to own it she had to move right past step three and on to step four. And that was the step she had been trying to ignore.

Taking the emotional energy spent on the one who had died and reinvesting it in another relationship or relationships terrified her. There were still times when she felt the loss so deeply it was hard to breathe. Then there were other times when she had to pull out Sam's aftershave to remember what he smelled like.

That was one of the reasons she'd moved to Sequoia Lake and purchased Sam's childhood home. She wanted to be surrounded by parts of Sam that weren't a part of their marriage. Sacramento reminded her of their problems, but Sequoia Lake reminded her of the man she'd fallen in love with. The man she wanted Paxton to know. But moving on and reinvesting were two different things.

The first was necessary to find peace. The second felt as if she were being disloyal.

"So you want someone who has deep ties to the community?" she asked.

Nicole gave Liv's packet one last glance, then picked it up and held it out to her. "That is the *only* thing missing on your résumé that would make you my top choice."

Liv looked at the résumé. To most, it would be a series of hire and end dates with a collection of skills and hundred-dollar words. To Liv, she knew that between all the recent employers and references was a complicated story of love, sacrifice, frustration, and loss. But it was the blank part on the last page that had her straightening her shoulders. Because that was the part of the story she had yet to write.

And it was up to her how it would play out.

"I see your concern," Liv said, taking back her application. "What you need, then, is for me to bring this back to you with more extra-curricular activities and community connections. When do you need that by?"

Nicole lifted an impressed brow. "I need to bring my final decision to the board the first week of August, and I'd like a week or so to weigh my options."

"It will be on your desk by the end of next week."

She would make sure of it.

◆ ◆ ◆

Commit today, forget tomorrow.

It was the one rule Ford Jamison swore by. A balancing act that had pulled him through some of the worst shit-shows of his life. First in the army, then as one of the top K-9 trackers for Washoe County Search and Rescue out of Reno. He was Washoe-SAR's Hail Mary call, their great white hope, the one guy who could turn a worst-case scenario into a rescue. And he had—a dozen times over.

He celebrated the successes as much as he mourned the losses, but he never let either of them detract from the next search. Until he'd made one bad call—and forgetting became impossible.

Which was how he found himself eighty miles from home in the small mountain town of Sequoia Lake participating in a training exchange program with the local team, Sequoia Elite Mountain Rescue.

Participating? Ford snorted as he turned his car down a pine tree–lined road, because that made it sound voluntary. When in reality there had been nothing voluntary about it. Pissed that he'd skipped out on his type-one certification, his boss in Reno had sentenced him to desk duty in the same small town he'd been trying to avoid when he'd missed his certification.

He either needed to find some closure and get his head back in the game or risk losing a career he loved. Which was a hell of a lot better than risking lives.

Something he'd promised himself he'd never do again. So he didn't even roll his eyes when he pulled up on a residential search in progress that a Boy Scout could handle.

The call had gone out over the wire as a missing female—LuLu, a five-year-old with golden hair, last seen wearing pink bows and a tutu, was suspected to have wandered off from her front yard earlier that morning—but Ford knew the moment he rolled up on the scene that he should just keep on driving.

Because on the porch, dressed in curlers and a fuzzy robe, was the grieving mother clutching a stuffed toy in one hand—and a pink leash in the other. Making Ford wonder just how many legs this LuLu walked on.

And if the FIND MY BABY flyer with the picture of a prissy purse-dog in bows nailed to a nearby tree wasn't enough to let him know this was his "Welcome to the Department" party, then his boss of less than a week smiling like a smug prick certainly was.

Harris Donovan stood on the porch waving him over, a familiar shit-eating grin on his face.

Ford and Harris went way back. All the way to Ford's first day at the police academy when Harris, a senior, thought it would be funny to screw with the new kid's GPS. It had taken Ford two months of changing out brake pads to afford the GPS handset—and six hours to complete a sixty-minute hike.

Ford failed his first in-the-field assignment, and the two had a come-to-Jesus meeting—Harris telling Ford he needed to lighten up, and Ford introducing Harris to his right hook. They were both sentenced to twenty hours of volunteer time picking up trash on one of the trails they'd trained on, and they were serving their time when they came across an injured father with his son.

Harris's confident charm allowed him to connect immediately with the kid and earn the father's trust—a necessary skill for any first responder. While Ford's relentless nature and attention to detail turned what could have been a holiday tragedy into a family reunion that made national news. That's when Ford switched his focus from SWAT to search and rescue.

He wasn't interested in a reunion with his own father, not anymore. But bringing other families together always took him one step closer to filling that empty hole deep in his chest. Until Ford had been forced to make an impossible call—and he still wasn't sure if he'd made the right one.

"You stay here while I see what's going on," Ford told his copilot and partner, who sat in the passenger seat, his eyes on Ford.

Bullseye was stubby, tubby, and sixty pounds of wrinkles, with ears that hung to the ground. He was part shepherd, part sloth, but all bloodhound when it came to tracking. He also objected to being sidelined—something Ford could relate to.

"Sorry, man, but we both know what happened the last time you ran across a stuffed animal you just *had* to smell."

Ford had ended up playing doctor to the pretty nurse he'd set out to avoid—and missed the morning debriefing. Which was probably why he'd been the only person called out to today's search.

Not that he was complaining when the alternative was sharing coffee with a woman he had no business sharing anything with. Unless it was the truth.

And that wasn't going to happen.

Bullseye gave Ford a convincing look that he was all business. Too bad his body vibrated with excitement the second he saw the old lady waving that doll.

The dog could pick up a week-old scent in the middle of a bacon factory and not lose focus. But put him in front of something fuzzy that looked as if it needed to be rescued and added to his ever-growing flock of stolen goods, and Bullseye went nuts. Because he didn't work for treats or dog toys like normal dogs. Nope, that dog was a klepto and would climb the Himalayas if he knew that at the top he'd get his reward—a fuzzy trophy in need of saving.

Bullseye had a box full of trophies he'd collected over the years, and if Ford tried to remove even one, the dog wouldn't sleep until he found it.

A Beanie Baby in Ford's pocket was effective for a simple door-to-door urban search. When it was a high-altitude search with rough terrain and difficult conditions? Bullseye demanded a real game of find the fur-baby. And when a search turned into a recovery, Ford had to pull out the big guns: Lambkins. Bullseye's number one choice in tchotchke therapy.

Carrying a stuffed animal should have been easier than carrying a stash of jarred baby food. But strapping a wheel-size bubblegum-pink lamb puppet with a matching tutu and cotton-ball fur to Ford's back-pack was a hell of a lot more embarrassing. Especially when done in front of some of the goliaths of the SAR world—who responded with offers of lotion and mood music.

Ford preferred to refer to Lambkins as a chew toy. Only that was as ridiculous as slapping a John Deere logo on a Speedo and calling it manly. But pink lambs and baby talk happened when one adopted a service dog trained by a day-care provider who specialized in wanderers.

"All right, but one tail wag before it's playtime and you're back in the car. Understand?"

"*Woof!*"

Ford clipped on his harness, and the two hopped out of the truck.

"I know she's a wanderer, but she's been gone over an hour, and she never skips her breakfast," the older woman cried. "Not when it's beef and peas."

"Don't worry, Ms. Moberly, I've called in the best tracker we have. If anyone can bring LuLu home, it's this guy," Harris said in welcome as Ford walked up the cobblestone walkway. "Meet Ford Jamison, the department's newest community-outreach officer. And his partner, Bullseye."

Bullseye sat at attention, his chest puffed out, belly dragging the ground. Ford managed not to roll his eyes at the mutt as he tipped his hat in greeting. "Ma'am. I'm actually head of the K-9 search division out of Reno."

Ms. Moberly pressed a hand to her chest. "So you specialize in find-ing canines? Thank the Lord." And there went a quick sign of the cross. "When I called Harris about my LuLu disappearing, he told me that he had the perfect person for the job." She looked at Harris with hero worship. "I didn't know you were going to bring him over from Reno."

Harris rocked back on his heels. "Only the best for our residents. Now why don't you tell Ford here what you've been telling me."

The woman's eyes went wide as she turned her focus to Ford. "My LuLu hasn't been missing the necessary twenty-four hours to coordinate a full search party, but she's a special-needs dog—got the depression pretty bad—and I read on the website that you waive that rule for a special-needs child."

"But LuLu is a dog," Ford pointed out.

"With the depression," Harris reminded, and Ford gave him an *Are you kidding me?* look. To which Harris replied with a *Welcome to desk duty* tip of the hat.

"She needs her pill." Ms. Moberly looked around and then leaned in and lowered her voice. Bullseye leaned in too, and when he realized that she wasn't handing over the stuffed animal, he plopped onto his belly with a sigh. "Last time LuLu stopped taking her medication, I caught her paws deep in a box of chocolates. By the time I got to her, her muzzle was covered in the poison, and we had to pump her little belly. The vet shaved her naked, made her so self-conscious she wouldn't even go to Wag and Waddle until it grew back."

"Maybe she was just hungry."

"She wasn't hungry—she was ending things. Death by chocolate. It's what the ladies at Wag and Waddle call it when they think LuLu can't hear them, but she knows she's being ostracized." She clutched her chest. "Dear God, do you think that's why she left? We have Wag and Waddle in an hour."

Ford channeled his people skills and offered a small smile. "Ms. Moberly, couldn't LuLu be hiding inside? Maybe she found a warm corner and curled up and fell asleep. Or maybe she's at the neighbors' house."

Ms. Moberly's gray bob danced around as she shook her head. "I checked every inch of that house and even offered up bacon. Nothing. And she doesn't like the neighbors—they have cats. She's scared of cats."

Probably because the cats heckled the poor dog for dressing like a ballerina.

"Strangers too." Ms. Moberly froze. "You don't think she was snatched by a stranger, do you?"

Ford and Harris exchanged looks, but it was Harris who spoke. "Do you?"

"Well, I don't know, but if that would speed up the search party, I will have it known that LuLu is a front-runner for this year's Wagon Days Darling. If she's selected, she'll ride in the float with the mayor."

"Wagon Days Darling is a big honor around here," Harris said ever so helpfully.

"The biggest," Ms. Moberly agreed. "Which is why I wouldn't put it past Dorothy Pines to dognap my LuLu to get an edge up. She was the one who started the 'death by chocolate' campaign against us when LuLu was first tapped to enter. And now we find out she's a finalist and she goes missing. Don't you see the pattern?"

All Ford could see at that moment was Harris's smug grin. "There could be a lot of reasons for LuLu's absence, but if you suspect theft, then you'd need to contact the sheriff's department."

Ms. Moberly shook her head so fast her gray halo danced. "Absolutely not. Have you seen the sheriff's dog? Tyke is nothing but a big bully, likes to sniff my LuLu hello even when she hides behind my feet. Do you believe that no means no, Mr. Jamison?"

"Of course he does, ma'am," Harris said, and Ford wanted to punch him.

"Then you'll understand why I called your office. I won't have that dog taking advantage of LuLu's weakened state when we find her. Not when this sweet thing here is ready for action."

Ms. Moberly leaned over and gave Bullseye a head scratch. Bullseye didn't even bother opening an eye. He was already asleep. "Now, you might want a notepad and pen so you can take notes. I saw on *Criminal Minds* that in a missing-person situation, it's important to walk through their final days."

"LuLu's a dog," Ford repeated as Harris took a notepad from his chest pocket and handed it to Ford.

Ford ignored this. "Could you excuse us for a moment?" Before Ms. Moberly could argue, Ford grabbed his "boss" by the back of the neck and walked out of ear range. Bullseye rolled onto his side and farted.

"Look, I'm sorry for missing your briefing," he whispered. "It won't happen again. So you can stop with the whole first-day prank wars."

"No prank, Jamison. We got a call. You were on the schedule. I thought, *How lucky are we to have a K-9 officer on our team today?*" Harris laughed. Ford did not.

"I'm the head of the division." Well, he was back home, where he wouldn't have to deal with this kind of crap. "And I'm here to consult on recruiting and organizing your new volunteer K-9 team and maybe find some lost hikers. I *train* dogs—I don't find them."

"You're here because you decided to play hooky on the biggest test of your career, and your boss sent you to detention—in my department. So you get to play community-outreach director while you're here, which means riding the desk and the occasional callout." Harris gestured to the manicured lawns, neatly kept houses, and newer SUV parked around the cul-de-sac. "So for the next three weeks, this is your community. And it's time to start reaching out. Making connections. Building bonds." He leaned in. "You can start with Ms. Moberly."

"Making nice with the residents isn't really my thing." It was why he'd stuck with the more extreme cases. He had an innate confidence to him that worked in rescue situations. Small talk with townsfolk? That was not on his list of skills.

Although he'd done some pretty good small talk earlier that morning. His body was still humming from the encounter.

Harris hooked his thumbs through his belt loops. "Great time to turn your weakness into your strength, then. Practice makes perfect."

"Do you have any other fortune-cookie advice for me?"

"How about *beggars can't be choosers*, so gear up," Harris said, pointing to the mountain range behind them. "Because until you decide to stop bailing and haul your sorry ass up Canyon Ridge and pass your certification, this is as exciting as work will get for you."

It wasn't the hike up one of Sequoia Lake's most treacherous peaks he was worried about. It was spending twenty-four hours up there alone, looking down on the site of the accident that had changed everything, with nothing but his memories and what-ifs to keep him warm.

"I didn't bail. I was doing a search at the mudslide in Montana," Ford pointed out.

"A search you volunteered to go on even though you knew your yearly test was that weekend," Harris said. "And you didn't tell me that Sam Preston was the victim of that car crash two winters ago that went from rescue to recovery when the big snowstorm hit."

Ford froze at the name he hadn't heard since all the media had died down more than a year ago.

"Yeah, that was the same look I had when Bob from Reno called to see if I could offer some air support on a search, then asked me if I knew I'd brought on the guy involved with Sam's recovery."

"It was a recovery and a rescue. His son made it out."

Barely. Ford had found Sam and his son in a cave, a quarter mile from the accident site. Sam was in critical condition, Paxton hardly old enough to understand what was happening. And both were at risk from the elements.

It had been touch-and-go for a while, and when the temperature dropped to freezing, Ford began to doubt if any of them would make it out. A therapist would argue that he never had. That a piece of him was still back there.

A piece he was hoping to reclaim by coming back to Sequoia Lake.

"Does his widow know you were the responding officer?" Harris asked.

"No," Ford said sharply. "And I intend to keep it that way." Which was why he'd backpedaled over buying her coffee.

He knew walking up to that counter exactly whom he'd encounter. Prepared himself for the familiar rush of guilt that came whenever he'd caught a glimpse of Sam's family on his visits to the area over the past couple of years. But nothing could have prepared him for the spark of attraction he'd felt.

"Good luck with that, man." Harris laughed. "This is Sequoia Lake you're talking about. Gossip is like gold in this place. A bear can't shit in the woods without the town calling a council meeting to discuss it."

"Well, there will be no discussions here. I won't be around long enough to create any buzz."

"Hate to break it to you, but the gossip mill started churning the moment you were spotted flirting with the town's favorite single mom this morning. I give it until dinner before people claim that destiny placed you in the rental right down the lake from her."

Ford snorted. "It wasn't destiny."

"Right. Bob didn't think so either. Just like I don't think he sent you here to ride the desk to scare you into getting recertified," Harris said. "I think he sent you here so you'd have to face the one site you've been avoiding."

"I've worked in Sequoia Lake on over a dozen searches with you since then."

"All of them were type-two searches, and none of them lasted more than a few days. You do the search, disappear for a day, then burn rubber out of town." His friend's face went serious. "Hell, I don't think you've spent more than a week anywhere in the past few years."

That was how Ford liked it. As long as he kept moving, the what-ifs couldn't pull him under. As for the disappearances, that was repentance.

"So you want to be straight with me? And don't give me that BS story about Bullseye needing some time off after the search in Montana."

Ford looked over at his dog, eating up the attention he was getting from Ms. Moberly, and felt his heart go heavy with concern. Ford wasn't the only one struggling with the job.

Bullseye was more than a trailing dog. He was one of the top air-scenting dogs in the country. A talent that had them at the top of the national registry list to call when a natural disaster hit.

Bullseye could detect a body fifteen feet underground and know with a certainty if it was a person or a corpse. Each rescue lit Bullseye with excitement, but recoveries took their toll. And the Montana job had more recoveries than rescues. The last being a seven-year-old boy named Thomas.

It wasn't normal for Ford to know the subject's name in this kind of search, but he'd seen a weeping mother standing helpless by an ambulance, staring at the site where her house had once stood. So when the search was over and the small body was recovered, Ford had done the one thing he'd promised himself he'd never do again.

Instead of moving on to the next case, he'd spent a week looking into the boy's life. Knew he'd liked *Star Wars* and played T-ball and that his favorite subject in school was science. Knew that he wanted to be a fireman when he grew up, like his dad. And even before his boss called to chew him a new one for missing his certification again, Ford knew he was in up to his neck.

His inability to let go started when he'd met Sam down in that frozen ravine. Listened to the stories about his wife, witnessed the deep love and commitment to his small son. It was what had driven him to leave Sam behind and get Paxton to safety. It was what had fueled a two-year-long promise—that was going to end this summer. Ford was going to make sure of it.

"We both needed a break," Ford admitted. "And we'll both be back on our A-game, ready for Canyon Ridge before the summer ends."

Harris studied him for a long, hard moment. Ford didn't know what he was looking for, but clearly he didn't find it, because he said,

"Well then, you might want to grab your notebook. Looks like you've got a missing dog to sniff out."

Ford held up his hands in surrender. "I should have told you about the connection to the town, but if I limited jobs based on distance to past subjects, I'd be living in Alaska." He paused. "No, wait, spent five weeks there during that avalanche."

"Point taken."

"Good, then can you drop the hazing bullshit and give me a real job?"

"Since you're no longer a high-mountain rescue officer, this is as real as it will get for you," Harris pointed out. "As for the hazing, as soon as you find LuLu, I need you to pay a visit to the assisted-living home on the west side of Lake Street. Mr. Gordon in room 34 has wandered off again."

"Alzheimer's?" Ford asked, because although it wasn't the kind of search he usually headed up, at least this subject walked on two legs. "I'll get right on it."

"Oh, and you might want to check the senior center. It's casino day."

Ford made a note. "Is he a gambler?"

"Nope. Bring a blanket, though," Harris said with a tip of his hat, then headed toward his department-issued Jeep. "The last time this happened, he forgot his pants and ended up mooning the ladies. From the front."

CHAPTER 3

Liv had become a pro at making lemonade out of all of the lemons life had thrown her way. But today, she was certain she'd need something much stronger.

She'd made it through a six-car pileup that backed up the ER for most of the day, a child-neglect case that resulted in casting a four-year-old's arm and making a call that she was sure would rip apart a family. Then spent her lunch finishing up paperwork and brainstorming how, between the hours of midnight and three a.m., Liv was to become Mercy General's social liaison without breaking down.

But after receiving a call from home, Carolyn explaining how Paxton had barricaded himself in his room after camp, not even coming out for one of his grandma's famous peanut butter cookies, Liv realized how close she was to tears.

Especially right then, with only a stubborn vending machine separating her from the last Hostess cupcake in the entire hospital. She'd checked. Which was why she'd dug up her last four quarters from the depths of her purse and put them in the machine.

"I paid the toll, now give me my cupcake," she said to the machine, even giving it a little shake. But the cupcake didn't move, just sat there, all alone, stuck between the Plexiglas and the faulty release coil.

The rational thing to do would be to inform maintenance that the machine next to urgent care was broken. They'd file a report and send someone down to fix it—in the next few hours, if she was lucky.

Liv didn't have a few hours. And she wasn't feeling very rational. Nope, rational had flown out the window the moment her mother-in-law had called and Liv realized that her son needed her at home but she was stuck here at work. Normally, she'd ask to leave early. But today wasn't a normal day.

Not only was the hospital short-staffed, but Liv had just thrown herself into a professional ring where the competition was racking up endless hours of OT, not requesting family emergency TO. Leaving her with ten minutes left of her break and her sugar fix just out of reach.

Which was why she enlisted her foot. A few swift kicks to the bottom corner of the machine shook the cupcake until it was dangling from the end of the coil release, but it wasn't enough to break free.

Liv glared at the machine, punched in the buttons again for good measure, and then stared longingly at the lonely cupcake. She shook the machine. Nothing.

Shook it harder—still nothing.

Dang it.

This was going to require a more direct approach. And possibly a set of medical forceps. Which was how Liv ended up on her knees, right arm jammed into the dispenser door, the metal tongs a scant inch from the plastic wrapper of the cupcake.

She worked quickly, hoping to finish before a patient noticed her on the floor, performing surgery on a vending machine. Given how packed urgent care was today, the odds were against her. Which meant she might have to admit defeat.

Only Liv was tired of feeling defeated. She needed a win. Even if it was in the form of chocolate cake with marshmallow-cream filling.

Liv quickly scanned the waiting room, nearly wrenching her arm out of the socket when she caught a glimpse of the officer standing at the nurses' station. Dressed in a crisp pair of uniform pants, a matching shirt that had the Sequoia Elite Mountain Rescue logo on the pocket, a department-issued gun on his hip, and a set of well-toned arms that had been wrapped around her just hours earlier.

Liv swallowed hard as he approached the counter. Because it wasn't just any officer. It was Officer Cub Candy, and he was chatting up Nurse Brandy, a recent graduate who was finishing up her residency at Mercy General. Brandy was twenty-three, perky, and the perfect cub-size treat.

Liv was long past perky. A mature woman who was down on all fours wearing cupcake scrubs and fighting with a vending machine.

Ford said something cheeky, Brandy giggled, and Liv rolled her eyes. Not at Brandy, but at herself.

With a smile that said, *Hey, big guy,* Brandy looked at the monitor and clicked away on the keyboard. Ford offered her up a smile and rested a casual hip against the counter—as if he had all day.

Liv had less than a few seconds before he noticed her.

With one last snap of the forceps, she went after the cupcake, catching the lower edge of the wrapper—and Ford's attention, which zeroed in like a heat-seeking missile.

One look into those intense eyes and a rush of heat lit her cheeks—and other, more concerning, places. The former wasn't all that surprising, seeing as she was facing down an armed officer with her hand stuck in the proverbial cookie jar. The latter was as irritating as it was liberating.

Her first reaction was to ignore him—she'd paid for the cupcake, after all—but since that was as likely as tuning out a Chippendale at a ladies' luncheon, she ignored the tingles and gave him a cool smile. "Afternoon, Officer Jamison."

"Nurse Cupcake," he said, all kinds of professional, even though his eyes were filled with warmth and amusement. The closer he came, the louder his boots clicked against the tile floor, and the faster her heart raced. "Are you okay?"

Liv was tempted to ask him what he defined as okay, then remembered she had roughly seven minutes left of me-time and didn't want to spend it trying to read between the lines. She'd had a day full of that.

"Medical emergency," she said, giving a gentle tug, which did nothing more than lodge the cupcake farther.

He looked at the cupcake and grinned. "I can see that. Lucky for you, I've had extensive medical training."

She remembered just how skilled his hands were. Just like she remembered how he'd asked her to coffee and then gone cold the second she'd mentioned her son. "Not necessary. One more tug and I've got it."

"Why fight when all it takes is a little nudge in the right direction?" Ford said with a clarity that made him seem a decade wiser and capable of handling anything that came his way. He might look like a playboy, but Officer Jamison was a full-fledged badass who put his life on the line regularly.

He pulled a bill from his pocket and slid it in the machine.

"I already paid for it," she explained, going silent when he pushed the button and the coil receded, freeing the cupcake.

It dropped to the bottom of the machine with a small thud. Then he stuck another bill in the coffee machine. "Decaf or regular?"

"I'm fine," she said, pulling her arm free.

"You were trying to pry a cupcake out of a vending machine with a set of tongs. I think we passed fine."

Liv was so far past fine that when he offered her the cupcake and one of those smiles he seemed to give out so freely, her body quivered.

Stupid body.

"Thank you," Liv said, taking the treat.

Their fingers brushed and—*wham!* That quiver became a racing current of electricity that sparked.

Liv didn't move. Heck, she could barely breathe through the tsunami of sex-starved hormones flooding her body as if the levee had finally given way.

Clearing her throat, Liv dusted off her knees and told herself to get a grip. He was just doing what heroes did—saving a damsel in distress. And while the idea of being a damsel had once appealed to her, she no longer needed anyone to save her. Liv was more than capable of saving herself.

"Like I said, medical emergency." She opened the cupcake and took a bite, moaning when the sugary goodness melted in her mouth.

Ford's deep brown eyes met hers and held. "Long day?"

"The longest." She took another bite and struck absolute heaven in the form of marshmallow-cream filling. "But nothing a cupcake can't fix."

◆ ◆ ◆

It was going to take a hell of a lot more than a cupcake to fix what was wrong with Ford.

He hadn't set foot in this hospital in a long time, in any place that had to do with the accident, for that matter. Not once since making the call that took Sam's life.

And then Paxton's voice.

Which had been *numero uno* on his list of reasons to avoid type-one searches in this area. But today it wasn't the lingering what-ifs messing with his head. No, that honor went to the stubborn and sexy woman licking frosting off her lips. Leaving him to wonder if his attraction to her had something to do with their up-close-and-personal meeting earlier or the fact that as Sam's widow she was off-limits.

Ford had always had a hard time with limits. The harder the limits, the less time it took to break them. But this was a line Ford didn't want to test.

"Sorry," Liv said as she licked the icing off her fingers. "I should have offered to share, but it was a whole-cupcake kind of emergency."

"What kind of man would stand between a woman and her medicinal sugar fix?"

She snorted. "You'd be surprised."

"I'm full of surprises," he said, and she released a startled laugh. It was a great laugh, Ford decided. Raw, unexpected, and so bright his chest lightened. Damn, she was beautiful.

Add that to the playful smile she sent his way, and sparks ignited in places that had no business heating up. He didn't understand what was causing the strange pull, and he wondered if it was a one-sided deal.

"You're full of something," she finally said, tossing the wrapper in the trash can next to the machine, proving that, clearly, Nurse Cupcake wasn't buying what he was selling. "What are you doing here?"

Excellent question. One he wasn't ready to answer. "I was dropping Mr. Gordon off—"

"Ohmigod. You were Flash Gordoned?"

"Flash Gordoned?"

"Yeah, Flash Gordon is what we call him. He's a regular," she said. "Used to be some kind of exotic go-go dancer in Vegas back in the sixties. He usually comes in with one of the trainees, though." She looked him up and down. "Are you a summer trainee?"

He crossed his arms and might have flexed a little. "Do I look like a rookie to you?" Liv's expression said she wasn't sure. "I'm not a rookie."

In fact, he had a reputation for being one of the most skilled type-one SAR officers in the Sierra Nevada. Had more successful high-risk rescue cases under his belt than anyone in the country. When shit got real, guys like Harris looked to Ford for direction.

He'd worked hundreds of rescues over the past eight years—most of them dangerous, a few of them suicide missions. Ford never gave up, never backed down, and never doubted his decisions.

Until he was forced to sacrifice one for the safety of many. For Liv, that would be the only decision that mattered. So why did he care if she thought of him as a rookie?

Because it did. And now that he'd met the woman whose life he'd inadvertently changed, her opinion of him mattered as much as fulfilling the promise he'd made to Sam. And wasn't that one hell of a fubar in the making.

"And for your information, I got stuck with Flash because I assisted in an emergency surgery and missed morning briefing," he informed her.

She bit her lip. "Oh."

"Yeah, oh."

"I'm sorry about making you late." She sounded genuine, but it was hard to tell since she was still grinning over him getting stuck with Flash Gordon. "Had he gone full monty, or did you get to him before he started singing 'Flash Gordon'?"

"The boom box was going strong, but he was struggling with a pair of shimmery booty shorts that could double for a headband when I got there," Ford said.

"The gold ones?" she asked, and he closed his eyes and gagged a little. "You're lucky it's not Fourth of July. He brings out the Let Freedom Ring banana-hammock," she said, and to her credit, she didn't laugh. "You were Flashed because you were helping me." Her elegant hand rested on his forearm. "I feel bad."

Bad was the last thing Ford felt. Not when her soft fingers were touching his skin, radiating through his body and waking up every nerve ending.

"I was Flashed because Harris is a prick," he said, taking a step closer. "And even if I'd known the consequences for missing the morning briefing, I still would have helped you."

"Because you like being the hero?" she asked quietly, tilting her head closer until he could smell the light floral scent of her shampoo.

"I go where I'm needed because it's my job," he said, delivering the same old explanation in the same old *No biggie* tone he used when it came to women.

But he had a feeling Liv wasn't like other women. She focused on the small things other people tended to dismiss, and she was perceptive as hell. So when she silently studied him, her discerning gaze so intense, Ford felt as if she were filtering out the bits of truth he kept hidden behind the cold, hard facts.

And when he was about to break eye contact, her lips curled slightly and she shook her head. "You picked your job because you need to be needed," she said, but there was no judgment in her statement. Just a deep appreciation, as if she too understood the calling that drove him. That instinctive response to rush toward the fire when everyone else was running away. "Mr. Gordon is all settled, yet you're still here."

And she was still touching him. "I'm here to find out how *our* patient fared from this morning." His answer was light, breezy—and not what Liv was looking for.

Sticking her hands in her pocket, she gave him an equally light and breezy smile. "He made a full recovery, just in time for the first day of superhero camp. Did I thank you?"

"You did. Then there was the rookie comment."

"An honest mistake," she said sweetly, leaning closer. And damn she smelled good. Like sunshine, frosting, and hot-woman good. "But I must admit, I'm impressed. Emergency surgery, cupcake extraction, and elderly care all in one day."

"Don't forget finding Ms. Moberly's missing maltipoo, LuLu."

That got a grin from her. "Is there anything you can't do?"

"Besides convince a pretty nurse to have a cup of coffee with me?" he asked. "I'm not all that good with open wounds."

She studied him from those insightful, warm caramel eyes that seemed to hide as much as they revealed. Good thing Ford's secrets were buried too deep to be found. "Then I guess a career change into medicine isn't in your future?"

"I've been told I give a stellar sponge bath," he teased, but she didn't laugh. She was too busy trying to figure out what wounds he was hiding.

"Nurse Preston to exam room six. Nurse Preston. To exam room six," a voice came over the intercom. "Code Flash in exam room six."

"Thanks for the cupcake," she said.

"What about the coffee?"

Liv pushed the button on the coffee machine for leaded and then handed him the cup. "It's not Shelia's coffee, but it'll keep you wired until midnight. And lucky for you, there are lots of pretty nurses here."

Feeling decidedly put in his place, he watched her scrub-clad backside disappear down the hallway, and he admitted that while that might be true, there was only one Nurse Cupcake.

CHAPTER 4

"I'm sure he was just testing his boundaries," Liv said to the 120 pounds of coiffed hair and *When I was a mother* censure staring her down from the other side of the kitchen island.

Carolyn Preston was as known for her generous nature as she was for her unsolicited advice. She'd give a stranger her last dollar—and then her opinion on how to fix his life. She was an expert in every field, quoted Wikipedia as if it were delivered on stone tablets, and insisted on making tuna casserole even though she knew Liv hated tuna.

She was Paxton's biggest advocate, Liv's biggest critic—and back from Palm Beach for the summer. When word reached her that Liv needed a sitter, Carolyn had packed up and rented a place across town—even though Liv had offered her the guest room. Liv appreciated the help, but the self-help pamphlets, which were strategically placed throughout the house, she could do without. Saturday night, after a particularly craptastic day at the hospital, she'd reached for her secret stash of red velvet cupcakes only to find a bag of gluten-free bagel chips in their place—and an article on the deadly history of Red Dye No. 5. That morning she'd found her laundry clean and folded on her bed, with a book titled *The Proper Widow's Handbook to Grieving* lying atop her black lace nightie.

"I considered bringing the cookie to Paxton's room, but what would that teach him?" Carolyn threw her hands in the air as if this one cookie was the difference between Paxton speaking or not.

"It was just his first day of camp," Liv said, hanging her bag off the back of a kitchen chair and heading straight for the fridge. "You know Pax—he has to warm up to the idea."

"He doesn't need to warm up—he needs to toughen up," Carolyn said, sounding more upset than angry. "And giving him these pep talks in front of his peers isn't helping him any."

Liv gave her a big eyebrow raise. "Are you checking up on me again?"

"Of course not!" Carolyn sounded offended, as if she hadn't tailed Liv to the therapist's office, only to interrogate the poor therapist about her grandson's condition after they'd left. "I just asked the counselor when I picked him up if you were hovering."

Liv reached past the soda and grabbed the bottle of wine in the back. "What do you want me to do, slow the car down to a soft roll and kick him out?"

"You can park, but maybe let him walk into the building himself. That's what I did with Sam. He cried himself sick when I dropped him off at preschool, but instead of coddling him and rewarding the negative behavior, I gave him the confidence to handle it on his own. And I think Sam turned out just fine," Carolyn said proudly.

Sam had turned out to be a brilliant surgeon who was confident and resourceful and had this amazing ability to connect. It was what had drawn Liv to him in the first place. The way he could focus solely on one person, in the moment, made her feel special—safe. It was this intense tunnel vision that had allowed him to earn his patients' trust and grow his practice so fast.

But over time, he began to give so much of himself to his profession that there wasn't enough left over for Liv and Paxton. A problem that was at the heart of nearly every argument they'd ever had.

Including their last.

Liv plucked a wineglass from the cabinet and sat at the counter. "Paxton isn't like Sam. He's his own person, and he needs to heal in his own time."

"Well, while he's hiding away from everyone, the world is moving on. I just don't want him to get left behind."

Liv wanted to point out that her son was probably hiding because of the awful tuna smell wafting from the oven, but she didn't say anything. Mainly because she was too angry over the whole "world moving on" bit.

Maybe for other people moving on was easier. For Liv, the journey had been painful and hard-earned, so she couldn't fault her son for resisting. He hadn't just lost his father—he'd lost half of his little world. And every step forward meant one step farther from that peaceful, happy time. Farther from the dreams and a future neither one of them wanted to say goodbye to.

Her marriage might not have been perfect, but it was hers. And she'd loved Sam—even when he'd driven her crazy. She often wondered if that was the problem. That if things had been perfect before their time together had come to an end, if their family had been solid, then maybe moving on wouldn't feel like such a betrayal.

Liv had still been mourning the dreams she'd had for their marriage when the sheriff showed up on her doorstep and took a sledgehammer to the already splintered foundation.

She was doing her best to piece together the fragments, but there were missing pieces, and she'd accepted that. Her world would never be the same, but at least it was starting to resemble something close to normal.

A new kind of normal, Liv liked to think of it. They might not function like other families, but they'd both gotten dressed this morning and left the house. That constituted forward progress, in her book.

"I know, and he'll get there," Liv promised. "It will just take longer and have a few more bumps in the road than most kids. But you had to have known that when you signed him up for the camp."

"I didn't sign him up for that camp," Carolyn said, as if horrified by the idea.

Surprised by this information, Liv clarified, "You said he needed to go to camp, be around kids."

"Yes. Music camp or science camp, something that would give the boy structure, direction. Not a free-for-all fun day where the biggest achievement is who can belch the loudest."

Liv would be thrilled if Paxton won a belching contest, because that was what most six-year-old boys did. But right then, she was more interested in who had covered Paxton's tuition. Needed to know why she'd received a letter from the local parks-and-recreation office stating that Paxton had been gifted a coveted spot in the summer camp. And why Carolyn had insisted on spending the summer here when she'd been so anxious to leave Sequoia Lake not so long ago.

"So you didn't pay for his camp as an early birthday present?" she asked, because if it hadn't been Carolyn, then who was their fairy godmother?

Ever since Sam's death, little presents had shown up on Liv's doorstep. Paxton's birthday, Christmas, even Easter. It was never anything extravagant, just perfect little presents to make the holidays easier to swallow.

Liv had asked her friends, coworkers, even the ladies from Living for Love, but everyone had sworn that they weren't the secret Good Samaritan. The only person left was Sam's mom.

"Of course not. Had I known he'd be gone all day and I would be nothing more than a chauffeur, I would have planned more day outings with my friends."

"Carolyn, I didn't intend for it to feel that way," Liv said.

"I know you didn't, but I came here to spend a few weeks with my grandson, help him adjust before kindergarten." Carolyn went silent, and Liv's warning bells started ringing. "Not that it matters. He said he didn't want to go back to camp."

Liv perked up. "He said that?"

"Yes. Why do you sound so happy?"

"Because he talked to you after a rough day. That's huge!"

Paxton had left with his dad a healthy, talkative three-year-old, excited for a white Christmas at his grandparents'. And he'd come home a boy who was terrified to speak.

On rare occasions, when Carolyn had spent a significant amount of time with him, he'd speak to Liv in front of Carolyn. But he hadn't communicated directly with Carolyn since before the accident.

"He was talking to that dog of his. I was just the eavesdropper," Carolyn admitted.

"He was talking to you," Liv said gently. "Using Superdog Stan is his way of working through his anxiety."

"You said the same thing when he insisted that a caped dog flew down from the sky to rescue him from the accident." Carolyn's tone was terse. Full of judgment.

"That story is how his little brain dealt with such a tragic loss. He'll outgrow it." It was the same thing Liv had been telling herself since first hearing Paxton's account of the rescue. If anything, he'd become more insistent that the imaginary dog was real.

And that, more than his silence, worried Liv.

"Well, something needs to change, because I told him not going back wasn't an option." Which would have made Pax feel even more anxious.

"How did that go over?" Liv asked.

"He locked himself in his room," Carolyn said, busying herself with brushing imaginary dust off her cuff.

"He works better with options." And before Carolyn could regurgitate all the research on the safety created by setting boundaries and how effective tough love could be, Liv added, "But I'll talk to him."

Compromise, Liv told herself. It was the only way they'd get through this as a family. Carolyn wasn't trying to be difficult—she was just trying to help. She'd lost her son that day, and all she had left of him was Paxton. Liv could relate to her need to control.

Liv poured herself a glass of wine. Carolyn raised a big questioning brow. "Oh, do you want a glass?"

Carolyn looked horrified—and a bit judgy. "It's not even five o'clock."

Liv looked at the clock—*damn*, only 4:25—and set the glass down. Plastering a smile on, she said, "Thanks for helping out today. He may not have expressed it, but he loves it when you come over."

"I love him and just want to see him flourish like . . ." Carolyn's voice trailed off, and her face filled with heartache and worry. "Like a normal boy."

"I know," Liv said, wanting the same thing but unsure of what normal even looked like when a kid lost half of his world.

With a shaky nod, Carolyn picked up her purse and keys off the counter. "I put a casserole in the oven, a scrapbooking flyer one of the moms gave me is on the fridge, and remember, I'm visiting with friends in Tahoe City for the next couple of days."

"Have fun." Liv felt the air lighten, the sun grow brighter. Two whole casserole-free days on her forecast. "I swapped shifts with Margery so I can pick him up from camp."

Olivia thought about the other moms who would be there, most likely the same moms who had been in Paxton's preschool, and she cringed. Maybe he could skip tomorrow. It wasn't like George Washington had gone to superhero camp, and he'd created a nation.

"Tell Paxton Grandma loves him and hopes he goes back to camp." So much for playing hooky.

"Will do. And Carolyn," Liv said right as her mother-in-law was about to leave the kitchen, "I miss him too."

Carolyn paused on the threshold and slowly turned around. "Thank you," she said quietly. "Sometimes it feels as if I'm the only one who's still hurting."

"It will always hurt," Liv said, her hand going to her ring finger, a brief moment of confusion still coming when she found it naked. Her heart racing as if she'd lost it. "But as time goes on, the hurt is what triggers the good memories."

The debilitating pain that made breathing difficult would lessen until it became a warm ping in the back of her heart. And it was only then that she'd realize that love didn't hurt, but the act of trying to kill it did. And once Carolyn stopped trying to drown it out, she'd find her peace—just like Liv had after her mother died.

Liv waited until Carolyn was pulling out of the driveway before fishing her cell from her purse. She took a long swallow of wine, then called backup.

"How did camp go?" Avery said in greeting. Liv let out a sigh. "That bad, huh?"

Telling herself that it was five o'clock somewhere, Liv took a sip of wine. "He's hiding in his room."

"If I was forced to spend the afternoon with Carolyn, I'd hide in my room too."

Liv laughed, and it felt good. Then she immediately sobered. "It's not that. He told her he didn't want to go back to camp."

"What are you going to do?" When Liv remained silent, Avery said, "You know that he's going to be fine no matter what, right? He will get through this because you're a good mom, who will be right beside him every step of the way." Avery's conviction came from someone who had faced death and kicked its butt. They'd met the first week Liv had started at Mercy General. Liv had been working in the ICU, and Avery was waiting on a kidney transplant. They connected over shared loss of a loved one and bonded over a love of cupcakes. "And didn't his doctor say that nearly all kids outgrow this?"

"Yes," Liv admitted. "But maybe holding his hand will prolong his healing time. Or maybe I'm pushing too hard too soon." So what if he started kindergarten at seven? Why was that such a big deal? "Or what if I'm doing everything wrong?"

"What if you're both just having a rough day and all you need is some time to process?" Avery said, and Liv wanted to cry.

"What if you're wrong?"

"I can't be," Avery said with conviction. "Because Paxton is loved. And he's safe. And you will both come out of this stronger than ever."

Liv did love him, with every ounce of her soul, but she sometimes wondered if that was enough.

Liv opened the oven to check the casserole. The second the scent hit her nose, she gagged and then slammed the door shut. "Want to come over after work for dinner? There's plenty."

Avery paused. "Why do I get the feeling there's a casserole involved?"

"And wine," Liv said cheerfully.

"No way. I just got a new kidney." Liv's friend hadn't just received a new kidney. The miracle transplant had given Avery a future that didn't have an expiration date stamped on it. "Without a spare, I'm not willing to risk it. Life's too short for one of Carolyn's concoctions."

Words to live by, Liv thought, fanning the pungent air. When that didn't help, she lit a candle.

"Plus, I'm checking off another wish in my living journal. Rhonda Sparks spent all year working on a signature dish for that Sequoia Lake's Hottest Chef contest, but she's in the middle of her radiation treatments and can't stand the smell of food. I said I'd use her recipe to perfect the meal and enter it for her."

Shortly after Avery was given a second lease on life, she'd created a living memory journal filled with the wishes and dreams of women who would never get their second chance. Living out their dreams was Avery's way of honoring them—and paying forward all the love and support she'd received through her recovery.

"What are you making?" Liv asked into the mouthpiece.

"Rhonda said her favorite episode was when the person made a flat-iron steak with a red pepper sauce, cayenne sweet potato mash, and green beans with bacon," she said. "I'm doing a practice run. My kitchen is a disaster, but the red pepper sauce is amazing."

Liv's stomach growled at the thought of a home-cooked meal that didn't involve canned fish. "If you need a judge—"

A loud crash came from upstairs, followed by a child's cry. Liv's skin prickled, and all the exhaustion from earlier was replaced with heart-pumping adrenaline.

"What was that?" Avery asked, since the sound was invasive enough to be heard over the phone. She might have even heard it across town.

"Paxton," Liv hollered as her feet sprang into action. She was up the stairs and rounding the hallway when she heard another scream. She burst through the bedroom door, her worry clogging her throat, and then she came to a full stop.

Because there on the floor, peeking out from beneath a fort made of Superman sheets and a matching comforter, were two sock-free feet, a thin beam of light, and a big bushy tail—that moved. But it wasn't the unexpected sight of a dog in her house that had her pausing. It was the sounds coming from inside the makeshift hideout.

It was so foreign she had mistaken it for a cry for help, when in fact it wasn't a cry at all.

"Liv?" Avery said, and Liv could hear her friend's keys jingling in the background, as if she was already heading over to the emergency.

"It's fine," Liv said, her voice wavering. "Pax is. I thought he was screaming, but . . ." She trailed off, unable to speak through the sudden shift in emotion.

"But what, Liv?"

"He's reading and laughing," she whispered. From the empty juice box and cookie crumbs, she guessed that he'd somehow managed to sneak a few of Carolyn's cookies into his room. "He's in a fort with a dog, reading from his comic books and laughing."

Like a normal kid.

"But before he can release the poison"—Paxton's voice was muffled from beneath the covers—"Superdog flies through the air and says, 'Drop the nuclear kibble, Mammoth Mutt!' But Mammoth Mutt doesn't. He sticks his big tooth right in the middle of the bag to rip it open when . . . *bam!* Superdog snags Mammoth by the collar and ties him to the telephone pole with a laser leash."

"*Woof!*" The tail-wagging increased with excitement.

"I can hear him," Avery whispered. "He sounds so happy."

"He does, doesn't he?" Liv said, thinking about how withdrawn he'd been lately. She must have spoken too loudly because the reading stopped and so did the wagging.

There was some movement inside, then a whole lot of commotion, and like a heat-seeking missile, a black nose poked out in Liv's direction, followed by two wet, black eyes and the biggest ears Liv had ever seen.

"*Woof! Woof! Woof!*"

"When did you get a dog?" Avery asked.

"We didn't."

"Oh boy." There was a silent pause where Liv could hear glass bottles clanking through the phone. "Carolyn, casserole, and another stray? I hope you have more than one bottle of wine to wash down this Monday."

Liv should have been furious. She and Paxton had decided that they'd wait until he was older to get a pet. Her son might be quiet, but that only gave him more time to plot and scheme. Which was how she'd wound up sharing a shower with a garden snake and her morning coffee with a raccoon who had moved into her pantry. If they didn't have a serious talk, she was going to wind up sharing her bed with a mountain lion.

For some reason the image of the big mountain man from that morning popped into her head, and she found herself smiling. An honest-to-God smile.

Finding Superdog Stan posing as roadkill should have ruined her day. In the past it would have set her back ten steps. But a chance encounter with a charming man had changed all of that.

It wasn't the flirting, although that had been fun—a little too fun. It was how he'd looked at her, treated her, as if he thought she was interesting. As if she wasn't broken.

He didn't ask her how she was holding up or if she was sleeping at night, because he didn't know to ask her those things. Didn't know her past. Which was a gift in itself because it allowed her a small glimpse of the woman she wanted to become—gave her hope that she was on the right track.

And the confidence to apply for the Mobile Medic position.

"You know what? I'm going to toast this Monday and celebrate it with pizza from Mile High," Liv said.

"Pizza?" Her son's freckled face appeared where his feet had been, and then he smiled, big and bright and so beautiful. "What about Grandma's tuna casserole?"

"That depends," Liv said, her tone dialed to litigation attorney.

He went so serious she wanted to laugh. "On what?"

"On if you'd rather have pizza with cupcakes afterward."

Paxton popped up on his knees, and the dog followed suit. Only the dog was so tall he pulled all the blankets up with him. "Lemon with raspberry frosting?"

Yellow and red. Superdog's colors. Liv smiled back. "Why not? Life's too short for casserole."

Paxton didn't comment on the *Life is too short* part, but the promise of no casserole had him crawling out from his hideout and wrapping his arms around Liv's waist. The dog shot across the room and raced at Liv, sheets trailing behind him.

He was like a potato with toothpicks for legs, but he moved with the speed of a cheetah. And right when she thought he'd jump on her, Paxton said, "Sit."

And bless his little wagging tail, the dog sat.

So when Paxton looked up at her with his big baby blues, so similar to Sam's, she felt her chest catch, and he asked, "Can we keep him?"

Liv made a big deal of looking at the dog's collar. It was bright orange with, thankfully, a golden name tag dangling from it. "Looks like he already has a family, and they're probably worried about him."

Paxton thought about this for a moment and then bounced on his toes. "What if we can't find his family? Can we keep him then?"

Liv knelt and got eye level with her little guy. "His tag has his owner's name and number on it." Scrawled right under the name, BULLSEYE. "So I don't think he will be hard to get ahold of." In fact, one glance at the owner's name, and Liv knew exactly which house Bullseye was calling home for the summer. Just like she knew why the thought of dropping him off had her heart racing. "Plus, we talked about this."

"You said when I got bigger. Look." Paxton pointed to the new pencil mark on the door frame. Since this used to be Sam's room, it was right next to his father's growth marks. "Dad was only here when he got Stanly Dog." Stanly Dog was Sam's childhood pet, more of his best pal, really. And Paxton's stuffed toy's namesake. He had been a giant white shepherd with big black eyes who could do a zillion tricks and looked a lot like Paxton's favorite superhero. "And I'm all the way up here."

All the way up here constituted a quarter of an inch, but to a kid who ranked in the tenth percentile in height and weight, that quarter inch was a big deal.

"Pets are a lot of responsibility, sweetie. Between you starting big-kid school in August and my work schedule, it wouldn't be fair to the dog. Maybe when things settle down. Okay?"

Paxton nodded and let out a sigh twice his size. All of the excitement he'd had a moment ago vanished, and in its place was a quiet resignation that had Liv's soft underbelly rolling over.

Liv couldn't give him a dog of his very own right then, but she could give him a fun night—something comforting to hang on to while they talked about going back to camp. "Although, I don't see why he can't stay for dinner."

Paxton's face lit up. "Really?"

"Yes, but after dinner he goes home."

"Did you hear that? You get to stay for pizza!"

Bullseye barked his thanks, and Paxton jumped up and down, but all Liv heard was her son communicating with someone other than his mother.

◆ ◆ ◆

Two hours and a glass and a half of wine later, the sun touched down behind the Sierra Nevada, painting the sky a bright orange. From her back patio, Liv could see clear across the lake to the gas lamp–lined main strip of town.

The water was still tonight, barely lapping at the dock a few yards away. A warm summer breeze whispered past, rustling the nearby ponderosas and scenting the air with pine and easier times.

She'd made it through another day. The pizza box was empty, Paxton was in his room getting ready for bed, and all that was left to do was take their dinner guest home. But as Liv walked down the shoreline, her bare feet sinking into the warm sand, Liv realized she had several problems all at once.

Problem one: the dog.

Bullseye didn't belong to just any neighbor. Per his owner's name on the tag, which she'd rechecked three times to be certain, it appeared her furry dinner guest was staying at the old Keller cabin, meaning he belonged to her newest neighbor. Mr. Jamison, the tall, dark, and too-dangerous-for-her-good-sense neighbor. A fact that had driven her to distraction all through dinner. What were the chances that *his* dog would end up at *her* house on the same day they met?

Which led her to problem two: the chances were slim to unbelievable.

She was just supposed to walk up his steps, knock on his door, and give him one of those *You're never going to believe this* stories? Because he was never going to believe her. Sure, he could think the situation was nothing more than a crazy coincidence. Or he could think of her as plain old crazy.

After blurting out that she was his neighbor and knew exactly where he lived—not to mention the not-so-subtle groping—she wouldn't be surprised if he thought the lonely widow had seduced his dog into her house with the promise of bacon and belly rubs to stage another run-in with the town's newest bachelor.

Finally, there was problem number three: no one appeared to be home.

She walked up the back steps and peered through the window into the house. It was completely dark.

With a sigh, Liv thunked her forehead against the glass. She had a dog that didn't belong to her, a son who needed a pep talk about the joys of summer camp, and there was no sign of life inside the house.

After knocking three times, Liv admitted defeat and looked down at the runaway at her feet, whose tail wagged happily. "On the bright side, problem three eliminates problems one and two."

Bullseye looked up at her as if to determine what they were going to do next.

"Mr. Keller used to leave a spare key on the porch," she said, searching the top ledge of the door for the spare key. Nothing.

"If we find it, I can let you inside, go home, and nobody will ever know the difference."

"*Woof!*" Bullseye said, objecting to being left alone. The dog had a point. For all she knew, Ford worked the night shift.

"Fine, but sitting on his porch until he comes home isn't an option."

In complete agreement, Bullseye tugged on the makeshift leash—a scarf from Liv's knitting period—and headed toward her house.

"Oh no." She tugged on the scarf, but he kept walking, his big furry butt waddling with purpose. "Dinner with you was bad enough. You ate all the pepperoni and didn't even clear your plate."

He whimpered and dropped to his belly, resting his head on his paws, his eyes looking up at her through long lashes.

"You can drop the cute act," she said, leading him back to the porch to check under the flowerpot. "It isn't working." It was totally working. "Paxton needs a good night's sleep, which he won't get with you sharing his bunk. And there is no way you're sharing my bed with all that dirt on your paws. You need a bath, and I've been dreaming about my own tubful of bubbles all day, so you're out of luck, pal."

She pulled out her phone and pressed the button. "Siri, how do you pick a lock?"

"Let me check my sources," 007 said—and she pictured the latest Bond with the buzzed hair and big biceps. *Not as big as Ford's,* she thought. "Okay, here is what I found on the web. A video of 'Nine Easy Steps to Pick a Lock.'"

She looked at Bullseye. "I'm more of a nuts-and-bolts kind of girl." She pushed the button. "Let's go with the nine steps to pick a lock."

"All right, here is the article."

Liv heard footsteps behind her, followed by a husky, "Being more of a visual guy myself, I have to say I'm a little disappointed, Nurse Cupcake."

Liv swallowed, while Bullseye started barking and yanking on the leash like he was at Disneyland and the gates had just opened.

Eyes glued to her phone, she stopped Siri's little B&E lecture and slowly craned her head up as a pair of bare feet came into view, followed by a wetsuit that did little to hide the hard, coiled muscles beneath. Her gaze and heartbeat rose in unison as she straightened, because the wetsuit was unzipped, dripping wet, and hanging from his lean hips— leaving nothing but tanned skin, a set of abs that were drool worthy, and a chest that begged to be petted.

Her finger tips tingled.

So did her thighs, because one well-orchestrated tug and she'd know what Man Candy wore beneath his suit—if anything at all. It hugged his body so tight she couldn't imagine room for much else.

He cleared his throat, and Liv tore her gaze away. Big problem there, because their eyes met and held, hers like a deer in headlights, his twinkling with humor. And then he let loose that smile, the one he'd flashed her earlier that morning, and Liv's body crackled with excitement.

"And while my bath is on the smaller side, I wasn't joking about my sponge-bath skills," he said, the summer night taking on more heat. "In case you were interested."

CHAPTER 5

After a decade of dealing with panic-driven subjects, Ford had more than earned a PhD in nonverbal cues and body language. And Liv Preston was most definitely interested.

A nice thought, and had she been any other woman, he might have considered it. But she was a single mom, Paxton's mom, and they both had a heartbreaking past. A past he'd played a role in—and that made it impossible.

So this attraction between them would never go beyond flirting. "I wasn't going to steal anything, just returning your dog," she said. "He seems to have befriended my son."

With a grin, he pointed to the big pot on her right. "The key's under the fern. But next time you can just try the door. It's unlocked."

"Oh, I promise there won't be a next time," she said, shoving some kind of braided leash made from yarn at him.

"Too bad." Ford stuck his board in the sand, resting one arm at its peak. "Because I can't promise you the same. Once Bullseye here finds a friend, he has a hard time letting go." Not wanting to get into where his dog had learned that, he squatted down to give the mutt a *Good job* pet. After all, by tracking the scent from the stuffed dog earlier that morning, he'd found his missing subject.

Just like he had two years ago when Bullseye had found Paxton and his dad in that cave.

"I'm sorry if he's a little sticky. He may have had some peanut butter cookies. And maybe a cupcake, but I made sure that dessert was served after dinner." She said it as though she'd hosted his dog for a playdate.

"Dinner being?"

"Pizza. But I don't think the cheese settled so well." She waved a hand in front of her face and grimaced.

Ford laughed, then leveled the dog with a look. "One funny sound and it's the garage for the night."

Bullseye averted his gaze to study an ant crawling across the wood deck.

"Don't do that—I'm the one who offered it to him," she said, her heart in her eyes but some steel to her tone. "Just light a few candles and it's not so bad."

Ford smiled. He liked this compassionate-crusader side of hers. He also liked the sundress she'd put on. Light and flowy, flirting around her legs with every shift in the breeze.

If not for the lingering sadness in her eyes, she'd look like a sexy coed instead of a widowed single mother.

"Is your bed back on the bargaining table?" he asked, loving how her cheeks went pink. "Because I should warn you, he might look all sweet and cuddly, but he's a sixty-pound bed hog."

Bullseye jumped onto his hind legs and barked in offense, then placed his big paws on Ford's thighs. "What?" he said, turning his attention to Bullseye, ruffling his head when he barked again. "You didn't even bring any pizza home to share?"

"I brought this," she said, holding up a little Ziploc containing a half-eaten cupcake.

"There's a bite taken out of it."

She handed it over. "And all of the frosting is missing."

"So much for having my back," he said to Bullseye, who was too busy cleaning his paws to care.

"I have some leftover casserole in the oven if you want it," she offered, all neighborly like. "But before you say yes, it's only fair to warn you that by *some* casserole, I really mean the whole casserole. Because it was so bad not even the dog would touch it."

Ford picked up a piece of driftwood and tossed it. Bullseye took off, barking as if it were aliens coming to invade the planet. "Do you always warn someone before inviting them over to dinner?"

"I wasn't inviting you over. I came here to bring you a cupcake to say thanks for helping me out today."

He grinned. "Without frosting. Talk about neighborly."

"There's also the leftover casserole."

"The casserole that's so bad my dog wouldn't touch it?"

"I usually don't offer to poison my neighbors," she said through her fingers. "I'm just a little distracted by . . ." She flapped her hands at his chest, and there went her cheeks, flushing the most adorable shade of pink.

He lifted a brow. "My paddleboard?"

"No." This time the blushing was accompanied by a smile. "By all of the flirting and laughing. I'm not sure how to read you."

Join the club.

"Well, isn't that a damn shame," he said. "Because you have one hell of a laugh, and flirting is good for the soul."

It was good for the body too, almost too good. And if he didn't change the topic, Ford's bodysuit wasn't going to have enough room for his paddleboard. Because her eyes were locked on his mouth, and the way they dilated told him that she was drawn to him. The worst of it was, he was feeling pretty damn drawn to her.

And it had nothing to do with the promise he'd made to Sam.

Had she been any other woman, he'd see where that attraction led—which was usually a bed or the nearest flat surface. But this wasn't any woman, and he couldn't go there.

Ever.

"See, that," she said. "The whole *one hell of a laugh* thing—I'm not sure how to read that."

That she was hung up on it was interesting. Almost as interesting as the way she was looking at him. Not like he was some rookie, but as if she saw something in him that was somehow impressive. It was a look he could get used to.

He leaned against his paddleboard. "It's as straightforward as you bringing me a cupcake."

"Then let me clarify," she said seriously. "The cupcake was to thank you for helping me out with Superdog Stan and saving my son's first day at superhero camp. Even though I know it made you late for your briefing."

"Well, with superhero camp on the line, it was a no-brainer. First days are a big deal. How did it go?"

He asked it casually, as if they were two neighbors simply shooting the breeze on a nice summer's eve. When in fact, Ford had been looking forward to this day for months. Ever since he read about the program online.

The camp encouraged kids to find their inner superhero, while giving them a costume to role-play. *Fake it till you make it,* Ford liked to say. It was skill that had pulled him through some of his hardest times. And he'd hoped Paxton would find the same benefit. It was why Ford had enrolled him in the first place. His birthday present to Paxton. Not that Liv would know, because Ford hadn't signed the card. He never signed the cards. Just like he never stayed longer than it took to make good on his promise.

A promise that, up until today, had been nothing more than checking in on Sam's family from a distance. Making sure they were healing and thriving. And okay, whenever a holiday came around, and Ford found a trinket or comic book, something a father would gift to his son, Ford picked it up for Paxton—delivered from an anonymous sender.

What had started out as a onetime trip to Sequoia Lake to give Liv Sam's final Christmas present had turned into a two-year mission to find closure. But this was to be his last trip, so he needed to make sure that when he left, there would be no need to come back.

Well played, Ford told himself, because once he got past the reason he'd been sent to Sequoia Lake and became recertified, there wouldn't need to be another visit. Something that brought up a dump truck full of mixed feelings he didn't want to acknowledge right then.

It was clear that Liv was going to be just fine. She'd come a long way in the past year, and Sam would be proud. Oh, there were still a few hurdles she'd have to navigate, but Ford wasn't worried. Liv Preston was as tough as they came. She'd picked up the pieces and was moving forward. Which meant that Ford was free from his promise.

And at the perfect time.

He hated secrets—and this one was getting out of hand. Had witnessed firsthand just how destructive the cycle could be. Most folks were one dark secret from destroying everything that mattered. Playing the silent protector had taken its toll, and Ford was ready to relinquish the role.

Too bad that meant owning the past.

"I guess it went exactly how I pictured the first day going. Paxton, that's my son, doesn't do change well. He's had to adapt to so much change so fast. I think he's just rebelling," Liv said as if she wouldn't mind rebelling every now and again. "But tomorrow is a new day, which means a chance to make new friends, take new risks, and maybe come out of his shell a bit."

"He'll get there," Ford promised, because with a woman like Liv in his corner, there wasn't anything Paxton couldn't accomplish. Just like there wasn't anything positive that could come from prolonging this conversation.

Ford picked up his board. "Good night, Liv."

"Night, Ford." But neither of them moved.

Liv worried her lower lip while her gaze slid over his. And fair being fair, he did some gazing of his own, surprised to discover he couldn't look away. Sure, Liv had some kind of hold on him. But up close, she made his head spin so fast common sense was obliterated. Which was why he kept flirting with this particular woman even though logic told him it was a bad idea.

Even worse, it didn't feel like flirting. It felt more like connecting. A connection he suddenly wanted to investigate.

Not good, he thought. *Not good at all.* Because while he'd come to Sequoia Lake to find answers, when she smiled at him like that it stirred up questions that were a hell of a lot more problematic.

Ford told himself to take a step back, even as his feet moved forward.

"Woof!"

Liv braced herself as Bullseye, stick in his mouth, his sights locked on the pretty yellow sundress, charged up the beach with no intentions of slowing down.

"Sit," Ford said right before Bullseye would have lunged through the air and onto his new friend. Good boy that he was, Bullseye did as he was told, except the wet stick hit the ground, sending water and sand everywhere.

Bullseye looked at the stick, then up to Liv, his tongue panting in anticipation.

"First apologize to the lady for getting her dress wet." He gave a signal with his hand. "Then I'll throw the stick."

Bullseye lowered his head and nudged at her thigh with his nose in apology.

"It's okay, you were excited." She gave his head a pat. Lucky dog. "He was so obedient with my son. How long did it take to train him?"

"Two years."

Her eyes went wide. "That's a long time."

"Not for a search dog."

Understanding filled those pretty eyes. "He works with you, then?"

"Every day." Ford picked up the stick and threw it in the water. "Bullseye is a special dog with a lot of special gifts. But it took two years of intense training to get him ready for the field."

Bullseye swan-dived into the lake with all the grace of a rhino, and she laughed. "How do you know which ones are special?"

Ford watched the sun reflect off her hair, casting a soft glow around her, and said, "I know it when I see it."

CHAPTER 6

Smelling of iodine and still in her scrubs, Liv hurried to the back of the Bear Claw Bakery and plopped down at the end of the table, going low in the seat, a little breathless from her mad dash across the parking lot. She'd just finished a shift at the hospital and was gearing up for her second shift as president of Team Paxton Fan Club when she'd seen Ford standing across the street looking like sex on a stick.

The worst part was that he'd seen her. Not just a moment ago, but the other night on the beach. He'd blasted right past the grieving-widow exterior and spoke to that place, deep inside, that she purposefully kept secret. Even more terrifying, she liked what she heard.

She could blame the romantic backdrop of the sun setting over the deep blue lake for confusing her. But she was pretty sure it was the man himself. Which was why she'd spent the early part of the week avoiding him. A hard task since he lived just three doors down.

But when Liv set her mind to something, she saw it through.

Unfortunately, she chose to duck into the meeting place of the Women of the Wagon Trail—Sequoia Lake's version of the Daughters of the American Revolution. Made up from some of the town's oldest families, the WOTWT was the area's oldest society. And she'd sat down just in time for their weekly fund-raising meeting.

"What are you doing here?" Avery asked, looking at Liv as if she'd grown a third head.

Nope, just wings and feathers. And at any minute she was going to cluck like the chicken she was.

"I'm here for the meeting. Is it over?" Liv asked, looking around the café to find it oddly empty, then back to her two friends. Avery and Grace—the only two WOTWT members who seemed to be present.

Maybe her luck was changing.

"Hasn't started yet." *Or not.* "Irene was about to call the meeting to order when Mavis started harassing a couple of firemen, asking to sample their buns," Avery said, her hiking boots, khaki shorts, and fitted tank making her look like a real-life Lara Croft with long blonde locks. Which was fitting since she worked as an adventure guide at the local lodge. "Mavis took one look at their uniforms and thought they were the entertainment, so she started waving bills in the air, and chaos broke out."

Liv slung her bag over the back of a chair and took a seat. "Where are they?"

"Shelia kicked them out when someone started sampling buns without permission. Said they can't come back in until they promise to behave," Grace Mills, the third piece in their bestie sandwich, said. She was dressed in pressed capris, a light cream top with matching ballet flats, and a look of utter confusion. "What are you doing here?"

"It's the weekly Wagon Days meeting, right?" Liv asked, playing it cool and reaching across the table to help herself to one of the many cupcakes piled in the center of the platter. "I heard there was some kind of problem with the entertainment, and they needed volunteers, so where else would I be?"

Easier than explaining she was hiding from her sexy new neighbor.

Wagon Days was an annual fund-raiser hosted by the Women of the Wagon Trail, and it was their most honored achievement. It served as the biggest community fund-raiser and the most-attended family day of the year.

It was a time for neighbors to mingle and kids to run free. It was on old-fashioned town fair with more than a hundred food and craft booths from local vendors, a gold-panning contest, and even a cake-walk. The goal was to bring the town together to celebrate family, history, and nature the way the founders of Sequoia Lake intended when they settled this town. While raising much-needed funds for the local schools and churches.

Avery shot Liv a look. "Um, anywhere that doesn't involve talk of crafting, committees, and who's going to run this year's cakewalk."

Liv felt a rash break out on her wrist. "I don't see any glitter or glue guns. I'm on the Yahoo group committee for WOTWT—"

"Everyone in town is on the Yahoo group. It's not a committee," Avery interrupted.

"—and I happen to love cake." To prove it she snagged a cupcake right off Grace's plate and sank her teeth into the gooey treat, moaning with pleasure. "God, that's good," she said around bits of key-lime cupcake. "So is there a sign-up list going around?"

"It must be low blood sugar," Avery said to Grace.

"Either that or she accidentally ate one of Shelia's special cupcakes," Grace said, guarding the rest of the cupcakes with her arms. "Because I could have sworn she just said sign-up list and smiled." She looked at Avery. "That is a smile, isn't it?"

Avery leaned in for a closer inspection. "I see teeth, but I'd say her lips are more curled than curved."

"Hello? Sitting right here," Liv said.

"We know," Avery said. "You are here, at a Women of the Wagon Trail meeting, of your own free will. An emergency meeting that will likely include people sharing their opinions in a loud manner and forced participation, and you're not looking for the nearest exit."

"When I mentioned it would be cheaper to sign up for my Sips and Splatters class rather than pop in every week, you said it was too much of a commitment," Grace pointed out.

Liv snorted. "You make me sound like I'm allergic to commitment." Which was ridiculous, because Liv was the most committed person on the planet.

As the daughter of two doctors, Liv had built her life around commitment. Always weighing her decisions in terms of achievement. Even before marriage, she'd only dated men who had potential to go the distance. She'd never had a fling, a hobby job, or even a phone plan that lasted less than five years.

"See." Grace pointed at her. "Just the word has you scratching."

Liv looked down and realized she'd been itching her wrist, so she sat on her hands. "Between Paxton and work, I never know what my schedule is going to look like. I didn't feel comfortable promising I'd be there if I couldn't be sure I wouldn't have to flake. So it is easier to pop in when I can."

Avery leaned in and asked, "So what has you popping in today?" *Besides avoiding a too-young man and all of his too-good lines?*

"I talked to Dr. Brown about the Mobile Medic position, and she said I have all the qualifications she's looking for." It wasn't a complete lie. Dr. Brown had said she needed to get involved in the community, and now she was sitting at a community meeting.

"Liv, that's amazing," Avery said. "It will give you the hours you've been asking for and the extra benefits for being full-time."

It was all those things and so much more.

"Except, she needs someone who is involved in the community. And since the other person on her list is Kevin Curtis—"

"Mr. Sequoia Lake Curtis?" Grace asked, plucking a second cupcake from the plate and handing it to Liv. "Seriously, senior year I was voted Most Likely to Study Abroad, and he was voted Most Likely to Be Mayor."

"Which is why I'm here." Liv licked the frosting off the top of the cupcake like it was an ice cream cone. "The best way to prove to her that I'm invested in this community is to help out with Wagon Days. And while I don't bake anything but cupcakes, and I can't craft," she said, convinced she sounded like the worst mother on the planet, "I make a mean Rice Krispies treat, and I'm as cool as a cucumber under pressure."

"A cucumber, huh?" Avery teased and let out a big yawn.

"Early morning at the lodge?" Grace asked.

"Nope. A couple of late nights with my sous chef."

"How did the iron steak and sweet potato mash turn out the other night?"

"Inedible." Yet her friend couldn't stop smiling. "I overcooked the steak, burned the sauce, and didn't even get to the green beans before Ty got home, looking like a rugged, hungry mountain man. So I made omelets in nothing but my heels and a spatula. According to Ty, I should check off another adventure in my journal, because he thinks I'm Sequoia Lake's hottest chef."

Liv remembered those early years, before kids and mortgages, when everything between Sam and her was so simple. Spontaneous and easy. Every little thing was an excuse to fall into bed together. They had miss-you sex, make-up sex, morning sex, mad-for-you sex. And her personal favorite, maybe-we'll-get-caught sex. Which happened often, but rarely happened in a bed. And they never got caught.

That was the Sam she'd mourned, the marriage she'd grieved. But the grieving had started long before the accident.

"Was there dessert? I mean, you don't have to tell me if you don't feel comfortable," Grace said, tearing off the top of her cupcake and flipping it over to make a cupcake sandwich. "But please tell me. The closest I've come to sex on a stick was eating a Fudgsicle while watching the lawn boy manicure my hedges."

"Why don't you ask Liv?" Avery said, skewering Liv with an amused look that sent her pulse skyrocketing.

"Why me? A Fudgsicle makes my vanilla ice cream sundae sound tame," Liv said coolly. Only her palms were starting to sweat, and her cheeks felt awfully red for a girl who hadn't spent much time in the sun.

"I was talking about you playing doctor with Cub Candy the other day—"

"Cub Candy with the abs and perfect butt?" Grace asked.

"I had an emergency. He happened to pass by and lent me his finger," Liv said, and Grace's mouth fell open. "He was helping me stitch up Superdog Stan!"

"What exactly was he helping you do on the beach at sunset, then?" Avery asked.

"Nothing," Liv said, but Avery wasn't having it.

Giving another yawn, her friend sat back in her chair and settled in for the long haul. "From what I heard, it looked like a whole lot of something was going on."

And since Avery had more sources than the local newspaper, Liv knew there was no point in lying. "Fine. I came home to Paxton hiding Ford's dog in his room, so I went over to his house to return him. Ford was there, and I thanked him for helping with Stan, then apologized for my son being a pet-tomaniac. No big deal."

"Even a blind woman would agree that Cub Candy in nothing but lake water and a wetsuit is a big deal," Avery said.

Liv held up a hand. "Can you please stop referring to him as a cub? It's not like he's a coed guy spending his summers paddling around the lake and picking up on sun bunnies."

He was spending his summer rappelling from mountains and rescuing coeds. Big difference. Or so she'd told herself every night when she'd fallen asleep thinking about just how hard those glistening abs would feel—above her.

Both women exchanged a pointed look that, combined with the snorts, had Liv squirming in her scrubs.

"From what I understand, he was too busy eyeballing you to even notice the sun bunnies," Avery said.

"He wasn't eyeballing me. He was just making me laugh, flirting with me to get a reaction." And her body had reacted all right. Revved up as if it had never seen a half-naked man before.

Not like him, her girly parts whispered. Because while Sam had been handsome in a distinguished doctor way, he'd never looked as if he lifted logs for sport. Sam was a surgeon with a one-track mind and a soft touch.

There was nothing soft about Ford. Even his name suggested molded steel and firing pistons.

"According to Ty, the only thing Ford was interested in making was moves on you."

"God, I wish someone would move on me," Grace said. "It's been so long I don't know if my body would know how to move back."

"How would Ty know if he was making moves?" Liv asked with an exaggerated eye roll, even though something about Ford making moves her way sent her stomach into a free fall.

"He was paddleboarding with Ford, doing his male-bonding-with-the-new-team-member thing," Avery said. "He claims he waved to you, but you were too busy drooling over Ford to wave back."

Good God, had she been that obvious? And in front of his new teammate?

Tyson Donovan wasn't just Avery's husband. He was also head of the technical rope team for Sequoia Elite Mountain Rescue. He was the coordinator for the local team and ran most of the searches in the area. He was on the fast track to coordinating the entire Sierras.

And Liv was on the fast track to developing a serious crush on his newest coworker. Not all that unexpected when one came eye to pec with something *oh so* tempting three times in one day. Plus, Liv hadn't been tempted by another man since college when she'd met Sam, so the attraction had caught her by surprise. "Making moves is like breathing for a guy like Ford," Liv said. "Trust me, he isn't interested in anything more than a little flirting with a cougar."

Grace snorted. "If you're a cougar, then I'm a saber-toothed tiger."

"Half my age plus seven is the cougar equation," Liv pointed out, reciting one of the dozen or so *Cougar Life* blogs she'd stayed up late reading.

"That only works if you're over forty, and last I checked you weren't anywhere near the big four-oh."

"Maybe not, but I'm closer to cougar than coed," Liv said, trying to remember the last time she'd had the energy to paddleboard after a full shift at the hospital. The closest she'd come was lifting the couch to find the remote. Had it not been *Bachelor* Monday, the only heavy lifting she would have done was with the Costco-size bag of Red Vines licorice hidden in her bedroom.

"Before you start checking the mail for your AARP magazine," Avery teased, "I will have you know that Ford is twenty-eight."

"Twenty-eight?" Six years' difference wasn't so bad, Liv thought as she took a sip of her lemonade. Twenty-eight meant they were almost in the same decade. *Almost.*

"And he's sexy, single, and a stand-up guy," Avery added, as if she were reading his profile off a dating website.

"He looks more like an up-against-the-wall kind of guy to me." Grace shrugged. "But what do I know? I've been divorced for more years than I was married."

Avery considered this for a moment, then scrunched her nose. "He looks like more of a kitchen-counter guy to me, but that could be last night coloring my opinion."

Liv could picture him as both, but what had her heart going thump-thump was that he'd also be a sweet lover. She could see it in the way he looked at her, how gentle he'd been helping her at the craft store. Ford would be considerate and thorough and—oh my God, did she just moan?

"Even though he's older than I thought, he's still six years, one marriage, and thirty-six hours of labor younger than me," Liv said, feeling the wrinkles set in.

"There's always Chuck from Bunny Slope Supermarket," Grace offered, and Liv shivered—and not in the same way she shivered when she thought of Ford.

Chuck was balloon-shaped, balding, and the town butcher. He was also fifty and convinced that Liv needed a man to bring home the country-cut bacon.

"Ford is looking better and better," Avery teased. "Plus, he's on loan from Reno and leaves at the end of August, making him the perfect summer fling."

Liv's heart stopped, and she choked on a piece of ice. "I don't think so."

"What if you give him a kiss and see how you feel after?" Grace asked, eyes wide with excitement at the idea.

"Because the last man I kissed was Sam," she said, a wealth of conflicting emotions churning in her belly. "And kissing someone else would change that forever." And when something had the power to change forever, Liv had become gun-shy.

"Plus, I have my hands full with work. Paxton's still taking in stowaways, only this time it wasn't a stray. Carolyn is in town, her helicopter-grandma blades going a zillion rotations per second. And Ford and I are in completely different phases of our lives."

He was living life single and fancy-free, and she was a single mom who had lived more lives than she'd ever hoped to.

"Avery said a summer fling, not matching headstones," Grace reminded her.

"And being in different phases makes this perfect." Avery shook her cupcake at Liv. "Remember when we sat in my hospital room while waiting for the transplant results and made a promise? We vowed we were going to stop letting fear and outside limitations decide our future. To go after life at full speed and find some happiness." Avery's tone was soft but serious. "I believed you, so much that I dove in without looking and found my way. I found Ty." She took Liv's hand. "Now it's your time."

"Ford is not my Ty, and I barely have time to breathe. And what about her?" Liv pointed at Grace. "She was there too."

"Don't throw me under the bus just because you know she's right," Grace said defensively. "But if it makes you feel better, we can tackle my disaster of a life right after you find your smile." Grace's hand went in a circle to encompass Liv's face. "And I'm not talking about the plastic *everything's peachy* one you give everyone around town. But a real one, like you wore a second ago when you were talking about Man Cub. I'm not saying a fling is the answer, but you need to make a bold step."

"I dropped Paxton off at summer camp even though he was one blink away from a meltdown. That's a bold step." One that had her looking at her watch.

Avery's hand came to rest over the face of Liv's watch. "You have twenty minutes until you need to go back to being Supermom. Right now we're talking about you being bold."

"Bold is convincing my scared, crying kid it will be okay and driving off while his little eyes followed me out of the parking lot . . ." Liv swallowed down the overwhelming sense of helplessness that had haunted her all day. "I told him it would be a great day, even though I knew it would suck."

"That is a bold mommy move," Grace agreed quietly, her eyes a little misty. "I wouldn't have been strong enough to drive off."

Liv's went misty too, because Grace knew just how painful the inability to protect a child could cut. She had tried for years to have a family, only to have her dream of motherhood end seconds before it was supposed to begin. It took days for her to admit her baby was gone and months for the sorrow to fade enough to leave her house. In the end, Grace found herself divorced and childless, in a home built for a family.

"I almost turned around," Liv admitted.

"But you didn't—you showed him that you believe in his strength. So even if it's an awful day, he has the confidence that he can push through it," Avery said. "And before you know it, he'll be jumping out of the car, excited to see his friends."

"What if he doesn't?" Liv asked, as terrified that day would never come as she was that it would.

"He will. The more he steps out of his comfort zone, the more he'll come to understand that sucky days happen, just like magical ones." Avery leaned in, her tone careful. "It's going to be up to you, though, to show him it's okay to wish for the magical ones. And to enjoy them when they come."

"What does that mean?" Liv said, her voice a little cutting. Because she worked hard to make every day magical for Paxton, and her friends sounded as if she were holding him back.

And that hurt.

Avery and Grace were her two closest friends. Had been since Liv started at the hospital. Avery had been in long-term care waiting on a kidney, Grace had suffered a shocking miscarriage, and Liv had buried her husband. They'd connected over cupcakes and bonded over loss, eventually promising to be one another's lifelines.

Although right then, it felt as if they were lifting the rope just out of reach.

"Only that you deserve some magic." Avery's face softened. "I survived because I received a kidney transplant, but I am living because my mom showed me how to be more than a survivor—she showed me how to be a warrior," Avery said, her voice so full of conviction Liv felt her chest swell. "That was her biggest gift to me. And it's a gift you can give Paxton."

Avery took Liv's hand. "You are an amazing mom and friend, and your devotion to Paxton is breathtaking. But you are more than a mom and a widow, just like he's more than his condition. You deserve to have things in your life that make you happy."

Liv wanted to be happy—she really did. But she didn't know how to do that without losing focus. She'd pieced their lives back together like a patchwork quilt—she'd found a job, figured out how to change a flat and fix the garbage disposal, and even weathered two winters at high altitude. But happy? That still hadn't happened.

"Which is why I want to volunteer to help with Wagon Days," Liv offered. "I hear they need some extra hands. I happen to have two available." She wiggled them for show.

Her friends looked at her as if she were crazy.

"What? It's a great way to get involved in the community," she defended.

"You do know that the State Line Seniors are hosting the first annual Carson City Campout and Carnival the same weekend as Wagon Days?" Grace asked.

"How is that an issue?"

"Because the State Line Seniors have been trying to one-up the Women of the Wagon Trail since the state line was drawn," Avery pointed out. "They hired some fancy carnival company to bring in rides for the kids and a paintball alley for the teens and dads. They booked Adelle to perform and even got Cesar Millan as a judge for their Pets on Parade."

"The dog whisperer to the stars?" Grace asked, shaking her head. "There goes the Wagon Days Darlings for the parade."

"Did you say Adele?" Liv asked, wondering just how connected these State Line Seniors were—and how bad it would be if she found herself in Carson City.

"Adelle Lewis," Mavis said from behind, a group of blue-haired biddies standing in her wake. "She was Miss Nevada 1956. Won her crown by maneuvering her baton and tassels in a perfect horizontal twirl. But her real claim to fame is her immunity to gravity."

"With Adelle and her tassels, we'll lose the Moose Lodge, Senior X-Treme, and the Sequoia Senior Guard," Patty Moberly said, coming forward. "The carnival rides take away the families, and without them our parade is sunk, and LuLu has worked so hard."

"The parade is the kickoff for the weekend," Shelia, the head of the parade committee, said, stepping out from behind Mavis. "It's what gets people in town and ready to spend a day at the fair. Without a parade there is no fair. The schools count on the money. Last year's event funded the kids' music program."

It also funded the academic-outreach program for kids who had a hard time merging into mainstream schooling. Kids like Paxton.

"Which is why we need to rethink our game plan. Give residents and tourists a reason to come here," Irene, the Wagon Days chairwoman and Avery's mother-in-law, said.

"Maybe we can bring back the Mango Mamas. I heard that the lead singer is almost recovered from her stroke," Shelia suggested.

"Their mangoes are too ripe to stand up to Adelle's tassels." Mavis shook her head. "We need an overhaul."

"Wagon Days is in three weeks, and there isn't time to change everything." Irene held up a three-inch worn leather binder. "This is every contact, sponsor, committee list, map, and booth that has been approved for this year's Wagon Days." She slid it across the table. "I'm not willing to do everything needed to change a year's worth of work."

A symphony of *amen* and *uh-huh* arose, and the room filled with suggestions and opinions, people dividing into two sides, arguing about patchwork quilts versus a party barge.

Liv wasn't crafty or into boating, and she didn't know who the Banjo Brothers with the flaming fiddle were, but there was one thing Liv did know. Years in the ER had taught her how to manage and solve problems.

As Dr. Brown had pointed out, Liv was great at finding common ground. What she needed to work on was her ties to the community. And maybe this was the way to do both.

She ran a finger down the spine of the binder and felt her heart give a little jump. Because it was more than lists and ideas—it was three generations' worth of stories and friendships and traditions. Traditions Sam had been a part of.

Traditions she wanted her son to experience.

She picked up the binder to flip through it. The corners were worn, the leather touched until it felt like butter. But inside sat a treasure trove of connections and opportunities. Opportunities to grow and build roots, two things her little family needed.

"I'll do it," Liv heard herself saying. She even looked down to realize she was standing, her hands sweating from the sudden shift in attention. Meaning she was the center of everyone's attention.

Instead of smiles of delight, Liv was met with horrified gasps, and Gretchen, their oldest member, checked her hearing aid. "Didn't the girl just move here?" Gretchen asked.

"Two years ago. Long enough to appreciate the traditions, but fresh enough to have a new perspective," Liv said, wondering when she'd become the kind of person to get involved. She looked at her friends. "Right?"

"You still walk around like a deer in the headlights when it snows and a neighbor asks if you need your driveway shoveled," Avery said innocently.

"Because I can shovel my own driveway." And clean her own gutters, mow her lawn, and when she really wanted to have fun, she changed the oil in her car. "And with your help, I can make this event representative of the entire community. The founders as much as the newest generation."

"We need some young families to breathe new life into the event," Mavis agreed. "Leapfrog races and panning for gold aren't doing it anymore. Kids nowadays want interaction, adventure, thrills, and unless we give them something new, the State Line Seniors won't be our only problem."

To Liv's surprise, a wave of bobbing gray buns flew through the room. A burst of warmth skated through her body, and deep down, Liv knew this moment was important. For the town and for her.

"What if we sprinkle some new booths in, add some local celebrities to the parade, and find some entertainment that would appeal to the whole family? If we play to our strengths, we can figure this out."

"Backwoods Brewhouse has more than a dozen local craft brews on tap. I bet a craft beer booth would bring in the male demographic," Avery said with an encouraging wink.

"People always tell me that they'd love to see more notable artists come," Grace added. "If we played this off like more of a craft beer and art festival and less like a small-town fair, I know of several artists who would show up."

Shelia frowned. "But we are a small town. That's what makes us special!"

"What makes us special is our community." Liv looked at the group, and a small spark lit in her belly. It wasn't just hope, it was a challenge. And Liv loved a good challenge. "There isn't a resident in town that one of us isn't connected with. Why not ask them and then plan a day that speaks to everyone?"

"I think we just got ourselves a new entertainment chair," Mavis said, and the circle of smiles was enough to make Liv feel as if she'd gained a gold star of approval, but that didn't mean the commitment was any less terrifying.

"Finding help in this town is easy," Irene said. "Especially with those mommy friends of yours."

"Mommy friends?"

Liv didn't have many mommy friends. Most of the moms in town with kids Paxton's age were CMOs. Career mommy officers who played

Supermom by day and Wonder Wife by night. Liv was a single working parent who pulled split shifts to pay the mortgage and fed her kid cheesy noodles and nuggets because she forgot to go shopping.

CMOs and SWPs didn't live in the same space-time continuum, which was why Liv's two closest friends were career women.

"If we have any hope of relating to the next generation of young families, we need to hear what they have to say," Mavis explained. "And who better to do that than one of their own?"

"And that would be me?"

◆ ◆ ◆

Liv was still thinking about what Avery had said when she pulled up to the park. One glance out the window told her that she'd need more than a binder and a little magic if Paxton was ever going to find his permanent smile.

In the distance, she spotted a group of kids in blinking tennis shoes and brightly colored capes racing around in circles playing a complicated version of freeze tag with lightsabers and balloons. Their laughter carried throughout the park and penetrated Liv's chest, swelling up until she wanted to cry.

Oh, Pax, she thought helplessly, watching her little boy in his red Superboy cape and brave smile, pacing the perimeter of the park—all alone.

Where was his team? And where were the counselors? And why weren't the other mothers getting involved?

If that hadn't been her son wandering alone, Liv would have pulled Paxton aside and told him to invite the new kid into the group. But the CMOs just stood at the other side of the parking lot in coordinated sports tops, grouped around their hubby-maintained SUVs, talking about the latest trick to get kids to eat broccoli.

Liv wanted to call bullshit.

The superhero camp brochure promised positive social interaction, team building, and fun. Lots of fun for all. Even the shy ones. The only thing Liv saw was one big suckfest!

Unfortunately, Paxton agreed. His posture said it all as his blinking shoes scuffed the ground, while he held Superdog Stan to his chest as if it was his only friend in the whole world. It wouldn't be so bad if Paxton preferred to be the lone wolf, but he didn't. Her son was bright and beautiful and craved connection.

He just didn't know how to go about it.

The camp counselor, Captain Jason, a local firefighter dressed in a costume that was somewhere between Hercules and George Jetson, called them in, and the kids went rushing to the picnic area, which was decorated to look like the Hall of Justice. Captain Jason handed out red and blue handkerchiefs, dividing the group into two.

One by one the kids took a side until there was only Paxton left. His eyes were big with want, but when Captain Jason held up the two handkerchiefs, Paxton froze.

"You got it, baby. Just point to the red one." Liv knew he wanted the red one—red was Superdog's color—but he didn't even move when Jason waved it his way.

Liv opened the door, ready to scream that he wanted red, when she paused.

One of the other boys, Tommy, a neighborhood kid with whom Paxton sometimes shared comic books, grabbed the red handkerchief and waved him over. Liv held her breath as Paxton picked up the pace and raced across the field. But instead of standing next to Tommy, her son took the material and then stood a few feet behind. Holding himself apart from the group.

Liv glanced at the moms on the other side of the parking lot, and a wealth of guilt welled up, filling her chest until all the denial and anger and helplessness she'd clung to spilled out, leaving nothing but acceptance.

And the reality that maybe the girls were right. She'd been so busy watching out for Paxton, she hadn't realized that Paxton had been watching her.

Liv had moved him here so her son could grow up in the town his father loved. In a place that valued family and friendship. Yet neither of them had allowed themselves to enjoy everything Sequoia Lake had to offer. They'd been too busy trying to survive to have fun.

And they both desperately needed to stretch their wings and find some fun.

Liv glanced in the rearview mirror and cringed at the woman she saw looking back. The messy bun, the tired eyes, the hollow smile. And the wrinkles.

She leaned forward to inspect her forehead. When had those appeared?

Fingers on her temples, she tugged and tugged until they flattened out, and then she smiled her brightest smile.

"Now you just look scared." She let go and watched them bounce back into place, cursing gravity.

Riffling through her purse, she applied a layer of lip gloss, then let her hair free from the messy bun and narrowed her eyes—getting up close and personal with herself. "Your son needs to be a warrior, so time to get busy fixing that."

Liv gave her hair a little fluff and put a welcoming smile on her face. She was done hoping and praying for tomorrow to be better, so she was going to bring the better.

Feeling stronger, she hopped out of the car, and when her foot hit the asphalt, she felt something deep inside shift. And when she took that first step, it wasn't just a step, it was a strut.

A *Mama's almost got her groove back* strut that took her across the parking lot and straight for her biggest insecurity. The career moms who did it all and did it well. She was zeroing in, ready to put it all on the line, even if it meant hosting Scrapbook Saturdays, when a big man wearing a bright orange SAR shirt and department-issued ball cap pulled up in a Jeep.

"You look determined," came the masculine voice from within the car. "Where are you running to?"

Harris peeked his head out the window, and Liv's heart gave a disappointed thump.

"I was going to go talk with the other moms while I waited for camp to let out," she said. Harris looked at the other moms, then back to her, and raised an amused brow. "You know, in case they're looking for a backup cutter for Scrapbooking Saturday."

He hopped out of the Jeep, and *woo wee*, was the man big. Funny, built, and did amazing things to his uniform. Half the town was in love with him, and the other half were men.

"Scrapbooking Saturday has been moved to Tuesday nights at my place because it conflicted with summer T-ball practice," he said, resting a hip against the grill, dead serious. "You're always welcome to join in. You can even bring Paxton. The kids all play in the backyard."

Oh yeah, when he wasn't flying his chopper and saving lives, he was the single parent to an adorable little girl, making him the complete package. Only, for whatever reason, his package didn't do anything for her.

"I'm not really into scrapbooking, but I'm branching out."

"I have more stickers and paper than I could ever use." He winked. "And I make a great cosmo—just ask the ladies."

"I bet." Liv laughed easily. She knew Harris well enough from the kids' preschool, but he was also related to Avery's husband, so they socialized from time to time. "Is Emma enrolled in superhero camp?"

"Yeah, and Friday is my day to bring Popsicles, but we won't be here. I was hoping to see if someone would swap days with me."

Liv put on her best *one with the community* smile. "Well, I don't have a Popsicle day. I could fill in."

"No Popsicle day?" he asked in mock horror.

"I was late in signing Paxton up for the camp, so I didn't make it to the parent meeting. Actually, I was surprised when they called and said they had an open spot, all paid for. I heard that this camp had a waitlist that's like a year long."

"It does," Harris said in a tone that she couldn't decipher. "Moms start registering their kids before their second ultrasound. I guess you just got lucky."

"I know," Liv said. "So since I didn't get an official day, I'll just take yours, if you'll do me a favor." Harris lifted a brow. "I'm helping out with Wagon Days, creating a new and improved family fun zone, and I need help with permits and crowd control. Irene's binder said that was all handled by Sequoia Elite. Will you help me with all the paperwork?"

His lips tilted up at the corners. "As long as you don't yell at me like you did when I tried to carry your trash cans up your driveway."

"I didn't yell," she said. "I was just letting you know that I was getting to them and they were on the list."

"It was almost time for the next garbage pickup." She didn't even bother to argue, and that seemed to appease him. "Come to the station on Friday, and I'll help you file everything that needs filing."

"And I'll bring Popsicles," she said, patting herself on the back and telling herself that wasn't so hard.

"Oh, you can't just take my day. No, no, no. That's not how's it done. It all needs to be cleared through the TSP." When Liv just looked at him, he laughed. "The Stroller Patrol. It's on par with the president's cabinet, only instead of running the country, they run our kids' social lives. It's fascinating. You haven't lived until you've gone to a TSP meeting."

"I'm not really a committee person." Even though she'd just joined one. "I was just going to introduce myself."

"Good luck with that." Before she could ask what that meant, he threw an arm around her shoulder. "Afterward, we'll talk about your shirt."

Liv looked down. "What's wrong with my shirt?"

Harris didn't answer, just dragged her toward the group of moms, who all perked up the second he came into view. The closer they got, the more animated the mothers became.

"Hey, guys," Harris said by way of greeting. "This is Paxton's mom, Olivia Preston. She's offered to cover my Popsicle day for me."

Liv waited for the polite nods, when instead, the head mom, an elegant brunette with perfect hair and a yoga butt, clasped her hands in delight. "Thanks, the kids really look forward to Popsicle day. I'm Kimberly, by the way, Will's mom, and this is Lara."

One by one, Kimberly named off every mother and respective child, then turned back to Liv.

"Nice to meet you all," she said, looking up at Harris as if saying, *Well, that was easy.*

She went to move toward the field so she could see Paxton when Harris anchored her in place. "Liv is also in charge of entertainment for Wagon Days this year."

"Thank God they have one of us on the committee," Kimberly said as if Martha Stewart herself had appeared.

Liv looked at Harris. "One of us?"

"The TSP," he told her. "I guess you're an official member."

Liv almost asked if she was going to be pinned with a bright red TSP button, but she held her tongue.

"My boys want to skip it this year to go to the carnival in Carson City. They can't stop talking about the fire truck–shaped bounce house with shooting water hoses. But that drive with three little ones?" Lara shivered. "I'd rather give birth to the twins again."

"And she's talking natural birthing," Kimberly added.

Liv pulled out her cell, swiped to her notebook, and started a fresh list. "What would get your boys excited to go to Wagon Days?"

Kimberly looked at the other ladies and then let out an excited breath. "Fire."

Liv choked. "What?"

"Every year, on the weekend before school starts, we set up a huge tent on the lake so the kids can all play together one last time—you know, cement the summer bonds to make the first day less intimidating."

"That's a great idea," Liv said, thinking about last year's epic fail with preschool and how different it would have been if he'd had a buddy or two to walk into class with.

"Our moms did this for us, and we've kept up the tradition," Lara said. "We barbeque, do crafts, play in the lake, and then Harris does an evening bonfire."

"Don't make me sound like such a bro. I'm an expert at bead jewelry and bring a gourmet s'mores bar for the adults," Harris added.

"We've been trying to get something like this done on a bigger scale for Wagon Days," Kimberly said. "Maybe a make-your-own-superhero-cape booth or some kind of bounce house or maze."

"Bounce house and craft booth," Liv said as she jotted it down. "Would you guys be interested in helping run the booth?"

The women all shared an excited look.

"Olivia," Kimberly began, "you just tell us what you need and where you need it, and we will make it happen."

"Okay, then, why don't you start putting together your ideas." And then before she gave in to the urge to hide back in her car, she stuck out her hand. "And by the way, my friends call me Liv."

CHAPTER 7

"I heard you had a magical touch with the ladies," Dorothy Pines, current citizen in need, said, and Ford sighed.

He wanted to argue that it wasn't the touch that was magical but which lady he was touching that was the game changer. But since he was on the job, and the lady in question was a fifty-pound bulldog named Bubbles who'd gotten herself stuck in an air vent, he let it go.

It was Thursday, his shift was coming to a close, and this was the most exciting thing to happen to him since running into Liv on the beach three days ago. Not that he'd seen her since. She'd been playing a one-sided game of Hide-from-the-Neighbor.

On Tuesday she'd been watering her flowers when Ford stepped out on the deck. Liv dove behind the planter, only giving him a reluctant wave when Bullseye sniffed her out for a morning high five to the backside.

Yesterday, he'd spotted her pulling up to get Paxton from camp. She took one look at Ford and bolted into the Bear Claw as if hellhounds were on her heels.

"I'd suggest waiting until she comes out on her own," Ford said, repeating the same advice he'd given on the phone when Dorothy had asked to speak with the department's new K-9 rescue specialist. Harris had sent her call Ford's way, and Ford had thanked him with the finger.

Now he was ass up, with his head stuck in a wall vent, trying to sweet-talk a tank of a dog wearing a teal NAMAS-STAY tank top with matching booties to come out of her hiding spot, while a cluster of grannies in sweatbands and blue tips gathered around to watch the show.

"And here I thought you were the kind of man to take charge," Dorothy clucked.

Ford straightened to find Dorothy right behind him—and Bullseye blinking longingly up at her. "I'm smart enough to know when a woman needs time to warm up," he said. "And she doesn't want me anywhere near her ham hock."

"Well, if we leave her in there, she'll keep gnawing on that ham hock until her rump is too big to squeeze back out of the hole." Dorothy, relying heavily on the wall for balance, did some kind of front-bending yoga pose, then stuck the top half of her body inside the vent.

The bottom half had Ford averting his gaze. Covered in neon-green spandex and body glitter, Dorothy was showing enough saggy skin to make Ford shiver. Granted, she was the senior instructor at Downward-Facing Dog, a pet-friendly yoga studio on the west side of town. Senior in age, not experience, Ford suspected when she almost got herself stuck.

"Depending on how much she's already eaten, you may have to grease her up to get her out," an older woman in a leopard-print leotard and pearls said ever so helpfully from behind.

Bubbles had the body of a snow globe and the stubbornness of a pit bull, so Ford feared that if he didn't do something to appease Dorothy, he'd be called back out to grease down the dog and owner.

"How about I call animal control?" Ford offered. "They have these poles with leashes on the end. Maybe we can drag her out."

"She'll take one look at that dogcatcher's pole and dig her heels in," Dorothy said, standing back up. "It would be like trying to pull an elephant through a straw! Can you imagine?"

Ford took in the older woman's neon-green body suit and pink leg warmers and had a pretty good idea.

"You don't want a hairless dog walking the neighborhood, do you?" she asked.

"Uh, no, ma'am."

"Smart boy," she praised with a smile and a pat—to his tush. "That's why we called you and not animal control, right, ladies?"

Ten sets of silver halos bobbed in unison, and someone from the back said, "Also because we wanted to see if the town's Best Buns were as tight as they looked on Facebook."

Ford remembered the flash at the store the other day and ran a hand through his hair. "Like I explained to you on the phone, search and rescue doesn't handle animal cases."

"Well, Patty said you found her dog, LuLu, in record time, swore that it was a miraculous thing to watch."

Ford looked at the Taser on his hip, because that would be less painful than his week. Ever since word spread that he had rescued Ms. Moberly's dog, people in town had started referring to him as Officer Doolittle. Even the guys at the station had taken to hanging pictures of pets in costume on his locker.

"LuLu was hiding under Ms. Moberly's bed, chewing on a chocolate bar," Ford explained. "Bullseye here sniffed her out in two minutes flat. Nothing miraculous about that."

"Doesn't matter—it's all Wag and Waddle can talk about," she said, sounding put out. "Bubbles and I showed up to our weekly park date, and not a single person mentioned her new pageant outfit. They were too busy yapping about LuLu's return, as if Jesus himself had appeared with a doggy biscuit to give her the strength to hold on."

"That's some story," Ford mused.

"A winning story," Dorothy said. "Then a few days later, my Bubbles, last year's Wagon Days Darling runner-up, winds up in a grimy vent gnawing on a stolen slab of ham big enough to feed a whale. Which is what she'll look like if we don't get her out of there. This is her year, and Patty knows how hard Bubbles has been working to get her figure back after the last batch of puppies."

Ah, Christ. Ford knew where this was going. In fact, the entire situation was making his head spin. Or maybe it was all the sweatbands and saggy breasts on display. Either way, Harris was in for a come-to-Jesus meeting when he got back to the station. "So you think Ms. Moberly stuck Bubbles in the air vent?"

"No," she said on a sniffle, and Ford cupped the bill of his hat. "Bubbles went in there on her own to get a few minutes' peace from the demands of motherhood. But I think Patty saw the human-interest angle, knew it would give us an edge with the mommy demographic, and threw in the hot ham hock when I disappeared to call you."

"She cooked the ham hock in the five minutes it took to call me?"

"*Hot* as in stolen. She grabbed it right out of the butcher display over at the Bunny Slope Supermarket." The older woman looked overcome with distress. "Don't you understand?" she cried.

Ford was afraid he didn't. He didn't understand how he'd busted his ass to become one of the most sought-after K-9 rescue officers in the industry, only to be trapped in Mayberry handling neighbor feuds and dog-tampering cases.

Because you're scared of a damn mountain.

Not that it was a completely foreign concept. He'd felt trapped back in Reno. Staying there hadn't been an option. Reexamining old cases, second-guessing past decisions, until the second-guessing caused him to make shit decisions. Decisions that made him a risk to his teammates and subjects. So he'd come here, to close the file on the one case he couldn't seem to let go of. Only the case was closed, but he still felt trapped.

The truth was, Ford had felt trapped ever since his dad disappeared, leaving behind more questions than Ford could ever solve. Wasn't sure he even wanted to. Because what person would want to know, with certainty, that his father's love had limits? Or exactly what he was lacking that made him so easily disposable?

Douglas Jamison was a private man who one day decided domestic life wasn't for him, and he left behind a wife and son without warning.

Ford still remembered his mom pleading with the police to find her husband, swearing that there must be a problem because her husband would never run off and leave his son. The cleaned-out closet and missing personal items told a different story. A story Ford didn't understand until his mom admitted, many years later, that Ford was the result of a long-term love affair.

His father was a private pilot for an oil company who had another family on the other side of the country. When his wife discovered the truth, she gave him an ultimatum.

Ford was merely collateral damage.

Over the years, he'd watched in awe as people searched the globe for their missing loved ones. Ford's dad knew where his son lived, but he never once came searching for the missing love that had shaped Ford's life.

"Bubbles's campaign is sunk," Dorothy cried, gripping her chest with such force it challenged the support of her sports top and had Ford looking down, where he saw Bullseye studying the woman's fuzzy leg warmers—as if they were Lambkins's long-lost cousin.

Ford gave a stern look and shook his head. Bullseye ignored this, his eyes trained on the pudgy old lady with nuzzle-worthy legs.

"I can already see the headlines in the *Acorn Gazette*: 'Pageant princess blows the crown for a piece of cheap meat.' I bet Patty's already given them the ex-ex"—*sniff, sniff*—"exclusive," Dorothy cried, Bullseye noticing the way her voice squeaked. Much like a chew toy.

"Nothing will turn off the mommy voters like a shoplifting sc-sc-scandal."

Head low to the ground, mouth twitching in anticipation, Bullseye slowly moved forward.

"Bullseye, no," Ford said sternly.

Bullseye stopped, his eyes darting from the pink furry legs to Ford with an excited *Baby?* look, to which Ford gave a *Lambkins is in the car* lift of the brow. With a dramatic huff, Bullseye hobbled over obediently and lay by Ford's side.

"I'll make sure there's no mention of the ham hock in my report," Ford said seriously, as if this were an actual case.

Dorothy stopped crying and dabbed her eyes. "Are you going to help my Bubbles, then?"

Ford cupped the bill of his hat and pulled it low. "On two conditions."

"Anything," she promised, taking his hands in her pudgy ones.

"Not a single mention of the words *miraculous, celestial, holy, godlike,* or *supernatural,*" he said, ticking them off on his fingers.

"How about *transcendent*?"

Ford shook his head. "Nothing that implies divine intervention or I will confirm the rumor that Bubbles was in possession of stolen meat."

A collective gasp filled the studio, and one of the ladies moved to light the sage candle.

"I have a jar of baby food in my trunk. Blueberry Buckle flavor, a search dog's biggest weakness. It can tempt even the most timid of dogs down a hundred-foot ravine." He stuck out his hand. "Do we have a deal?"

Dorothy studied his hand, pausing before she took it. "What's the second condition?"

Ford smiled. "You tell everyone who asks that it was Harris Donovan whose quick thinking and even quicker response saved Bubbles. And then you give them this number."

Ford scribbled down Harris's personal mobile number and handed it to Dorothy.

She stuffed the paper in her cleavage, then shook his hand. "You got yourself a deal. Now go and get my baby."

It took Ford two minutes and a jar of baby food to extract Bubbles from the vent, and another hour and a half to convince Chuck the butcher, who wanted his name in the paper, not to press charges against a dog.

Wondering if his day could get any worse, Ford headed toward the front of the market. He smelled like incense and cold cuts, his uniform was coated in dog fur, and his shift had ended well over an hour ago.

He picked up a six-pack from the refrigerated section, not sure what the rest of his night would entail, but he knew it would involve a hot shower and a cold beer.

However, as his luck would have it, he stumbled onto something much more interesting on his way to the checkout counter.

Liv was in the freezer section carting around enough Popsicles to feed a small nation and wearing a pair of sweatpants, a red tank top, and matching sequined Converses that made him smile. It wasn't the getup she'd sported last night in his dreams, but he wasn't complaining. Sure, the sweats hid any kind of curves he knew she had going on under there, but that tank top was soft, snug, and showing off her goods.

And that woman had some pretty damn fine goods. A little on the smaller side—and reacting to the chilled environment—but showstoppers all the way.

Ford considered telling her she'd be warmer if she shut the freezer door, but he figured it would make it harder for her to hide from whomever she was hiding from without the frosted door for cover.

In addition to the stealthy peeks she was stealing down the aisle, she was fighting to tug a giant box of Popsicles out of the fridge. The box was winning. In her defense, it was on the top shelf shoved to the back. Meaning that every time she got on her tiptoes to reach, her tank moved up and her sweats moved down, exposing an impressive strip of silky midriff.

Marina Adair

For a guy like Ford, all it would take was a single reach and grab, but since Nurse Cupcake didn't do well with outside help, he leaned a shoulder against the ice cream display case and took in the view.

She gave a little hop-and-squeal move that was all kinds of girlie and a tad bit adorable, causing the door to close on her and nearly shut her inside the unit. But instead of coming out, she plastered herself to the cold door and peeked through the window as if the grim reaper himself were standing on the other side.

"You can always just pull the fire alarm and run out the back," Ford suggested, and Liv jumped into the aisle, the door slamming shut behind her.

She looked down that aisle toward the back, where Chuck was packing giblets, then back to him. "You need to start wearing a bell."

"It wouldn't have helped anyway," he said lightly. "I'm that good." A smile tugged at her lips—not huge, but enough to know that she wanted to laugh. "Did Paxton bring home a penguin, or are you turning in your cupcake scrubs for Popsicles?"

"It's my week to be Popsicle mom," she explained, sounding slightly harassed. "Who knew there were so many different kinds to choose from? Sugar-free, gluten-free, nut-free, all-natural, artificial flavoring but not coloring, dairy-free."

"Can Popsicles have dairy?" he asked with a smile, noticing that all the BS from earlier slipped away until all he could focus on was how easy it was to be around her. He'd noticed it the other night on the beach but couldn't put his finger on what it was.

Soothing. Liv soothed his soul, silenced the what-ifs and vanquished the guilt. Which was ridiculous because being around her should cause all kinds of turmoil.

But it didn't.

"They can also be made in a factory that shells nuts and seeds." She looked up at him as if the fate of the world rested on this one decision.

"What if someone has a nut allergy? Surely they shouldn't be left out of Popsicle Day."

"Why not get a box of each, and then you'll be safe."

She looked at her cart, which had more boxes than kids in superhero camp. "You see my problem."

Ford looked down at her tank, which had SUPERMOM scrawled across the chest in red glitter. And poking out, just above the top curve of the *P* and first *M*, was hard evidence that she was super indeed. "Not a problem from where I'm standing."

Liv looked down and quickly crossed her arms. "Let me guess, you've got a cup of coffee to warm me up?"

"I was going to offer you a hand with the top shelf, but who am I to argue with a lady," he said. "Unless you'd rather ask Chuck for help."

"Don't even say that," she hissed, and before he knew what was happening, Liv had a fistful of his uniform shirt and had him spun around so his back was to the butcher counter, his body shielding her from view.

"What? He's nice, single, got a steady job, and with those meat cleavers for hands, he's defiantly not a rookie. I bet he could help a lady out."

Ford raised his hands to wave Chuck down, and Liv snatched them back.

"He could also keep my freezer filled with lamb chops and mincemeat," she said, peeking around Ford's arm. "But a steady supply of meat isn't what I'm looking for."

So it wasn't just Ford. It was all single men she avoided. Good to know. Not that it helped his ego any.

"What is it you're looking for, then?" he asked, and with a glare she stepped back. She was cute when she was trying to be tough. "Hypothetically speaking, of course."

That got a small smile out of her, but the sparkle in her eyes told him she wasn't falling for it. "It's been so long I don't even know."

"Okay, how about start by answering a few simple questions."

"What? Like favorite color, favorite food, favorite number?" She laughed. "There's more to connecting with someone than how they answered the latest Facebook quiz."

"I was thinking something a little deeper, like, 'Are you willing to have open conversations in order to connect with others?' But we can start with yours. In fact, I'll go first." Ford looked at her top. "At the moment, red, Popsicles, and no one really has a favorite number. Everyone knows the real question is favorite kiss," he said, and the moment the words left his mouth, he regretted it.

Liv froze, which was the exact opposite of what was happening in his chest. Because Sam had just entered the room. That was a lie—Sam had always been there. From day one. Ford had just vocalized what they'd both been ignoring.

"Liv, I—"

"No, go on, tell me how these questions will help me figure everything out." She folded her arms in a stance that was so far from warm and friendly Ford was afraid his nuts would get frostbite.

"Not everything," he said softly, apologetically. "But it might be a good starting point to talk about the kinds of things that pique your interest. For me it would be smart, sassy, and someone who can rock a pair of cupcake scrubs like nobody's business," he said jokingly, trying to get the lightness back. "In case you were wondering."

"I wasn't. But now that you mention it, I guess I like honest, easy to read, someone who doesn't have to rely on beef-rib bouquets or charming one-liners. It should just happen naturally."

Well, that went smoothly, he thought, looking down at the challenging spark in her eyes. Hating himself when he saw the raw ache behind it.

"Message received loud and clear," he said. "But you've got to start somewhere. I get that it won't be with me, but you need to put yourself out there."

CHAPTER 8

Friday afternoon, Ford arrived at the station expecting to find Harris busy in his office fielding calls from citizens in need. Instead, his desk was covered with missing pet reports dating back a decade, but Ford's boss was absent. Maybe on a call. Which meant that Ford was free to eat his lunch in peace.

Only when he got to his office, Harris was sitting behind his desk, feet propped up, with a blonde in his lap. A giggling pixie of a blonde with big blue eyes, wearing ballet shoes and a tiara.

"Hey, Emma," Ford said to Harris's daughter, who was already scrambling off his lap trying to get at Bullseye. But unlike other kids who would launch into a dog, Emma stopped at Ford's feet and looked up, her hands behind her back, little hips swaying. "Mr. Ford, can I play with Bullseye, or is he still working?"

Ford looked over at his dog, who hadn't worked a day since they'd arrived, and said, "He's on a break, so have at it."

Emma bounced on her toes, the skirt of her dress moving like a pogo stick. "Can I take him into Daddy's office?"

Ford looked at Harris and gave a smug-ass grin. "I don't see why not. It's probably quieter in there, more room to play too."

"I have a bunch of files on my desk," Harris said.

Ford waved a hand and sat down in the spare chair. "She'll be careful, won't you, Emma?"

"Very," she promised, and looked up at the toughest son of a bitch Ford knew, decimating him with a single dimple. There was something so comical—and endearing—about watching it.

Harris's world revolved around someone small enough to fit in a rucksack.

"All right, but only for a few minutes because we have to leave for dance soon." Which explained why Harris's SAR uniform had been replaced with sweatpants and a SHE'S MY SUGARPLUM FAIRY T-shirt.

Emma raced out the door with Bullseye hot on her trail. They hadn't even slammed the office door when Emma pulled out her favorite Disney doll, and Bullseye let out a contented yowl.

Ford looked at Harris's pink knee brace and smiled. "Who's the princess, you or her?"

"It's her first dance class, and parents are encouraged to join their kids. Emma picked out the brace," Harris explained. "And since I'm Emma's only parent, that means I get to spend my afternoon off doing pirouettes or some shit. And tonight, when you and the guys go to the bar to watch the game, I'll be at home playing Emma's version of *Chopped* because I haven't gone shopping. Do you know why I haven't gone shopping?"

Ford felt like a jerk. "Because you've been busy fielding calls about lost pets?"

Harris rested his elbows on the desk and leaned in—so close that Ford could see he meant business. "No, because if I had gone shopping, then there would be no need to make a mash-up of food for dinner. And Emma's favorite dinners are mash-ups, like coconut-crusted chicken and chocolate-chip mashed potatoes. Do you understand what I'm saying?"

It was obviously a rhetorical question, because Harris didn't wait for an answer.

"Being a single parent is hard. Rewarding, but hard as hell," he said. "It takes sacrifice and worrying—a lot of worrying about if you're doing the right thing. Because the kid comes first, always, even before your own happiness. Which can make for some pretty lonely nights. So lonely, sometimes—"

"Whoa," Ford said, standing. "Are we talking about your sex life? Because I'm not cool with knowing how you spend those lonely nights. If you need a sitter, just ask."

"I'm talking about how you spend *your* nights, Ford."

"Again, not comfortable with the direction of this conversation," Ford pointed out, unsure if he was amused or confused by the direction the conversation was taking.

"Well, it's about to get a hell of a lot worse than uncomfortable." Harris slid a letter across the desk toward Ford, but he didn't let go. "I had a chat with one of the moms at Emma's camp the other day. I didn't know that her son was enrolled because she wasn't at the parent meeting. Seems that there was a lucky spot that opened a few weeks before camp started. It got me thinking, what are the odds that the camp I was talking to you about and happened to mention a random opening was filled by Sam's son?"

"Fuck." Ford sat in the chair and leaned back.

"Oh, you're more than fucked, because this just gets better." This time Harris let go of the file, but Ford didn't need to look at it to know what it was. A clear sign that his time here was up.

"I can explain," Ford said.

"I hope to Christ you can, because I'm not sure there's a way to explain how the camp tuition, of a kid you rescued, was covered by an anonymous donation that—oh, and here's where the fucked comes in— you used Washoe County Search and Rescue funds to cover." Harris shook his head. "What the fuck were you thinking?"

"It wasn't department funds," Ford pointed out. "It was my money. I can prove it. I just sent the money order in an envelope with department letterhead so she wouldn't know it was me."

"Oh man," Harris said, slowly sitting back with the biggest *Oh shit* expression Ford had ever seen. "This is more screwed up than I thought. This isn't about Sam. This is about Liv."

"What? No. This has nothing to do with her." And everything to do with that freaking promise he couldn't let go of.

"Sorry, man, I don't believe you. Because you're running around like some JV player trying to impress the homecoming queen."

His friend's lack of faith hurt like a double shot to the chest. Especially since Ford had meant it when he said it, but suddenly it felt like a lie. And wow, he felt like an idiot.

Had he come here to Sequoia Lake with the goal of swooping in like some kind of fly-by-night hero and impressing her? Damn straight he had, because if he did manage to impress her, then maybe she'd manage to forgive him. And eventually he could forgive himself.

"I don't want her to think of me as some hotheaded rookie who made an impulsive decision that ended up costing her husband's life," Ford admitted. "I hope she never finds out what happened that day, but if she ever does, I don't want her to think that her husband was lost because some FNG didn't know what he was doing, didn't understand what was at stake."

"You might have been new to the team, but you were far from a fucking new guy, Ford," Harris said evenly.

Ford swore and rested his head in his hands. He took a deep breath, but it didn't help. Nothing helped. The anger and frustration and guilt—a hell of a lot of guilt—had coiled in his stomach tighter and tighter until he'd gone numb with regret.

He'd tried to ignore it, tried to bury himself with work, but that hadn't helped either. Which was why he'd missed his certification. Ford could hike up that twelve thousand feet and sleep in subzero temperatures a million times over, but it wouldn't change that night. Wouldn't give him his unflappable calm back. Ford would always question his intuition, his decisions, and hesitating wasn't an option when in the field.

Problem was, the field was the only place Ford excelled. And if he couldn't let go, find some sort of peace with memories so he could sleep at night, then he was going to lose that too.

"I sent the chopper back," he heard himself say. "When we got the call, we were briefed that it was a single male in his midthirties who'd skidded off the mountain and down into a ravine. We knew he'd left his car on foot and was probably headed toward one of the caves by the river for shelter."

Ford blinked away the image of the accordioned SUV, hood dug into a snowbank, the windows missing, the doors and roof shredded from the hundred-foot slide down a jagged mountainside. He would have thought it was bad intel if they hadn't seen the footprints leading away from the wreckage.

"The chopper lowered me down right as word came that the storm had turned. I knew if the team didn't get out right then, they'd be stuck." He looked up and met his friend's gaze head-on, ready to accept whatever came at him. "I sent them back to base camp."

Harris blew out a pained breath. "You made the right call. Safety first, subject second. If they'd stayed, then another team would have been sent out and in danger as well."

"I saw the empty car seat," he admitted. "I saw it and could have called them back, but I thought, *What kind of asshole would have his kid out at three in the morning in a storm like this?*" Ford choked on a humorless laugh. "The kind of asshole who was trying to get his son back to his mother for Christmas morning."

Ford had just come off a three-day search in a nearby mountain range and was so tired he'd forgotten it was Christmas Eve. It wasn't as if he had family to rush home to spend the holidays with. But Sam had, and he never made it.

"That's every rescuer's worst nightmare. A call nobody wants to make, but you made it, and you made the right call."

"How do you know?" Ford yelled, then cupped the bill of his cap so he didn't have to look at his friend. Because what guy wants to lose his shit in front of his buddy?

And just great, now Harris was standing and coming around the desk to sit in the chair next to Ford. Like he thought Ford was a delicate flower.

"Because I know you," Harris said simply, and Ford's throat tightened. "And I know that valley, how hard it is to navigate a Bell Ranger through there when the winds are whipping, and how dangerous it would have been to try to land in that storm. And if you still don't believe me, then know this—any other search team on the planet wouldn't have plowed into that storm and come out with a survivor."

Ford waited for the guilt to subside, waited for his heart to finally catch up with his brain and admit he'd made the right call. But whatever freedom he'd hoped would come from this confession never came. "I start to believe it, and then I get called out to some site, and once I hear that a kid is involved, I start thinking about Paxton and how Christmas will forever be the day his dad died, and all of the what-ifs and doubts come back."

"You start giving in to the what-ifs and you'll never get out from under them," Harris said.

Ford slid him a sidelong glance. "Every time that kid sees another dad, takes up baseball, makes it through his first day of school, he's going to wonder about his dad. He won't be able to let it go, so I guess it's only fair that I can't either."

Harris turned his body toward Ford and rested his elbows on his knees. "Because of you he gets to play baseball and go to his first day of school. And he's got an amazing mom who loves him. Emma's only got one parent, and trust me, that kid is loved."

"He barely smiles."

"Neither do you."

"He doesn't talk."

"And Emma can talk a doorknob deaf. Kids are different. And every call-out is different, which is why when you hand over your case file at the end of a rescue, you hand it all over. You walk away and know that you did all you could do. That job is finished."

"It doesn't feel finished," he said. "I made a promise to Sam that I would make sure Liv was okay."

Harris laughed. "Have you met the woman? She is the most stubborn, independent person I've ever met. Well, besides you."

She was also the loneliest. Looking at Liv was like looking at his mother. Too proud to take help, too tired to enjoy her life. She'd always said she'd get to the fun part later, but Ford had been a wild kid, and for his mom, later never came.

He refused to do that to another woman.

"Independent doesn't mean happy," Ford said.

"So, then, what's your plan?" Harris asked. "You make friends with the kid, flirt with his mom a little and make her feel special—"

"What's wrong with making her feel special?" Ford argued, his shoulders tensing. "Everyone wants to feel special, and there's nothing wrong with flirting."

"She's not just anyone, and you're going back to Reno in a few weeks," Harris pointed out, and Ford felt his hands tighten. "Then what? The next birthday or holiday rolls around, you send another unsigned gift?"

Ford dropped his head in his hands again, because no matter how much he wanted to deny the scenario, he couldn't. Past actions—and a ton of desperation—had him asking, "What do you suggest?"

"Have you considered telling her the truth?"

Ford looked up through his brows. "That I made her husband a promise that turned me into her mystery benefactor?"

"I was thinking more of an *I'm the one who rescued your son, and your husband loved you.* But coming clean is always a good thing when it involves a beautiful woman."

"I don't want her to relive his death." *And hate me.*

"But it's okay that you do?" Harris asked. "Because that's selfish thinking, man. The longer you hold on to this, the longer your team goes without its leader. Sam didn't make it, but Paxton did. What other kid is going to need you when you're riding a desk and handling missing senior calls?"

Ford would find a new career before it came to that.

Harris let out a tired breath. "I can't believe I'm going to say this, but what if you got to know her a little? Let her get to know you. She can see you're a skilled officer, and you can see that she's doing fine. Then you can walk into that certification clearheaded and guilt-free."

"Are you saying I'm not fired?" Ford asked, wondering when another few weeks of settling dog disputes had become important.

"Not yet," Harris said with a smile. "As long as you promise not to mess with the single-mom code."

"I'm not into single moms or taking advantage of vulnerable women." Although Liv hadn't looked like a mom the other night in her sundress and bare feet.

"You think Liv is the vulnerable one here?" Harris let out a big, obvious laugh and clapped him on the shoulder. "Man, good luck with that."

◆ ◆ ◆

Two hours later, Ford was still trying to figure out what Harris had meant by his comment. Not that he was going to ask the prick, since

Harris had Ford reviewing a pile of volunteer forms for the new K-9 trailing team.

Harrison wanted a solid team of ten identified by the time Ford left, but after flipping through the applicants, he knew he'd be lucky to find one person who had the time to dedicate to becoming a solid team member. It wasn't qualified applicants he was lacking. There were a dozen or more who were fit outdoor enthusiasts—and working sixty-hour-a-week careers. What he needed were people who had the time to train their dogs and the flexibility to drop everything at a moment's notice for a call-out.

He was just finishing up a call to Ms. Pines, who was asking if he'd received the flowers she'd sent for helping rescue Bubbles, when there was a knock at the door.

Ford looked at the horseshoe of white lilies in the corner of the room, then at Bullseye, who was eyeing the cluster of THANK YOU helium balloons that Ms. Moberly had sent more than an hour after the flowers arrived.

Another knock sounded.

Needing a vacation from his vacation, Ford said, "Come in."

The door opened, and in walked the prettiest bouquet he'd ever seen. Liv looking fresh-faced in a yellow sundress with tiny little white flowers on it and even tinier straps. In fact, the whole thing seemed to be held up by this belt that was thin enough to snap with a single tug, and it was fastened right under her morning glories.

Holy hell, her morning glories—something Ford was doing his best not to notice, but when they were placed on display the way they were, it made not looking impossible. So he gave himself one glance, a split second to take it all in, in one of those forget-what-you-saw kind of situations that made his head spin.

And okay, maybe it was two seconds, but Ford was a morning-glory aficionado—and Liv deserved a blue ribbon.

"Nurse Cupcake," he said, standing, uncertainty weighing heavily.

Bullseye let out a joyous bark and raced over to give her a big doggy welcome to the office, which included running around her legs and getting hair all over her dress. Not that she seemed to mind.

"Hey, Bullseye," she said, giving him a big scratch that had the dog's eyes rolling back into his head. One last belly rub—lucky dog—and Liv straightened. Her expression was as uncertain as Ford's heartbeat. "I didn't mean to interrupt."

"Just being the department receptionist."

She smiled, small, but it gave him hope. "I came to ask some questions about permits, and I saw you in your office and decided to see if you had a minute." She looked around the office, her lips curving when she saw the balloons. "But you look busy. Was there a funeral I didn't know about, or did I miss your birthday?"

"More like I got stuck in the middle of a feud," he said, feeling himself relax.

"Yes, the great Baby Bubbles in the Vent rescue—I heard about it from several of my patients," she informed him primly. "There's even talk about selling Team Doolittle T-shirts at Wagon Days."

"Please tell me you're making that up," he moaned.

"Sorry, you're a big-time hero around here."

Ford considered her warm smile and found himself hoping that if she knew the truth she'd still think the same. For some reason, the idea of disappointing her was worse than saying goodbye. "That's a direct result of Harris being an ass."

"That's the result of you being kind." He rolled his eyes, and she laughed. "What? You've made an entire group of residents feel safe and heard. It's sweet."

"Sweet?" he choked. "Somewhere across town Harris just high-fived himself."

She laughed, then leaned in, showing him a little slice of her morning glories encased in black lace. "Most guys would love to have their own fan club."

The only fan he was interested in gaining after yesterday's slip was Liv. Admiration came from compassion and understanding and usually led to respect. And Ford needed her respect to convince her to slow down long enough to enjoy the life she was working so hard to build.

"I'm not most guys," he warned her.

"I've noticed that." She took a deep breath and let it out. "Which is why I wanted to apologize for how I reacted yesterday at the market."

"I was out of line," he said honestly.

"No, you were just being honest," she said, and Ford felt the guilt clog his throat. "I'm not ready for an open conversation because that would require me to be open. And opening up is scary. Which is why I snapped at you."

"You don't have to apologize."

"Yes, I do." She met his gaze head-on. "You said some really sweet things to me the other night, and I didn't know how to handle it, so I hid. But I'm tired of hiding, which is why I've come up with a plan to put myself out there, and I need your help." Liv pulled two files from her purse and held them to her chest. "Based on how I reacted the last time you tried to help, I would understand if it made you uncomfortable. So if you say no, you won't hurt my feelings."

"There you go with the warnings again," he teased, but his shirt felt a little tight around the neck.

"I just like to be up front so no one feels obligated."

Ford didn't feel particularly obligated to anything at the moment. Even his promise to be a stand-up guy for Liv. He was too busy watching the way she worried her lower lip, her eyes never leaving his as if she preferred to see what was coming. Her posture was sturdy, ready for whatever was around the next corner. It was as impressive as it was disheartening.

"As long as there's no casserole involved, we're good."

Liv laughed. "I needed that."

So did he. His chest felt as if it were about to explode with tension. "What's going on, Liv?"

"I need a favor," she asked, and Ford was on board with whatever it was. Because Liv was a petite powerhouse with melt-your-soul eyes and an easy grace that reminded him of a warm summer day in the Sierras. Tempting combination for a guy who'd made a career out of walking into the eye of the storm.

Which was the only reason he could think of for why he said, "Whatever it is, I'm in."

"Really?" she said, her shock causing her to sputter a little. Ford did a little sputtering of his own, because this was exactly how he'd gotten in this mess in the first place. "I haven't even told you what it is."

"You don't have to," he said, doing what Harris told him to do. Get to know her. "You asked, and I said yes."

"But what if I was asking you to come mow my lawn shirtless so I can watch you while I eat a box of Fudgsicles?"

He thought about that and grinned. "Would you return the favor?"

"No," she said quickly. Too quickly, plus the spark in her eyes said that she wasn't as opposed to the idea as she'd thought. And Ford had to admit that Liv was tougher than he'd given her credit for.

"Would I at least get a Fudgsicle when I was done?"

She shook her head. "That would lead to flirting. And while flirting is your second language, it leaves me feeling off balance," she admitted, her tone so genuine his chest clenched. "So if you say yes, then there will be a strict no-flirting rule in effect because this is too important of an opportunity for me to complicate."

Liv's smile didn't falter, but there was something about the way she held the papers to her chest, something as uncertain as the emotion in those big brown eyes that had his warning bells blaring. Maybe it was the way she pulled back inside herself, her emotions rounding down until it was as smooth as a lake, without even a noticeable ripple. Or the fact that she was staring at his mouth. But the easy humor faded, and Ford felt himself being sucked in.

"I'm in charge of entertainment for Wagon Days," she said, and the look of abject horror on her face made him want to laugh.

"I haven't been in town long, but even I know that most women would give their favorite handbag to be approved."

"My favorite handbag is a canvas tote from Bunny Slope Supermarket, and I'm not most women."

"Is that another warning?"

"Just being up front. From my experience, misunderstandings tend to complicate things more."

Her comment should have turned him off, but instead he wanted to see just how complicated things could get. Which was the one thing he'd promised Harris he wouldn't do.

Ford rested his elbows on the desk and leaned in. "So how can I help?"

"Be the celebrity judge for the Wagon Days Darling pageant."

First doggy yoga and now this. Ford dropped his head back against the chair and closed his eyes. The guys were going to give him so much shit.

"And before you answer, remember you already said yes," she reminded him. "But it isn't a big commitment. All you have to do is watch a bunch of dogs parade in front of you, then interview them, and announce the winner at the start of the parade."

He opened one eye. "You want me to interview a dog?"

"I think you interview the owners about their dogs. But hey, you're Officer Doolittle, so you do what feels right."

"Whatever feels right, huh?" he asked, and when she smiled, releasing a sassy grin in his direction, doing the wrong thing had never felt so good. "Fine," he said, resting his forearms on the desk and leaning forward. "But it will cost you."

"Oh," she said softly, and the growing panic in her eyes at the idea of owing him one surprised him.

Yet the way her breath quickened when she did one of those *pretend not to look at his mouth* glances intrigued him. "Cupcakes. One of the fancy ones you had the other night. With all the frosting intact."

She let out a startled laugh. "You drive a hard bargain, but my mom warned me about sharing my cupcake secrets. You tell one person the secret, and the next thing you know everyone in town is using your recipe, and everything that was special is now commonplace."

"I guess your mom left out that the special ingredient is you," he said, watching her closely.

"That," she said a little above a whisper. "That scares me."

"Scares you or challenges you to see yourself differently, Liv? Because that's a big difference."

She thought about that, then finally sighed. "I'm not sure."

He softened his expression. "Then I won't say it again until you're sure."

"I like predictability," she admitted, knowing that they weren't talking about cupcakes any longer. "But I'm starting to see the appeal of the unexpected."

"Your binder says different," he said, looking at the stack of lists and spreadsheets clutched in her hands. They were itemized, color coded, and had more blank boxes than checked ones.

She looked at the dog-eared and worn pages and sighed. "This right here is seventy-five years of history and traditions that prove predictability is overrated." She opened the file and pulled out a stack of printed emails and blog posts. "I looked at what they've done in the past for Wagon Days, and I get why they needed some new ideas. And since the biggest party I've ever planned included myself, Paxton, and his grandparents, I talked to my mom posse."

"You have a mom posse?"

"It's something new I'm trying," she said. "Only it turns out mom posses have ideas. Lots of ideas. And they aren't shy about sharing them."

She spread the contents of the file across his desk, and Ford felt his eyes blur over. There were sketches, magazine clippings, lists, and even color swatches. "Is this a community event or the inaugural dinner?"

"I'm not sure," Liv said. "But I promised to make this Wagon Days amazing, so I have to bring the fun back to the event. Except fun involves a lot of opinions, suggestions, and paperwork."

"I've become a ninja at paperwork. Maybe I can help you with some of it."

"And what will that cost me?" she asked, but instead of looking suspicious, she looked genuinely interested.

"This one's on the house." Ford grinned and picked up a stack of kid-friendly craft ideas to flip through them. "There must be five dozen ideas here."

"And that's just the Stroller Patrol and Living for Love. I haven't talked to the senior center, the Wag and Waddle, or any of the other local clubs." Liv opened the second file and handed Ford a smaller, more realistic stack. They were permit forms, already completed and waiting for a signature. "Here are the top five ideas and the list of local businesses who have agreed to donate the supplies."

He glanced at the firms and gave a low whistle. "When were you appointed?"

"Wednesday."

Impressive. In two days, she'd managed to organize a team, secure donors, and complete the majority of the paperwork for the county. Some of his search teams in Reno weren't this prepared.

"But the new paperwork needs to be signed and in to the county by Tuesday morning. Which means I need to get someone from this department to sign off on it before the city will consider granting me the permit."

She sat back and quietly encouraged him to read the forms. Her eyes following his every move and her teeth worrying that lip again made concentrating on anything else damn hard. But he warriored on.

He turned to the second page and met her gaze. "A bounce-house lagoon and kid-zone island?"

"Yeah, the Stroller Patrol didn't have to worry about gaining departmental approval." She snatched the packet back and handed him a new one. "These are the ones I thought would get kids excited, make parents feel comfortable, and be a slam dunk for your department to approve."

She leaned in to point to the first one, and it took everything he had to keep his gaze on her face, because the V-neckline of her dress puckered, giving him a lovely peek of silky skin and the scalloped edge of what he knew was the black lace from earlier.

"This one is simple," she continued. "It's just a giant tent at the end of Lake Street for a make-your-own Wild West badge for the little ones. I already have the team to run it, and Mavis will donate the fabric. I just need a signature."

"Easy." He scribbled his John Hancock and flipped to the next page. "A s'mores bar?" He looked up at her through his brows. "A raging fire on the middle of the beach is your idea of a permitting slam dunk?"

"A controlled fire on a safe section of the beach, and yes, I thought it would be a fun nighttime thing for the whole family," she explained, her face so animated he couldn't look away. "Ned from Neddy's Lumber and Garden Gnomes offered to donate the wood, and Bunny Slope Supermarket will donate the rest. All I have to do is find the right location."

"And get safety-first Harris to agree to an event that includes giving fire and sticks to a sugared-up pack of preschoolers." He set the papers down. "He'd never sign off on this, and he'd have my ass if I did."

She crossed her arms a bit smugly and said, "Then why did he suggest it?"

"Harris suggested a bonfire and s'mores bar?"

"Adult s'mores bar, but I went with the family-friendly experience," she explained, and Ford corrected his earlier assessment. She wasn't impressive. She was a force.

Nurse Cupcake might be a tiny thing, but she had a will big enough to save the world and enough soft curves to make things interesting.

"Well then, we'll make sure Harris is listed as the officer in charge," Ford said, scribbling his good buddy's name down in the respective box. "What's next?"

"Just wait," she said, flipping the page, the spark in her eyes telling him this was the one she'd come up with. The one that had her smile on full tilt.

She sat back, patiently waiting for him to read the outline. He loved how her eyes followed his every move, proving that her earlier huff was for show, because she was as excited as a kid on Halloween.

Ford got to the grand finale and looked up. "You want to do a fireworks show? You do know that we're in fire country, right?"

"Keep reading—there's more." Her elegant finger pointed to the schedule of events that was long enough to fill a state fair.

He closed the packet and looked her in the eye. "What's your goal here?"

"A perfect old-fashioned carnival to honor the founders of Sequoia Lake, with some added modern pizzazz for the newer generations. A perfect old-meets-new day of fun for the entire family," she said, as if she had this in the bag.

It was complete bullshit, of course, which made him even more eager to help. Her voice was all sweet enthusiasm and big dreams, but her uncertainty was right there beneath the surface, if one knew what to look for.

And when it came to this woman, Ford knew what to look for, and right now she was too busy troubleshooting to have any kind of fun.

"Been rehearsing that long?" he mused.

She sighed. "It sounded good when I pitched it in the mirror today. Better than the whole 'I need to prove to my boss that I can be a company girl.' To do that, I need to prove I'm a community girl and kick the Carson City carnival's butt with the best Wagon Days since its inception."

"That I can help you with," he said. "But the petting zoo, milk-can toss, and gold panning are way too mother-approved to beat out a paint-gun alley with glowing pellets," he said, and she opened her mouth to say *fireworks*—he could see her lush lips forming the sound. "And wagon rides down Main Street and fireworks are permitting nightmares—and not the answer."

She sat back. "Since when did you become an expert on what kids think is cool?"

"Since I started volunteering at a junior search-and-rescue camp a few years back."

Liv looked impressed, as if thinking maybe she'd been wrong about him. "What are you thinking?"

"A challenge course where families and kids work together to complete different obstacles." He took out a pencil and began to sketch a basic map.

Liv leaned in while he was writing, resting her elbows on the other side of the desk and scooting her chair all the way forward. When he finished, he flipped it toward her.

"A log ladder, a mini rock climb, and is that a zip line?" she asked, clearly impressed. And Ford liked impressing her too damn much. "Wow, this is like those team-building camps."

"We could do ground-based courses for the kids and higher events with harnesses for fifteen and up," he explained. "The thrills of a carnival, only in a back-to-nature kind of way that the founders would have loved."

Liv studied the map, her smile becoming more and more real at the idea. "It's like our own little Wild West." She looked up. "But wouldn't this be a huge undertaking? Wagon Days is in three weeks, and even though I want to go big enough to make a splash, I don't want to promise the world only to deliver a petting zoo."

"Every spring, my department teams up with Sequoia Elite to run a junior search-and-rescue camp outside Reno for at-risk kids. We do zip-lining, obstacle courses, and team-building events. We could easily do the same thing here, right by the lake." When she didn't look convinced, he said, "You asked for my help—let me help you."

Liv considered his words for so long one would think he'd asked her to a lace-only sleepover instead of offering to lend a hand at something he happened to be good at. It was going to come down to what she was more afraid of: underdelivering on the town's expectations or letting someone new into her world.

"Help is a new concept for me," she admitted. "But that's what this is about, working with community officials and residents, right?" She released a breath and smiled. "How do you guys plan this course?"

Ford smiled. "Come here."

Ford opened his browser, and the site loaded right as Liv rounded his desk. "Look at this," he said, scooting his chair back so she could slide up to the desk, so close he could feel her body heat.

It couldn't be helped. His office was small, overflowing with flowers and balloons, leaving little room behind the desk. Normally, Ford would have moved out and given her the chair, but she moved in so fast he didn't have time.

"Are these pictures from the camp?" she asked.

"Yes, and all the equipment you see is owned by the department, but Sequoia Lake Lodge has everything we'd need to replicate this. We could even add in a little hiker 101 training to make the moms happy," he said, wondering if she was reneging on the no-flirting rule, since her thigh pressed against him when she bent over to get a better look at the monitor.

He could feel her breathing change, but she didn't move.

"It looks like it requires more than just a ton of equipment." She reached for the mouse, their bodies pressing closer until her hair slid over his forearm. It was silky and smelled good enough to bury his face in.

But she'd said no flirting, and he'd honor that.

"Wouldn't we need trained personnel to run it?" She tapped the screen. "This camp looks like it has one instructor to every ten kids, and we're hoping to have hundreds of kids, all day. Do you have enough people to run that?" she asked, her face willing him to say yes, but preparing herself for the disappointment.

Ford didn't want to be another disappointment. She was putting herself out there, getting involved, asking for help—and he wasn't about to shut her down.

Not when she was so close he could feel her breath mix with his when she spoke.

"We'd have to create a course that required the fewest amount of department hands to run it." Reno was just over an hour away. He could talk a few of his buddies into helping, if necessary. Plus, that's what Harris had told him to do—get to know the lady. "And prove we have enough extra medical personnel on hand for the permits to go through."

"I bet I can get some of the hospital staff to volunteer their time," she said. "My boss wanted a creative way to introduce the Mobile Medic team to the community. I can't think of a more fun and positive first impression to the families in town." She smiled. "This might actually work."

His desk, those lips, this insane chemistry. It could work, all right.

"One call, Liv, and you'd have everything you need."

"Are you sure?" she whispered, her tone saying she wasn't referring to the obstacle course anymore, but the obstacle that stood between them being friends and them being flirting friends.

She wasn't ready. He was leaving. And he didn't even want to think about Sam.

"Trust me."

"Because I don't want to get all excited only to have it blow up in my face," she said quickly.

"Like I said, any kind of fire is out of the question," he assured her. "But making this the best summer on record—I'm all in."

Before he knew what was happening, Liv straightened right as Ford stood, and Bullseye—taking the commotion to mean that it was cuddle time—bolted out from his bed and underfoot.

Liv's foot, to be exact, causing her to collide with Ford's chest. Her one delicate hand went around his neck, and the other pressed against his chest. His hands were no better, as they slid around her waist to steady her, and Bullseye jumped up on both of them to get his group hug on.

"Leave the lady alone," Ford said, batting Bullseye to the ground and telling himself to follow his own advice. But he noticed he still had one hand around her, spanning across her lower back, holding her to him—instead of holding her steady. Which was fitting, since there wasn't anything steady about Ford right then.

His head was spinning and his heart thrashing. He liked being close to her.

Too much.

"Sorry," she said softly, her voice nothing more than a whisper of breath, confirming that he wasn't the only one having a hard time with their no-flirting rule, and her magnolias were as magnificent as he'd imagined.

Checking himself, Ford stepped back, but the damage was already done. Every one of her soft curves was now imprinted on his body, which meant he'd never have to wonder again. Only the lack of wondering led him down a different path of wonder, which included nothing but those curves in his bed.

The pathway to trouble, he told himself, unable to tear his gaze away. And because trouble was a hell of a lot more exciting than filing papers, he said, "I'm not." And then because trouble loved company, he added, "So what time should I pick you up?"

"Pick me up?" she asked, and if she didn't look so completely adorable, he would have laughed.

"If you want Harris to sign off on this, then we need to be strategic on what we ask for and make sure we walk the area to foresee any pitfalls." Even though the only pitfall he could foresee at the moment was what was going to happen when she looked down and noticed that while he'd agreed to the no-flirting rule, other parts were protesting. "So when should I pick you up?"

"I guess this is where I say I'll bring the pizza," she said with a shy smile as she headed toward the door. Only to bump into it. "I have Sunday afternoon off, and Monday I'm working the swing shift at the hospital. Just let me know what works best for you."

Ford was about to ask her how he should contact her, but he was too busy admiring her sweet little jiggle as she opened the door and stumbled out of his office. He took in her lithe body, the way her dress hugged her hips as she moved, and how nicely it stretched across her exceptionally toned butt.

"*Woof!*" Bullseye barked.

He looked down at his dog. "Like you're one to talk."

CHAPTER 9

"I told you to get to know her, not ask her out on a date," Harris said into the headset, the wind and chopper blades muffling his voice.

"It's not a date," Ford shouted back as Bullseye barked into the wind.

Ford was leaning backward off the side of a Super Huey, Bullseye strapped to his side in a doggy Bjorn, with only a helicopter skid and a hundred-foot rope between them and rocky terrain.

Ty was already on the ground below, and because this was a joint training with CalFire, Harris was next to Ford, hooked into his rappelling gear instead of piloting the bird, and Bullseye was harness-on goggles-down, waiting for the go. Today's exercise was supposed to be fast roping into uneven terrain, but Harris was making it an exercise in patience.

Harris could be a whiner.

"As head of community outreach, this is what I do," Ford added.

Harris turned his head toward Ford, and even through his aviator glasses he could clearly make out a *bullshit* expression. "And you're doing it when her kid is at camp?"

"Tomorrow morning was the only day I'm in the office and she had free."

"If you don't stop bitching like a couple of girls and clogging the airways, I might leave you here until Monday," Ty said, his voice booming through the earpiece.

"As the father of a girl, I resent that, since it's always the big boys who have a hard time following instruction," he said, even as he looked at the training coordinator for the all clear but was signaled to hold until the other team cleared the landing zone. "And as a single parent, I can also tell you that if this kid-free coed outing involves a picnic, then don't be surprised if you show up tomorrow and she's dressed for romance instead of recon."

All guys who wore a department-issued uniform and gun had experience with badge bunnies—women who would do anything to marry into the lifestyle. Ford had had his fair share of flings and cons over the years, and he'd learned what to look for.

"Liv isn't the kind of woman to use her job to get a date," he said, confident in his assessment.

Harris gazed over the top of his aviators and looked at Ford. "Liv also hasn't gone on a date in over a decade." Even though Ford was sitting under a fifty-foot fan, he felt sweat bead on his forehead. "Yeah, so maybe you want to rethink your whole zip-lining outing."

Ford was tired of rethinking. He'd been doing it for two years without finding any closure. And if helping Liv with Wagon Days got him one step closer, then he was game.

"You suggested I get to know her, and she asked me for help with something that happens to be in my job description, so I said yes," Ford argued. "As for the zip-line request I put in, she wants to do a mini one for Wagon Days, and I thought using the department's training course would be a fun way to help her see the different kinds of courses we can build for the kids so she can get a better idea of what would work for the event."

"That's it?" Harris asked skeptically.

"That's it, man," Ford said. "But if you'd rather I call her and cancel so I can hold your hand while you clear some of those missing-pet cases off your desk, all you need to do is ask."

The training coordinator gave them the thumbs-up, then held up five fingers, ticking off the seconds before they began their descent.

Harris held up another finger altogether. "About those cases—you'd better focus on holding on to that rope, because if I make it down first, you're taking those back."

"And if I make it first?"

Harris looked at Bullseye and laughed. "Whatever you want."

Ford thought about the stack of applicants he had to call back and grinned. He might be carrying an extra sixty pounds in dog weight, but he also had the fastest rappelling time in his county. "You're on." Ford looked down at Bullseye, who was panting with excitement. "It's go time, buddy."

The coordinator dropped his last finger, and Ford pushed back off the skid and immediately let five feet of rope slide through his right hand. He was free-falling for a second before the rope tightened, swinging him and Bullseye up underneath the body of the helo.

With a final smile at Harris, Ford released his grip and quickly started descending. The air rushed past, pushing under his shirt and making Bullseye's tongue flap to the side.

"That better not be drool hitting my face," he said, but he was smiling because, *man*, he loved this. The rush, the weightlessness, the sense of freedom while being in complete control.

When Ford was in the moment, adrenaline pumping hard, he felt invincible.

And right then, nothing could touch him. Not the past, not the future, and certainly not Harris, who was a good ten feet above him, probably wondering how the fuck that had happened. Ford knew. Because while being tethered to a dog made the initial push-off more cumbersome, once they were hanging, that additional sixty pounds equated to one hell of a ride down.

And yeah, maybe Ford was easing up on the rope more than usual, but after this week he needed a win. So he didn't up the pressure until he was ten feet from touchdown. His feet touched solid rock, and he was unhooking Bullseye when Harris finally caught up.

Goggles and earphones off, Bullseye ran in circles, barking up a storm, excited for his reward.

"I've got some treats in my pocket," one of the other K-9 officers offered, but Ford shook his head.

"He wants something else. Don't you, boy?"

Breathing nonexistent, ears like a periscope, tail frozen, eyes locked on the tiny pink ear that was sticking out beneath Ford's vest harness, Bullseye gave a final bark and sat at Ford's feet.

Ford tugged Lambkins out by the ear, and Bullseye went stock-still. "Okay, here you go."

Bullseye looked at the proffered reward and threw his head back and belted out an argumentative bark, which echoed off the rocks and drew the attention of a few of the guys.

"Fine. Close your eyes, I give one distress call, then we're done," Ford said, and Bullseye dropped to his belly, placing his paws over his eyes.

Ford walked around in circles, crossing back over his trail several times to increase the difficulty, and then hid Lambkins in Harris's pack. With another crisscross of the area, Ford came back to Bullseye. Adopting the pussiest voice known to man, he said, "Help me, help me, Bullseye."

Bullseye sprang to his feet and, sniffer to the ground, followed the exact path Ford had taken, finding his prize in the pack in seconds. With the gentleness of a mother, Bullseye picked up his baby and proudly strutted among the men.

"What the hell was that, Daisy Doolittle?" Harris asked when Bullseye sat at Ford's feet to groom his baby.

"What?" Ford laughed. "Us kicking your ass, or the sound of the gigantic stack of volunteer applications hitting your desk?"

"Shit." Harris looked up at the sky, breathing heavily. "I'll make the calls, but you're running the meet and greet."

While Ford wasn't all that much of a department spokesman, he enjoyed working with volunteers and their dogs. Training dogs was a challenge that got him excited, and watching them deepen the bonds with their owners was rewarding. "As long as you give me volunteers who can be trained to help with basic stuff for Wagon Days, not a problem."

Harris studied him for a long moment. "There will be a problem if you don't honor the single-mom code."

"Jesus." Ford threw his hands in the air, then looked at Ty. "Will you tell him this is not a date?"

Ty grinned. "I would, but the only reason I'm here on a Sunday morning with you losers, and not at home with my smoking-hot wife, is because she's at Liv's helping her pick out what to wear."

Later that afternoon, Liv found herself back down at the hospital, arguing the merits of her idea, while Kevin shot a hole through each and every one.

"I think we need to take a step back and reevaluate the situation," he said, and Liv was surprised at the conviction in Kevin's voice. She hadn't expected him to flat-out reject her Wild West Roundup idea.

In fact, she hadn't even filed the permits, and already she knew she'd made a huge mistake.

She'd spent most of the weekend in the ER, fielding patients who were all suffering from different ailments but seeking the same outcome—a say in how Wagon Days was going to be run.

Once word spread that the event was under new management, people wanted face time with the newest chair. Most sought assurance that the event would reflect the town's history—or rather, each person's individual interpretation of the town's history—except Chuck, the butcher.

He'd come to talk about a history of a different variety—Liv's dating history. Which ultimately led to his idea for a "How to properly dress a hog" demonstration, with Liv as his number one assistant. But since Liv wasn't all that big on the idea of slaughter lessons as a first date, Chuck had left with his bouquet of hand-stuffed sausages and an apology on how dating a butcher went against Liv's recently adopted views on vegetarianism.

Now Kevin was so against her Wild West Roundup that he'd brought his concerns to Nicole. "If her new ideas for Wagon Days fall through or flop, that would be Mobile Medic's first introduction to the community."

"It isn't going to fall through, and there is nothing to reevaluate," Liv said assertively, part of her confidence coming from having someone in her corner.

She'd forgotten how that felt. Her focus as of late had been finding her footing so she could stand on her own. And she still was. Only today, she had someone standing by her side, in a sense. A sweet and sexy someone who not only made her smile, but made her feel special. And took an interest in her goals. It had been a long time since someone outside of her peers had taken the time to understand what she was trying to accomplish. For herself and her family.

"I was elected to head up the entertainment for Wagon Days, and I am heading it up." She looked at Nicole, who was leaning back in her chair listening to both sides as if she were the judge and jury. "You wanted to introduce the Mobile Medic and its team to the community in a fun and creative way, and this is the perfect opportunity."

"The perfect opportunity is waiting until after we finalize the staff," Kevin said, as if he considered himself a part of the bigger *we*, "then visit the schools to promote health awareness and back-to-school flu shots and vaccines." Kevin handed Nicole a flyer he'd taken the liberty to print up while Liv was cleaning up his exam room. "I've already cleared it with the superintendent, who is excited about the project and on board with helping spread the word about what we offer."

She was also Kevin's aunt.

"I didn't think a van full of needles was the first impression we were going for," Liv said, taking some ownership in the clinic's future. "Kids are already nervous about going back to school. My proposal lets us meet kids at a time when they are happy, excited, and feeling good. Which means they'll have a positive first experience with the clinic."

"It's a small detail that could have lasting effects on the way the kids perceive the clinic," Nicole agreed, and Liv had to stop herself from grinning.

"True, but pledging our support to an event that I hear is a long shot to be approved would have a lasting effect on how the board decides to fund us," Kevin pointed out.

"I'm already in the approval process," she said, telling herself that taking a hike with the gorgeous community-outreach officer, while not a date, was close enough to having this thing in the bag.

She had no idea how she was going to get the final sign-off, but Ford had been confident. And she was going to find enough volunteers to free up the officers to manage the course. Even if it meant joining every club in the county. All she needed was the medical personnel on hand.

And to think, this was all coming together because she had finally allowed herself to open up to someone new.

"I'm not asking you to sponsor the event," Liv explained. "I'm just asking you to give some of the staff permission to volunteer their time in an official capacity, and agree to have the Mobile Medic serve as the extra medic support for Wagon Days."

Nicole considered this. "This is one of the outreach issues Mobile Medic was created to handle."

"But the clinic won't be approved for service until the next board meeting," Kevin pointed out ever so sweetly.

"I can call a special meeting—that's not a problem. It's missing a great opportunity to serve the community because I was waiting for permission that bothers me," Nicole said, opening a journal and jotting down some notes. She looked up at Liv. "As long as you're sure you can get the permits, I don't see why we can't do a test run."

"That's fantastic," Liv said, moving to the edge of her chair. "I won't let you down."

"I hope not," Nicole said. "Once I call the board, they're going to be watching how you handle this new position and work with other groups in the community. This could be a big moment for you and the mobile clinic."

Kevin straightened in his chair, his *too cool to sweat it* 'tude fading. "I can't work that weekend. I'm already committed to run several other booths, and so is Brittany," he said, referring to the vocational nurse who was already placed on Nicole's team.

"I'll be coordinating the event, so I can't either, but I'm sure there are other nurses and doctors who would love the chance to work on the van for a day," Liv pointed out. "In fact, I bet I can find you a team before I go home today."

"That won't be necessary," Kevin said in a tone that translated into *Aren't you sweet*, and Liv understood why Ford took issue with the phrase. "I didn't want to say this, but last night one of my Moose Lodge buddies who works in the permitting office told me that you won't get your permit approved this late in the game."

"That's funny," Liv said, looking Kevin in the eye. "Who's your guy? Because my guy said it wouldn't be an issue."

Kevin grinned. "Well, *my* guy runs the Department of Community Development, which means he is the only guy who matters."

◆ ◆ ◆

It was a rare day in Liv's world when she was afforded the pleasure of sipping her morning coffee while it was still hot—and from an actual mug. Usually it was sucked down during her commute to the hospital. But since today was Liv's day off, and Paxton was already at camp, her plan should have been to enjoy her morning fix on the front porch and take in the rare silence.

The sun was up, the sky was the perfect color of blue, and several kayaks were already out on the lake. Liv let the breeze brush her face as she watched a flock of Canada geese who'd decided to cut their migration short and skim above the water's edge, flying under the new banner hanging in downtown.

It was so big that Liv could clearly make out every word, even from across the lake.

THE TRAILBLAZERS OF WAGON DAYS BRING THE LIGHTNING AND THUNDER BACK TO SEQUOIA LAKE. COME ENJOY THE CRAFT BEER, ART, AND ONE OF THE WILDEST ADVENTURES IN THE WEST.

An adventure that was sure to be Liv's last, she thought, hefting her backpack over her shoulder. She'd called the Department of Community Development first thing that morning. Even spoke with Kevin's guy, Harvey, who had sadly confirmed Liv's worst nightmares.

Her guy was full of shit.

While the sheriff's department signed off on any permits involving re-trafficking and crowd control, Ford had zero say in the final approval of permits. Something she would have known if she'd done her due diligence and research instead of up and changing direction based solely on the promise of a handsome man.

Ford's heart had been in the right place, of that she had no doubt. But it didn't change the fact that Liv now had twenty-four hours to come up with an alternate solution or she would miss the window to apply for the correct permits.

She wasn't so much mad at him as she was with herself for falling back on old habits. Which is why she'd texted Ford before she left the house and canceled their day. She needed to come up with a plan B, fill out the new forms, and get them in and approved ASAP. And that didn't leave time for a leisurely morning on her porch.

Especially charming and sexy ones who wanted to play hero for the day.

She needed to be her own hero, and this was her last chance to show what she was made of. Or Nicole was going to have to back Kevin's idea. It was the smart move. Kevin had the contacts, the necessary approvals, and the board's backing going for him. All Liv had was a binder of unvetted ideas and a twin-pack of Hostess cupcakes from her secret hiding spot—because, apparently, *her* guy was full of frosting.

The Women of the Wagon Trail were already hard at work on the event. News of the "Wagon Days Messiah" had spread like wildfire. Carolyn had found a new Crock-Pot recipe for tuna. And Liv still had to hike around the lake to do recon for an event that was likely to be canceled.

She looked at her cupcakes and wondered what the punishment was for eating dessert before eight in the morning. Double calories, she imagined, since that would be just her luck.

Maybe if she sucked down her coffee, the cupcake could be considered a breakfast pastry.

Liv set her backpack on the sand and tried to unhitch her thermos from the safety strap. It was childproof and secured tightly, so she pulled harder. With a frown—and a whole lot of bad words directed at whoever invented the idiotic idea of childproofing anything—she told herself that Paxton would never know and went straight for the sugar.

"I'm more of a bacon-and-eggs kind of guy, but for you I'd risk the sugar crash."

Liv looked over her shoulder, surprised to see Ford leaning on the railing of his deck, holding two cups of coffee. She was less surprised by the irritating tingles that started low in her belly. Surprise over her reaction to him had disappeared when she'd agreed to let some sweet-talking playboy distract her from her goal.

He was in nothing but a sleepy grin, yesterday's scruff, and a pair of worn jeans that hung indecently low on his hips—as if he hadn't bothered to button them. No shoes. No shirt. Just enough bedhead to make her wonder how warm his sheets still were. Which shouldn't have her body humming. But it did. And that made her nervous.

"Sorry, breakfast for one," she said, sticking half of the cupcake into her mouth, because if she was going to get that promotion, then she needed to come up with a plan B, and that didn't include the man who'd ruined plan A.

"That's a shame," he said. "Because breakfast for two is so much more fun."

"I don't have time for fun." She shoved the rest of the cupcake into her mouth, and it sank to the bottom of her belly with a thud. "But you enjoy your coffee."

"While your cupcakes were a breakfast for one, this coffee here is poured and ready for two."

"I've already got coffee." She nudged the thermos with the toe of her boot.

"Mine is piping hot and doesn't come with a screw top."

He held up the mug, and Liv nearly moaned as the steam rose into the morning mist. Her mouth watered.

"Coffee is coffee," she lied. "And mine won't accidentally burn me."

"Huh, you're one of those grumpy-in-the-morning people," he said, releasing double-barreled dimples. "Cute."

"I'm not grumpy." She was hurt. And felt foolish.

Liv knew better than to entrust her family's future to somebody other than herself. Not that she'd completely handed over the reins to Ford like she had with Sam. But when Ford had presented her with a simple solution that could solve all her problems, she'd naively bought into it. And almost blew her chance at a dream job.

"Oh yeah?" He casually rested his forearm on the railing, then eyed her backpack. "Then you want to explain why you texted a message canceling today, only to sneak out with enough gear to hike Everest? Most guys would take that personally." Bullseye stuck his head through the gaps in the railing and barked. "Bullseye agrees."

"I'm not sneaking, and I'd tell you it isn't personal, but that would be a lie. I've learned the hard way not to rely on people who make promises they can't keep," she said, sticking the remaining cupcake in her backpack and swinging it over her shoulder, the weight knocking her off balance. Or maybe that was the look of hurt in Ford's eyes at her words.

"What does that mean?" he asked, his tone going crisp like the morning breeze.

"That I was so focused on step four, I almost forgot I had to master step three first." And single moms with futures to secure had no time for distractions from fly-by-night heroes.

"Step three?"

"Making sure Paxton gets the childhood he deserves." She had to clear her throat before she could continue. "I had a plan and a direction, and maybe it wasn't as flashy as others, but it was a good one." More important, it was obtainable. "Now I have a bunch of people counting on me to deliver an event I can't possibly pull off, and a timeline that ensures whatever I do deliver will be a disappointment."

Even saying the word had knots forming in her stomach.

"With this Wild West–themed ropes course, no one will be disappointed."

"There won't be a ropes course," she said, looking up at him. "Not that my boss knows that. She's still holding out hope that her faith in me wasn't misplaced."

And Liv knew exactly what that felt like.

Setting the mugs on the railing, Ford walked down the steps until his feet were in the sand and he was inches from Liv. "Why won't there be a ropes course?"

"Because between crowd control and traffic control, there aren't enough officers to run an event that complex." Liv relayed the information she'd been told by Harvey at the Department of Community Development. "So if I want to still be in the running for my promotion, I need to simplify this event, get the forms down to city hall by five p.m., and make it exciting enough to bring the crowds."

"A ropes course will bring the crowds, and it can be simple." Ford looked down at his lack of attire, and Liv told herself not to notice how incredible he looked—or smelled. When that didn't work, she turned to face the water. "Just give me five minutes to get dressed, and I can show you."

When she didn't answer, he touched her shoulder. "Five minutes, Liv, and I promise you won't be disappointed."

But he wasn't just asking for her time. He was asking for her trust, and that was something she wasn't sure she could give right then.

"Don't worry about it." She gave a shrug to show him how this big issue wasn't all that big. "I work better alone."

"You'd work faster with someone who has done these kinds of things before." And although Liv was still watching the water lap against the shore, she could feel him move closer behind her. "Do you feel like you misplaced your trust in me?"

Liv wanted to say that she was still holding out hope too, but she knew she needed a more assertive emotion if she was going to salvage this event.

"Your confidence and charm is magnetic," she said, turning to glance at him over her shoulder, their eyes locking instantly. "It's easy to get caught up in."

"Seems like we both have the same problem," he said—to her mouth. And wouldn't you know it, little sparks of attraction shot straight down to her toes.

"Which is why doing this together is a bad idea."

"A bad idea is walking an hour around the lake with all of that weight on your back," he said, lifting her backpack off her shoulders. "Especially when we could take my truck and be there in ten minutes."

"I'd rather walk," she decided.

He studied her for a long moment, then shrugged one big shoulder. "Have it your way," he said, slipping the backpack on, his muscle bunching and coiling as he headed north along the shoreline.

With an excited bark, Bullseye raced behind him.

"Wait, I didn't say you could walk with me," Liv called out after him.

"We can discuss it on the way."

"You're half-naked."

Ford turned around, but he kept walking backward. "You can strip down to your lace if it makes you feel better."

CHAPTER 10

"Is this what you had in mind?" Liv asked.

Ford looked from the cluster of pine trees above the lake that Liv was pointing out, into her bedroom eyes, and admitted he was up to no good. He'd kept it casual as they'd wound their way along the lake's edge and toward the first potential ropes-course site. But the knowledge of just how good she felt by his side was almost as troublesome as the empty promise he'd made back on the beach.

He should have gone back to bed the second he read her text this morning canceling, taken the out the universe handed him, and run. Only running would have left Liv standing alone, and Ford couldn't stomach the idea.

Not when he'd spent most of last night going over the past two years. Every search, every call, every visit to Sequoia Lake raced around in his mind until the overwhelming itch to pack up and head into another storm became so acute he'd pulled out his bag at first light. But no matter how many times he checked his bag, he always felt as if he was missing something.

Then he'd seen Liv standing on the beach, staring out at the morning as if challenging it to come at her with all it had—her daily mantra—and he knew what was missing.

The fire.

Something Liv had in spades.

"The lakeside entry to Poppy Alley would be the perfect place to set up base camp," he said, letting Bullseye take the lead on the trail. "It's easy to get to, has a great view, and is visible from Lake Street and all of the booths. We can sell tickets right there." He pointed to the wooden walkway behind them that attached Lake Street to the water's edge.

"You sure know a lot about this place for being a transfer," Liv said, keeping pace with him. A miracle because her boots were more fashion than function. Same with the jeans, but the way they hugged that heart-shaped ass? Ford wasn't complaining.

"Bullseye and I come to town a few times a year," he said cautiously. "Sometimes to see Harris, sometimes to help with a search when they need a K-9 team."

"But you haven't gone on any searches this summer. Why?"

Oh, Ford had spent the entire trip searching. He just didn't think he was going to find what he was looking for on the job. Nope, he was pretty sure it went deeper than that. "If you ask my boss, it's because I missed an important test and they put me in big-boy time-out."

She laughed. "So judging dog shows and dealing with stubborn citizens is your punishment?" she asked as they reached a clearing in the outcropping of pines. "That must have been some test."

"It was *the* test," he confessed. "And for the record, I think stubborn is sexy on a woman."

"You're just saying that because you have your eye on my remaining cupcake," she teased.

"I'd have my eyes on more than your cupcake, but you laid down the no-flirting rule."

"I think you broke that rule when you asked me to go hiking in nothing but my secrets."

"Lucky you let me go back to the house and get dressed, then. Otherwise we would have gotten some strange looks when we drove through town. With you being overdressed and all," he said with a grin, remembering just how fast he'd gotten dressed. Liv had promised she'd wait, but he wasn't willing to chance it, so he'd tugged on the first shirt he'd found.

Good thing too. Because when he'd come back out, she was already walking down the shoreline. Clearly, waiting was not in her morning itinerary. Neither was talking.

Nope, Liv remained relatively quiet as they walked the short distance of the trail, bending down to run her hands along the carpet of bright orange poppies that covered the hillside and the valley around them. It wasn't until they reached a small outcropping of trees that she allowed herself to pick one.

She held the petal to her nose and breathed it in. Bullseye flopped on the ground and began rolling in the flowers.

"This is the perfect place for a family event," she said, turning around. "It's easy to reach—a two-minute walk from the main part of Wagon Days—but far enough out to feel like you're in another time."

Ford bent over to let Bullseye off the leash. Legs pointed toward the sky, Bullseye let out a yawn and closed his eyes.

"It's also private property, owned by Sequoia Lake Lodge, and I happen to know the owner," he said, referring to Ty and his parents, who would help in a heartbeat. All Ford had to do was ask.

"What about the permit issue?" she asked, taking in the sequoia trees and pines.

"By avoiding forest land and having the right personnel already lined up, there's no good reason for them to deny the permits."

She ran a hand along the trunk of an old oak, her hair loose and dancing in the breeze. "So when Kevin's guy said he couldn't sign off on the permits . . . ?"

"He's full of shit."

Her lips quirked. "He said the same thing about my guy."

"You have a guy?" he asked, liking the sound of that too much.

"I did yesterday," she confessed, walking to the edge of the clearing to look at the lake. "And it felt really good to not be on a team of one for a change." She turned and looked up at him, those big expressive eyes filled with gratitude and warmth, and Ford felt like a fake. He didn't deserve either emotion from her. And he especially didn't deserve the other thing he saw lurking beneath it all—trust. "You really meant that all it would take was me saying I needed help."

"I did, but don't let that fool you into thinking I'm some kind of hero, Liv," he said. "You need help, and I need to finish up here so I can get back to my life in Reno."

She leaned against the trunk of a nearby tree and studied him. "If this was just you doing your job, then why are you here instead of heading into the office?"

Good question. And one he didn't have an answer to. The only thing he knew for certain was that he was leaving in a few weeks, and this was the closest he'd come to finding peace in years.

"You're not the only one who needs someone in their corner," he said, picking up a stick and rolling it in his hands. "There's a lot riding on my ability to pass this test, and when I'm out here like this, everything doesn't feel so heavy."

She looked at him for a beat. Her eyes serious, assessing, and so soft he wanted to look away. "You don't look like the kind of guy to shy away from a challenge. So if it's not the challenge or the test that's weighing on you, what is it?"

"It doesn't matter," he said, tossing the stick. Bullseye halfway opened a lid, then closed it.

"It matters to me." Then she quietly added, "You know, going it alone isn't all it's cracked up to be."

He gave her a pointed look. "Ironic advice coming from you."

"I'm working on the reaching-out part. You're here, aren't you?"

"Only because you were afraid of what people would think when they saw me trailing behind you in nothing but jeans and bedhead."

"And because I know I can't do this all on my own," she said. "And that's a scary thing for me to admit."

"That you're on your own?"

She shook her head. "That I can't handle everything on my own, and relying on an outside factor for security takes me out of the driver's seat. The rules can abruptly change, and there's nothing I can do to stop it."

Ford's chest went tight at her admission. "Maybe we aren't supposed to stop it?"

"If you believed that, you wouldn't put your life on the line to save others," Liv said. "It's because we believe the way we do that makes us so good at our jobs. We're protectors—it's what we do."

"But you can't protect everyone," he said.

"Maybe not, but knowing you did the best you could has to be enough."

Ford had never considered how similar their jobs were. Just like he'd never considered how talking with Liv, about *this*, could feel so natural. "The weekend of my test I was at a rescue in Montana. A mudslide took out six houses in a cul-de-sac at the bottom of the mountain, including the home of a young family of four."

"Oh my God."

"The mom told the responding officers that she heard a loud noise in the middle of the night and went out to see what it was. I guess the husband had come home from work sick, so she didn't want to wake him. She figured she'd investigate the noise, and if it was bad, she'd wake him after. There wasn't enough time for an after."

"Was the family inside?"

"Sound asleep—they didn't even know what hit them. It was so dark the wife couldn't tell the difference between a wall of mud and the night. It took less than a second for all six houses to be completely buried under twenty feet of mud and clay."

"Were you there?" she asked, reaching out to place a hand on his arm, letting it rest there. There was nothing sexual about the simple connection, but it rocked him all the same. Reminded him of just how long it had been since he'd opened up to someone like this.

"No, they flew me and Bullseye out the next day." He remembered walking up on the scene, knowing he'd have to use GPS to even predict where the houses would have been. "It took less than an hour for Bullseye to identify the location of two of the bodies, but we couldn't locate the third. And that's when I noticed this kid. He was around eleven. All bony arms and legs, covered head to toe with mud, lying down on the ground."

"Oh, Ford."

He looked out at the lake, focused on the gentle ripples on the surface. "I went over to see if he was okay, and you know what he told me? That he'd snuck out that night to meet his friends. They were going to go watch the lightning storm from some peak, and he needed help getting back inside the house. He'd seen all of the mud, logically knew what it meant, but spent the night trying to crawl through it to be with his family."

What Ford left out was that he knew exactly how that kid felt. He'd been trying his whole life to crawl back inside a home that was safe and full of life. He understood how impossible a mission it would be.

"That must have been devastating," she said, and Ford realized her concern was for him, not the boy. "You're a fixer who was placed in a situation where there was no perfect solution. That would shake anyone."

"It isn't the lost ones that get to me." *Much.* "It's the not knowing that I can't let go of. I never get to see how my call or decision plays out over the long run," he explained, because while Liv was also a protector, she had the benefit of watching them check out of the hospital.

First responders weren't allowed that luxury. The second the ambulance pulls away, the story ends. Ford never knew if they made it to the hospital alive or how their lives went after they were released.

Being able to turn off when he clocked out was imperative for job longevity. Ford used to be able to flick that switch without hesitation. But most nights as of late, he couldn't manage to find the dimmer.

"You care," Liv said. "That's a good thing."

Ford looked up at the trees overhead and blew out a breath. "Sometimes I think I care too much."

"Not possible." She stepped into him until they were as close as one could get to a hug without moving their arms. "Your caring helped that family find closure."

He shook his head. "A body for the casket isn't closure. That kid and his mom will never be the same."

"No," she said, resting her other hand on his arm. "They won't, but I can tell you from experience that they will find a new path. It may take a while, but it will happen. It's taken me two years to get to this point." Liv paused to take a breath. "I lost my husband in a car accident."

"I know," he admitted quietly. Just like he knew this was the time to come clean. He couldn't sit by and let her talk about her loss without being honest about his role in it. "I'm so sorry, Liv. I don't know what to say to make this easier, but—"

"You don't have to say anything," she assured him, placing a finger on his lips. "Most of the time I don't know what to say, which is why I haven't brought it up. I like that you don't treat me different or look at me like I'm broken. It gives me the freedom to explore this new path, just like that mom and son will eventually explore theirs. And someday they'll even find peace with it."

"Have you?" he asked, desperate to see how her answer would change things. "Have you found peace?"

"Most days," she said. "In fact, one more step to go, and research assures me I will be back to normal. Whatever *normal* even is."

"How about today?"

Liv's lashes fluttered closed and she inhaled, her chest slowly rising and then holding. After a long moment, she opened her eyes and breathed, "Yes."

Ford couldn't explain what happened next, only that one moment they were talking and the next they weren't. Oh, there was plenty being said, just not with words. Liv's hand was no longer on his arm, but on his chest, and her back was pressed against the trunk of an oak tree.

His hands? Well, they were braced above her head. To an outside observer, it would appear as if he were caging her in, but the truth was, she was pulling him to her.

"Remind me again what step four is." Because Liv looked as if she were reconsidering her stance.

"Why?"

"I'm pretty sure it has something to do with what's happening right now."

Liv looked down at her hand, which had dropped a few inches south, and her breath caught. "Step four is taking the emotional energy I would have spent on Sam and reinvesting it in a new relationship," she said, as if reciting it from an article.

But her hands didn't move, he noticed.

"It's the hardest step, because it's saying I'm ready to move on, and that sounds disloyal. But it's also the most important step."

There wasn't much Ford wouldn't give to reinvest all the energy he focused on the past into a future with Liv. Hell, one night would go a long way toward soothing his soul. She was warm and open and one of the sexiest women he'd ever met. When he wasn't around her, all he could think about was seeing her. And when he was with her, he couldn't stomach the idea of leaving.

"You said earlier that you aren't ready for step four."

"I did?"

Ford was pretty sure she meant to word it as a statement and not a question. "Then why do you look like you want me to kiss you?"

"Do I?" she whispered, and that was definitely a question. He could see the conflict in her eyes, right below the nerves. Oh, and there was another emotion, potent and tempting as hell, lighting those golden pools. Need. There was a hell of a lot of need.

"Yeah, you do," he said, for her as much as himself. Liv's gaze dropped to his mouth, and Ford's heart hammered so hard he had a hard time thinking clearly. And he'd promised Liv that everything they did would be clearheaded. "So I need you to tell me that you aren't ready for this."

Because they were on the edge of something dangerous, something so combustible all it would take was one spark to ignite. And with his history with women, it was bound to burn hot and fast. But, man, he wanted some of that fire.

"Step four is about a new relationship." She looked up at him through her lashes. "It doesn't say anything about kissing." And on that last word, her eyes zeroed in on his lips and—*fuck me*—she wanted him to kiss her.

Only Liv was a single mom with a complicated past, which was new territory for him—territory he wasn't sure how to navigate. Flirting was one thing, but taking it to the next level when he knew he was leaving, knew she wasn't a casual kind of woman, was completely different— only she looked like she was about to prove him wrong by making the first move.

And God help them both if she did.

"Be sure, Liv," he warned. "Because once you go there, you can't come back."

She didn't make a move either way, and neither did he, instead waiting for her to decide. Watching her struggle with the finality of it all. Either way she went, one road would come to an end.

A gentleman would have ended it for her, but gentle was the last thing Ford was feeling. Not when he was a breath away from getting a taste of that peace he'd been so desperate to find.

And then it happened. He saw it in the way her body softened and her eyes bore into his. Yup, in one breath, Ford went from the unluckiest son of a bitch to walk the planet to the luckiest in a single, simple statement that changed everything.

"I'm tired of going back," Liv said.

It took about three seconds for it to register that while Ford stood under that old oak tree, the bark digging into his hands, less than five miles from the site that had ruined so much, Olivia Preston, the woman whom he couldn't get out of his head, was kissing him.

It wasn't one of those pent-up, get-down-to-business kind of kisses Ford had become accustomed to over the past few years. Nope, this kiss was completely foreign to him, in a way that was familiar and comforting. She brushed his lips once, then another tentative touch, and Ford gripped the trunk harder, wanting to let her set the pace. A pace that was so agonizingly slow, he thought he'd go crazy with want.

"Ford," she murmured in soft invitation, and he'd never RSVP'd so fast in his life. Cradling the back of her neck, Ford took over the kiss, languidly teasing and tasting until Liv let out a little sigh of contentment.

He slid his arms around her, pulling her close, and damn if she didn't rise on her toes to meet him. Pressing her lips to his in a kiss so sweet, something more than lust settled in his chest.

Ford knew right then, in that field, that when it came to this woman, it was the gentle that was going to kill him. One touch and he knew that nothing could be better than this.

CHAPTER 11

"It was just a kiss," Liv repeated for the third time that night, refusing to be one of those women who obsessed over ridiculous things—like how it had been three days since the kiss and Ford hadn't called. Not that she'd expected him to, or even that she would have known what to say if he had, since "Thanks" was the best she'd come up with.

But some kind of word would have been nice, especially since she hadn't seen his Jeep in the driveway.

"Then why did you scout out the bar before agreeing to come inside?" Avery asked, with a knowing grin.

"I was looking for Grace," Liv said primly.

"Grace is right there, in the same place she was two minutes ago when we were outside and she waved us in." Avery pointed to a booth in the far back corner. "Yet you haven't taken your eyes off the bar since we walked in."

Just like she couldn't get her mind off the way her body had melted when Ford's lips touched hers in a kiss that changed everything. It felt like the end and the beginning all at the same time, which probably explained the big, confusing knot of emotions in her chest that wound tighter every day that passed.

"Just reading the specials on tap tonight," she said.

It was Tap-That Thursday at the Backwoods Brewhouse. With half-price local brews, every stool was filled, and the bar was three deep—which made finding anyone difficult. Even the group of search-and-rescue guys gathered at the side of the bar in bright orange were hard to make out.

"Uh-huh," Avery said, calling Liv on that lie.

Not that it was a lie, really. Tonight was a celebration, and instead of going for her regular order of Riesling, Liv was determined to branch out, be adventurous. Which sounded like fun, except she couldn't stop wondering what had happened to her last adventure.

Earlier that day, Dr. Brown had submitted Liv to the board as a viable candidate, so keeping her focus was essential—and that meant keeping things professional. At least until she heard back on the permits. A hard task when she knew what his lips tasted like.

"You should consider the Flaming Pig's Ass—it will go with that goofy grin you've got going on," Avery said with a teasing grin, dragging Liv through the bar and straight for Grace, weaving in and out of the crush of people.

The open rafters, stacked-log walls, and vintage aging tanks displayed the deep roots of the historic mountain brewery, while the antler chandeliers and sleek leather furniture brought a hunting-lodge feel to the brewhouse turned bar and grill.

Grace sat in a booth covered in Liv's favorite fried foods, a bottle of champagne, and three glasses. Liv's chest expanded over the thoughtful gesture. It had been a long time since she'd had something to celebrate. Even longer since she'd had someone to celebrate with.

Liv had no sooner slid into the booth when Grace offered Liv a glass, then raised her own in toast. "To our friend Olivia. For moving up and making out."

Liv took her glass but glared at Avery over the rim. "Seriously? You told her?"

"Of course she told me." Grace clinked glasses. "Now, spill. I want to hear everything. Where did it happen? Who made the first move? What where you wearing? Is it going to happen again?"

"Poppy fields. Me. Clothes. And probably not." With that out of the way, Liv emptied her glass in one swallow.

"What do you mean *probably not*?" Grace sounded as if she'd just learned unicorns didn't exist.

"Just what I said." Liv grabbed a celery stick off the wings plate and dipped it in ranch. "It was an in-the-moment thing, the moment is over, and I think I'll skip the beer and go with a Riesling."

"Liv," Grace said in that nurturing tone that had the power to unlock people's secrets, so Liv shoved a carrot in her mouth, and then another, until it was too full to talk.

Her friends leaned back and sipped their champagne, content to wait it out. Liv swallowed and let out a big sigh. "He dropped me off at the curb and said, 'It was fun.'"

"No, he did not," Grace breathed, aghast. "He 'funned' you? That deserves a second glass." Grace didn't stop until the sparkling liquid was licking the glass's rim.

"No second kiss at the door, no 'Let's do it again.'" Nope, Man Candy had "funned" her and then didn't call.

This time Liv bypassed the veggie stick and went straight for a handful of fries.

"You did say you were looking for fun," Avery pointed out. "And before we bash the guy, did you want a second kiss?"

"Have you seen the man? Of course she wanted a second kiss," Grace said, but Avery's focus was locked on Liv.

Liv had done her fair share of dreaming over the past few days, and while part of her said she wanted another kiss—the naughty part—she had to admit that there was still some hesitation.

Sure, there was the expected guilt and the annoying flutters that wouldn't go away. But what had Liv rethinking everything was the sense of rightness she'd felt. In the moment and all the moments since.

How could kissing another man feel so right when losing Sam had been so incredibly wrong?

"You want a second kiss, right?" Grace asked, sounding confused.

"I don't know. The first one wasn't a premeditated kiss—it just happened." Even though he'd given her the chance to back out, the moment had already taken over. "But a second kiss would be a conscious decision."

A decision that when made with a clear mind would carry a weight she wasn't sure she was strong enough to handle just yet.

Her friends shared a look full of deep concern and worry. The one thing she hated more than being blindsided was making people worry about her. If Sam hadn't been so worried about her, he would still be around.

"Nothing you do will ever take away from what you and Sam shared," Grace said with gentle understanding. "He wasn't your first kiss, and it would be a waste of a big heart like yours if he was your last."

"He's no longer my last, but I'm scared of what happens when he's no longer my best," she admitted, because Ford's kiss had the power of a defibrillator—one zap could jump-start her heart.

"We're scared that you'll be so busy trying to do right by a man who is no longer here that you'll end up focusing on what could have been instead of what might be," Avery said.

"Trust me, surrounding yourself with memories isn't any way to live," Grace added, and Liv wanted to cry.

"Yes, it was Sam's childhood home, but we never lived there together, so they aren't my memories." Even as she said the words, Liv knew they were a lie. She was living with Sam every day. He was in every picture, every room, every decision she made. His memory even shaped how she'd approached her new promotion.

How would Sam do it? What would Sam think? Look what Sam's missing.

Her world was so full of Sam, there were times it didn't feel as if there was room for Liv.

Only she hadn't felt trapped with Ford. She'd felt free.

Problem was—attaching her freedom to a man who was destined to leave didn't feel like the fresh start she was looking for.

Avery's voice softened. "You once told me that I deserved to be happy, so now it is my turn. You, Liv Preston, deserve to be happy. Like glowing, you're so happy. Sam would have wanted that for you. Even if it meant sharing a second smoking-hot kiss with a smoking-hot guy."

Flutters took flight in her chest, and Liv had a hard time swallowing. Panic, hormones, and lust made for one complicated mess of emotions fighting for domination.

And just when she felt as if she were going to hyperventilate, Grace took her hand. "I did the intense forever thing too and got burned. Maybe not in the same way, but the loss was as painful. Wouldn't it be nice to experience the other side of dating? The side that doesn't have to be anything other than fun. No commitments, no expectations, no hurt feelings. All the benefits without the baggage."

While the thought of dating a rugged mountain man sounded exhilarating, a date with a kind man who made her laugh sounded equally as terrifying. Because while the first would be another small step toward moving on, Liv hadn't had a first date in so long this might as well have been her maiden sail.

And while she was open to a little putter around the lake to get herself reacquainted, she knew that with Ford it would be like chartering a speedboat set for open seas.

"I don't even know if he wants a second kiss," Liv said. "Which is why I'm going to just go with the flow and not obsess—that's the plan."

"Said every old cat lady ever." Avery reached out and loosened Liv's ponytail. "Your plan is going to land you in the friend zone."

Liv thought about how natural she'd felt with Ford, how easy it was to be around him, and found herself smiling. "You say that like friends is a bad thing."

"It is if you want to be kissed again." Avery gave Liv's hair a fluff and pulled it around her shoulders. "Now, what were you wearing?"

"A T-shirt and jeans."

"What happened to the dress we picked out the other day?"

"I was going hiking. It would have clashed with my boots." She left out the part where she'd canceled their date in a text.

Avery let out a long-winded sigh. "I'm surprised that with your Mom-A-Licious shirt, his dog wasn't the only thing jumping you."

"I didn't wear my Mom-A-Licious shirt." She'd worn her #LikeAMom shirt. "And my jeans make my waist look tiny and my butt look twenty." For a woman who was a few months away from being called midthirties, that was something to be proud of.

"Next time wear that blue top with the tiny straps that says 'I want to be kissed.'"

Liv knew the top she was talking about and felt a small thrill at the way the silk would slide against her skin. "The one I wore to your bachelorette party?"

"Oh yeah, that top looks great," Grace agreed, taking out a notepad and pen from her purse. "It takes you from a respectable B to a full C."

She looked down at her boobs and sighed. Not even a respectable B today. "The top got me zero action the last time I wore it."

"You weren't ready to be kissed, which is where the seven signs that you're ready to be kissed comes into play. Primping comes in at number seven," Avery informed them as if she were fluent in the language of seduction, when in reality she looked like a grown-up blonde Dora the Explorer.

Then again, the adventure guide was the only one of the three who was getting any.

"But it looks like I'm going to have to give you CliffsNotes, because Ford just walked in and is doing the same sweep you did."

Liv's stomach tightened, and she was about to turn around when she heard someone shout, "Ford, over here, man."

It was one of his buddies at the bar, calling him over, most likely for guys' night. Not wanting to draw attention, Liv sank down into the booth.

"That is the exact opposite of what you should be doing," Avery said. "No wonder why he didn't kiss you at the door. Now sit up and make direct eye contact and don't look away."

"Or I can respect that he's here for guys' night and talk to him tomorrow." When she wasn't in work scrubs with sprinkles on them.

"Or you can fluff your hair in his direction, sign five in letting him know you want to be kissed," Avery said, and both women started waving.

"Can you not?" Liv grabbed Avery's hand and lowered it to the table.

"Too late. He waved back to the crazy girls." It was only then that Grace put her hand down. "Aw, he's a keeper."

"What happened to just the fun side?"

"That was before I saw all his sides. They are equally impressive, and I give you permission to explore all of them," Grace said with a grin. "*If* you report back with details."

"He's here to see his friends," Liv said. "No more details to share."

"Actually, he's here to see you."

Liv didn't have to turn around to see who that gravelly voice belonged to, because her nipples went hard. Taking in a deep breath, she prepared herself for the impact and turned, but it was all in vain.

Grace was right—the man was smoking hot. In dust-covered boots, low-slung tactical pants, and enough testosterone to level a football arena, Ford was over six feet of unadulterated fun waiting to be tapped. Appreciating the way his work shirt clung to that very defined chest of his, she decided that fun was something she desperately wanted to happen.

"We're celebrating," Avery pointed out. "Want to join us?"

"Thanks, but I just need to talk to Liv," he said to the table and then looked right at her. His smile was dialed to flirt, but his eyes were serious. The kind of serious that made Liv's hands sweat. "Do you have a second?"

"A second kiss," Avery coughed, and Grace laughed.

Ford let the dimples pop out, but she could tell he had to work for that smile.

Liv cut her friends a hard glare, then stood. "Sure. I was going to get a beer at the bar."

Before Liv could respond, Ford had her hand in his big warm one, and he was leading her though the brewery, past the bar and his buddies—grabbing two bottles of beer on his way—not stopping until they were outside, the warm evening air surrounding them.

It was only in the light of the sinking sun that she realized just how dirty he was. He looked as if he'd been playing beach volleyball—fully clothed. His scruff was so thick it could be considered a beard, his eyes were tired, and his body language was on edge.

"Where are we going?" she asked.

He came to a stop on the side of the building and let go of her hand to cup the bill of his cap and pull it low on his head in an unconscious move that was all male and pent-up nerves.

"Ford, is everything okay?"

Setting the bottles of beer on top of a crate, he turned to face her. *Study her* was more like it. He slowly took in every inch of her, and a small smile touched his lips when he spotted her sprinkle scrubs. "I got you something."

To her surprise and delight, he pulled a small brown box from his jacket pocket. He held on to it, as if debating if he really wanted to let go, before looking up at her with his eyes and offering it to her.

"Is it a paperweight?" she asked, taking the box from his hand, trying to figure out what was inside, and telling herself not to get her hopes up. For all she knew, it was hooks or some kind of rappelling locks for Wagon Days.

"No, and don't shake it." Liv froze midshake and lifted a brow. "It's fragile."

Liv smiled for the first time since seeing him in the bar. Ford wasn't upset—he was nervous. Which was as ridiculous as it was cute, because watching this big, unflappable man struggle with giving her a surprise was endearing.

Breaking the tape with her nail, she slowly opened the lid, her hands doing some shaking of their own. Because inside the plain brown box, beneath the sheet of white wax paper and in a pink tin with little white nursing hats, was proof that Ford was one of the good ones.

"You brought me a nurse cupcake?" she asked, her heart melting over his thoughtfulness.

"I was in Shasta and found this cupcake shop with nurse cupcakes in the window. And I knew that today was a big day with your job." He shrugged. "So I swung by on my way out of town and picked one up for you."

"This is really sweet," she said, and he groaned at the word, but he didn't seem that upset. In fact, he actually blushed a little at her compliment.

"From you, I'll take sweet," he said, his smile faltering as the last word played off his tongue.

Hers disappeared altogether. Not because she knew, without a doubt, that she wanted to kiss him again. But because she'd take this moment over and over again.

"I don't know what to say."

In fact, it was becoming increasingly difficult to speak, period. Ford had gone out of his way to make her feel special, celebrated. Being on the receiving end of such kindness—and what felt a lot like caring—made her heart do crazy things.

"Nothing to say." He stuffed his hands in his pockets and rocked back on his heels. "I saw it and thought of you. I wanted to get you something to celebrate. Your boss called to confirm that the permits were in process, and I told her that I signed off and sent them to Harvey at the Department of Community Development. I also explained that everything is in order, and there is no reason they shouldn't be approved, but—"

"I know, she called me into her office right after she talked to you," Liv said, feeling a familiar rush of comfort that came from sharing. It seemed so simple, and for most people it was, but for Liv she hadn't had someone to share her day with in a while. "She told me that because we'd done such a great job with keeping the town's interests at the heart of the event, the Mobile Medic was officially cleared to work Wagon Days."

"The heart of it, that was all you," Ford said quietly. "I just helped with the paperwork."

"You more than helped. If it weren't for you pushing me to think bigger, Dr. Brown wouldn't have submitted me to the board as her top choice for the RN position."

"Congratulations, Liv." He said it sincerely, but there was a heavier emotion weighing down his words.

"I was going to tell you, but you haven't been home." Liv closed the lid and traced a finger across the seam. "You were in Shasta?"

"Yeah, a missing hiker. They needed a relief team, so Bullseye and I drove down," he said. "We found the hiker today. He'd fallen down a cliff and broken his leg, but he'll be fine. I just got back. Bullseye is in the car sleeping."

"You were out there for three days?" she said, noticing that he looked way too good for a guy who'd spent three days in the wilderness.

"Why?" He grinned, that charm in full effect. "You miss me, cupcake?"

Liv could have twirled her hair or one of the other silly things Avery would tell her to do, but instead she went for honest. "I did. More than I should have." And then because there was no point in playing coy, she asked, "Why did you come here tonight? Was it just to bring me a cupcake?"

Ford went stock-still, staring silently at her. She had confused him, which was fine by her since his little sweet gift had her so flustered she couldn't think straight.

"No," he finally said, and her body gave a little shiver.

The heat between them was so tangible it made it difficult to catch her breath. He didn't help the situation, letting his gaze purposefully fall to her lips, taking that shiver to a full-blown zing of anticipation. And when she realized he wasn't trying to hide his interest, she knew she had two seconds to make up her mind.

"Then why did you come?"

Without a word, Ford stepped forward, heading straight for her, his face taut, his brown eyes blazing.

This caught her completely off guard, and she took a step backward, her back coming flat against the wall of the building.

Grabbing the bill of his ball cap, Ford flipped it backward and closed the last breath of air between them. "I came for this."

Liv didn't have to ask what *this* was, because the second his fingers threaded through her hair, lifting her face to meet his, she knew she was ready. She wasn't sure what she was ready for, but she knew she wanted this.

He gave her a breath to think about it, just long enough for her to know she was tired of thinking. She wanted to feel.

And *my oh my,* did he feel amazing.

Strong and steady, moving with purpose. But she couldn't forget the tenderness. It was what had her head spinning. Had her rethinking why she'd been so hesitant to take this step.

One minute she was up against the wall, the next she was curled around his body, Ford's mouth needy and hot against hers. He teased the seam of her lips and then gently worked it open, and Liv felt all the air whoosh from her lungs as his hands slid down her back to that sensitive curve right below her shirt hem.

His fingers, those talented fingers, dipped under, gently skating back and forth across her bare back and around to her hip as he took her mouth in what had to be the most magical second kiss in the history of second kisses. A kiss that had the potential to last all night.

And the way he touched her, melting away her bones and every last one of her concerns, told her he was open to the idea. She just had to say the word.

But words were hard to come by since his mouth was fused to hers, in long, drugging kisses that had her heart pounding and her knees turning to mush beneath her. She must have wobbled, because Ford molded her hips with his hands and turned her, backing her up against the grille of his truck.

The heat still radiated off his engine. It was almost as intense as the fire that raged between them. Pent-up tension and bone-deep lust collided into one giant ball of chemistry that had Liv curling into him.

Her hands slid into his hair, and his went right to her bottom, cupping her backside in a confident and possessive way that had Liv moaning into his mouth.

Normally, that kind of thing wouldn't do it for her, but when Ford scooped her up and sat her on the hood of his truck, Liv was lost.

Lost in his taste, the way he touched her—in the way he made her feel. Sexy and strong and desirable.

She wound her legs around his waist, pulling him closer. So close there was nothing but the evening air between them. And man oh man, he smelled good. Insanely good. Like hot summer nights and life-altering adventures.

He felt even better. Solid and strong and—*right.*

There was that word again. Ford's arms were wrapped around her waist as if made especially for her. The way their mouths moved, slowly and languidly, perfectly in sync. It was as erotic as it was thrilling.

Liv knew that responsible Single Working Parents didn't leave their kids with a sitter to kiss sexy globe-trotters in public parking lots, but she wanted a few more moments under the stars. With his hands on her just like this.

The two of them.

No stress. No interruptions. No voices from the past creeping in. Just a moment to remember what it was like to be a normal woman. In the arms of an extraordinary man.

Ford must have felt the same because his kisses turned even hotter, trailing down her neck to the soft curve and lower. She let her head fall back, a breathy sigh escaping her lips.

"Ford," she whispered right as the back door of the bar opened.

Liv bolted upright as Ty walked out.

"Harris is looking for you. *Ah*—" Ty froze, and then a big smile spread across his face. "Hey, Liv."

Liv patted her hair down. "Hi, Ty."

"Bye, Ty," Ford said, his eyes never leaving hers. They were dark, heated, and completely wild. Just like her heart rate.

"And here I thought you were hiding from Harris, who found out about Shasta and is pissed, by the way," Ty said, his arms crossed as he leaned casually against the wall.

"Tell Harris I'll talk with him later," Ford said.

"That's okay," Liv said. Then to Ty she said, "We were just finishing up."

Ty looked at his watch. "Wow, that was . . . fast."

Ford shot him a death glare that would have made Liv pee her pants. Ty just shot him the finger.

Liv took in the scene, imagined what Ty must be thinking, and a strange heaviness settled in the pit of her stomach.

She told herself she hadn't done anything wrong. So what if Ty had gone to school with Sam and knew everyone's history? It shouldn't matter. She had mourned Sam and was ready to move on.

But no matter how she justified it, all she could think was that her first public sign that she was moving on happened with her sprawled across the hood of a pickup truck.

In a parking lot.

"My sitter is actually expecting me soon, so I have to be going," she said, taking a big step back.

"Let me walk you out," Ford said quietly, and Liv took another step back.

"We're already out." She looked up at the sky and then started walking toward the front lot. She held up the cupcake and over her shoulder said, "Thanks."

CHAPTER 12

It was past the lunch hour when Ford walked out of the Bear Claw Bakery, a hot pastrami sandwich in hand. Only instead of finding Bullseye in the Jeep where he'd left him, the dog was sitting on a bench in front of the shop, with a stray teddy bear next to him.

"Where did you get that one?" Ford asked.

Bullseye immediately began grooming his new friend.

"Not happening." Ford grabbed the stolen stuffed animal right as Bullseye was about to start gumming his ear. Based on the amount of saliva dripping off the toy, he'd already given him a tongue bath. "This doesn't belong to you, so tell me where you got it, and we are taking it back."

Bullseye looked up at him with puppy eyes, as if saying he had no idea what Ford was talking about. When that didn't work, he started howling. Loud and drawn out and a damn fine acting job. Everyone in the bakery looked out the window to see what the big, bad man was doing to that sweet dog.

"Fine, but if some kid goes to bed crying because he lost his Woobie, that's all on you." Bullseye didn't give a rat's ass. The second he sank his teeth into the bear's neck, Ford could have sworn he giggled, which wouldn't be a surprise since he was carrying the toy to the truck like a mama carrying her baby. Head high, spring in his step, tail straight up as if flipping Ford the bird.

Bullseye and Company jumped up through the open passenger door—the dog was too lazy to use the doggy door but he could open a truck door—and curled up with his new buddy.

With a stern look that was completely ignored, Ford closed the passenger door and then slid in behind the driver's seat and unwrapped his sandwich. The warm scent of freshly baked rye bread and melted cheese filled the car, and Ford's stomach grumbled. After three days of power bars and jerky, hot food was pretty close to heaven.

Not as close as kissing Liv, he thought, remembering the feel of her lips working his. She had great lips.

He was going for the first bite when someone tapped on the window.

Ford turned to find Harris's mug in the window, stank face in full effect. He was in athletic shorts and a DADDIES AGAINST DAUGHTERS DATING muscle shirt, and a couple of strands of sparkly beads were around his neck.

Ford ignored him and lifted the sandwich to his lips.

"We can do this here or while you're packing your bags."

Ford set his sandwich down and unrolled the window. "My mom warned me never to open my window to a man offering beads."

"It was Mommy-Daughter Day at Emma's dance studio. We were crowned Best Dance Duo, which means I get to throw the next class party, so don't fuck with me," Harris said, running a hand down his face. "And did your mom also warn you about what happens when you do an unsanctioned search without telling your boss?"

Ford took one last look at his sandwich and wrapped it up. "I had two days off, and a buddy from Shasta called asking for backup, so I went."

"On a type-two search. You aren't cleared for a type-two search."

"I went as a volunteer. On my own time."

"Thank God you didn't go as the SEMR community-outreach officer. That guy seems to have wandered off and left some moron in his place, because no way would my guy, who's one wrong move from mall security, gear up when he's been benched. By two departments." Harris was quiet for a moment. "I mean, that would be as reckless as trying to charm the panties off a citizen who's in the middle of an active project with the department."

"It's not like that."

"You brought her a cupcake! From Shasta!"

"They also had ones with little pacifiers on it," Ford said, resting his elbow on the window. "Want me to go back and get you one?"

Harris lifted a brow, and Ford let out a breath.

Ford was the easygoing one of his team. He had to be to do his job, and he took a lot of pride in his ability to not let things rattle him. This thing with Liv, though, had him rattled. And not in a good way. "It's not what you think."

"Good, because I'd hate to have to bring up the single-mom code again," Harris said, clearly not buying Ford's brand of BS. "Because kid-free coed outings that involve morning walks on the beach, coffee on your back porch, and locking lips are definitely off-limits."

"Ty told you?"

"You just did," Harris said, shaking his head. "This is Sequoia Lake—that kind of shit gets people talking and women thinking. And women like Liv are new to all of this. She didn't date a lot before Sam, and she hasn't dated once since. A kiss to her might mean something different than a kiss to you."

If his friend was going for the guilt angle, it was working. Ford had injected himself into a subject's life, then began steering it in a direction that was in his best interest and not hers, knowing he was leaving in a few weeks.

What kind of mess had he gotten into?

"She's in the driver's seat—trust me." And it didn't take a genius to figure out that, after last night, she was considering dropping it into a lower gear. He'd seen the look on her face, knew they'd gone too far.

"I bet that drives you nuts."

Ford rolled his head to the side until he met his friend's gaze. "Why do you think I took the search in Shasta?"

"I thought it was to piss me off," Harris joked, then went serious. Dead serious. "Remember, you have the ability to pull the emergency brake—"

"Which you think I should do because you're worried about her getting hurt."

"Sam and I played baseball growing up," Harris said. "So, yeah, when Liv came to town I made a point to get to know her, and since then she's become a good friend. So I will always worry about her." Harris rested his hands on the roof of the truck and leaned in. "Right now, I'm more worried about you."

"Me?" Ford laughed. "I have three more weeks in Mayberry, then I'll take my cert test, be back on the travel squad, and everything will be back to normal."

"Right in time for avalanche season," Harris said. "I guess you have it all worked out, then. Which explains why you tried to get a permit for a kids' zip line approved."

Ford straightened. "What do you mean, tried? Wait. Are you rejecting it?"

"You proposed a zip line and ropes course in Poppy Alley. For kids. To impress a girl." Harris snorted. "Of course I'm rejecting it."

"This isn't about impressing Liv. This is about finishing strong here, and my department does these kinds of kids' courses every year. A lot of departments do," Ford pointed out.

"We're small town, city boy." Harris laughed, and Ford wanted to punch him. "We don't have the kind of crew to work that kind of event right now."

"I only need six guys."

"You do realize you're asking for half of the local division?" Harris asked.

Ford hadn't considered that. He was used to Reno, where, between the outlying counties, he had access to more than a hundred deputies at any given time. And the ranking to pull guys as needed.

But he wasn't in Reno, and unless he got recertified, he'd be one of the guys getting pulled around. "I can call in some favors, bring some guys in from my department up north."

"Are you going to cover the overtime as well?" Harris asked. "With Wagon Days, our budget is already thin."

Right.

"What about department-approved volunteers?" Ford asked. "The way I laid out the course, I'd only need two extra officers to help with the zip line. The rest can be local guys who want to get involved with the event."

"So two guys are standing between you and—"

"Liv losing that promotion. That's all."

Harris thunked his head against the side of the truck. "Glad this isn't about a woman."

It wasn't about a woman. It was about a particular woman with melt-your-soul eyes and a rusty laugh who made Ford want to play hero. And he hadn't felt that urge in a while.

That was the problem with playing, he reminded himself. At some point real life levels the playing field, and all you're left with is a badge.

"I can cover two guys, but that's it. The rest will have to be volunteers. I'll take another look at the volunteer applications, and maybe we can get a few recruits to help with the simpler stuff to free up some deputies."

"Thanks. I owe you."

"And I will collect. But in the meantime, think long and hard about what you're doing," Harris said, and then with a smack to the roof of the car, he headed back to his Jeep, his beads glittering in the sunlight.

Appetite gone, Ford stuck his lunch back in the bag and started up the engine. Only instead of looking over to find his partner asleep on the passenger seat, he was met with nubby fur, two plastic eyes, and an opened passenger door.

"Bullseye," Ford called out, wondering what toddler his AWOL partner was mugging now.

Shutting off the engine, Ford hopped out and scanned the parking lot, the nearby stores, even going into Pins and Needles, because for all Ford knew, Bullseye was taking a crafting class on stuffed dolls.

Coming up clean and not wanting to be late to another briefing, he pulled out his phone and opened his Fido Finder, an app made by a search-and-rescue volunteer out of Montana to help locate scenting dogs—dogs like Bullseye who had a habit of following scents when not on the job.

Within seconds, a red dot appeared on the digital map, and Ford looked down the street toward the park. On the edge of the field, a boy stood petting Bullseye, who was practically sitting on top of the kid—like a professional search dog with his find.

Ford walked over to find a boy, clearly with the camp, wearing a red cape and shoes that blinked every time he hopped. And the kid was hopping as high as he could. With his arm in the air, a stuffed toy in hand, doing his best to keep it out of Bullseye's reach.

"If you sit on the grass, I'll give it to you," the boy said, but Bullseye just gave him a wet lick to the face. The boy laughed.

"Try using one-word commands," Ford said, then looked at the culprit. "Sit."

Bullseye sat still as a statue. So did the boy. His eyes big as saucers, his lips pressed firmly together, and clutching his toy to his chest in a defensive gesture that would have taken Ford out at the knees. Except the boy's identity had already leveled him.

Ford had caught a few glimpses of Paxton over the years, but the last time he'd been this close to the boy, Ford had been cradling him to his chest on a helicopter headed for Mercy General. Near hypothermia, spotted in his dad's blood, and tears staining his pale cheeks, the kid never made a sound. Not one during the entire twelve hours they were trapped in that cave.

He'd even cried in silence.

"Hey there," Ford said, crouching down to his level. "You're Paxton, right? This is Bullseye." Ford gave Bullseye a rewarding pat to the head, then proceeded cautiously. "I'm Ford, a friend of your mom's."

Ford waited for some sign on how to continue. Tears, fear, a spark of recognition. The first two made his palms sweat, but the last made him want to pack up and leave town. The kid gave him nothing to work with, leaving Ford with two choices: convince him to go back to camp or call his mom.

The first would be a challenge because Ford already knew how Paxton felt about camp—so thrilled he'd rather sit in a field alone. He didn't know Liv's schedule, so the second might pull her out of work.

And possibly blow Ford's biggest secret.

"Why don't we go find the other kids?" Ford asked, holding out his hand.

Paxton looked at it and then stuck his own thumb in his mouth.

Ford scanned the park, looking for a camp counselor who could explain how a kid was standing next to a busy street unsupervised. He spotted a cluster of capes and brightly colored tights on the jungle gym, a good football field away.

"Are you allowed to be over here?" he asked, and was met with silence. Time for a new strategy. Ford leaned in and whispered to his stuffed animal. "He's good, Superdog. You told me he was an accomplished superhero and that he wouldn't break, but I have to get Deputy Bullseye here back to headquarters, and I can't leave until I know the location of the camp."

Paxton didn't speak, but his eyes took on an excited twinkle.

Relieved he was getting somewhere, Ford quickly looked both ways, then as if imparting a direct order from Superman himself, said, "I need to get a message to someone in the camp. She has blue eyes, blonde curls, and goes by the name Ballerina Girl. Do you know her?"

Superdog remained tight-lipped on the subject, and Paxton kept sucking that thumb, but his head moved in a tiny nod.

"You do?" Ford made a big show out of wiping the sweat off his brow. "I can't tell you how relieved I am to hear that. They said you were good, but that's impressive." Ford pulled out his department-issued notepad and pen and scribbled a note. Folding it in half and half again, he scanned the park a third time. "Can you help Bullseye get this to her?"

Paxton looked at the note and then at the group of kids who were hanging from the bars and playing tag. He swallowed hard and then with a shaky nod, pulled his thumb out of his mouth and reached for the note.

"Thanks, Superboy." Ford handed him the secret message. "Now, she won't take it unless Bullseye gives her the secret handshake. Verification is important in our line of work." And because Ford knew that when it came to boys, the only thing cooler than superheroes and fast cars was a dog with a few tricks under his collar, he said, "Now, watch carefully. I'm about to show you the secret handshake. Ready?"

Paxton nodded, but his eyes were peanut butter on jelly, never looking away as Ford demonstrated.

Putting Bullseye on his leash, Ford stuck out his fist, made firm eye contact, and said, "Give me rocks."

Bullseye threw his head back and barked, then tapped his paw to Ford's fist. And then, because that was only the beginning, Ford made a sound of fireworks exploding, and Bullseye wiggled his paw as he pulled back.

"Like sparks of an explosion," Ford said, and Paxton's face lit with excitement.

Giving Bullseye a good rubdown, Ford handed Paxton the leash and then stepped back. "Now it's your turn."

Paxton tucked the note under Superdog's cape, Superdog under his arm, and then made a fist with his free hand. He looked at Ford, who gave him a go-nod, and he stuck it out for Bullseye. When the dog did nothing, Ford said, "Try it again, and this time say, 'Rocks.'"

Paxton's tongue peeked out in concentration, and he tried it again. With no command, Bullseye eyed the fist and let out a big yawn.

Paxton dropped the leash and toed the ground.

"Don't give up," Ford said, coming up behind him. "Bullseye wants to be your friend and trust you, but most of all he wants to give you what you need, but you have to tell him what to do." Ford stuck his fist out again, and Bullseye looked at him like, *Really, bro.* "He doesn't know if I want him to shake my hand or do the super handshake. That's why it's important to be clear about what you need. Now, make a fist." Paxton did, and Ford guided his hand forward. "Then you say, 'Rocks.'"

Bullseye let out a bark and then performed the trick, explosion and all.

"That was great," Ford said, and Paxton soaked up the praise. He didn't look at the ground or the sky—he looked directly at Ford and beamed so brightly Ford could feel the warmth seeping into his chest. "We used the right word, so he didn't misunderstand what we need from him. Now this time you take the leash and try."

Paxton looked back and forth between the leash and Bullseye, as though this were a trick to get him to talk, and if he didn't, their fun day would be ruined. Then he dropped the leash and stepped back.

Ford put a hand on the boy's slim shoulders. "You got this, buddy. And if you get nervous, just remember Bullseye's got your back."

Ford wanted to say he did too, but he was leaving, and the kid didn't need another person disappearing in his life.

"Now, get to it, Superboy," he said, using the name he'd called him that night, because silent or not, that kid had gone through an ordeal that most adults couldn't have survived.

With a breath big enough for Superman, Paxton stuck out his fist with force, pausing only to look over his shoulder at Ford, who pretended to be busy, making important notes in his pad.

Confident that he wasn't being watched, Paxton squared his shoulders. Ford did his best to give Paxton the room he needed, and that's when he heard it. A soft but fearless "Rocks."

It came out more *walks* than *rocks*, but Ford didn't care. Bullseye obeyed his command, and Superboy had overcome two pretty large obstacles today. His desire to find a connection was stronger than his fear of disappointing someone.

"Good job," Ford said, cool and confident as if he had no doubt in Paxton's skills, when inside he was shaking with relief. "Now go with Bullseye, and when you give the note to Ballerina Girl, let go of his leash and I'll call Bullseye back, but you need to stay there and keep an eye on Ballerina Girl until camp is over."

And wouldn't you know it, Paxton raised his hand like a salute, and then with the leash in his grasp, he raced off. Ford watched after him, his little shoes blinking as they got smaller and smaller, and the emotion in Ford's chest grew larger and larger until swallowing became impossible.

Because that little guy had managed to do the one thing Ford couldn't—accept that he needed connection.

◆ ◆ ◆

The sun was actually still shining when Liv pulled into her driveway. Because of a last-minute schedule change, she was able to get out of work two hours early—and make it home in time for family dinner.

Grabbing the pizza from the passenger seat, she walked around to the front porch. Paxton was sitting on the top step, wiggling with energy, as if he had to use the boys' room. He wore red tights, a blue shirt, and a cape tied around his neck.

"Mommy! You're home!" he said, full of excitement and animation. "I was waiting for you."

"I can see that," she said right as Paxton charged down the front steps and into her arms, clinging to her legs like a sloth. She bent down and gave him a big squeeze, holding him close so she could breathe him in. Only he was too excited to endure the hug, and he was already wiggling out of her arms. "Did Grandma tell you I was coming home?"

"Uh-huh. She also told me you were bringing pizza."

"And cupcakes. Where is she?"

"Talking to her friend." Liv hoped he was on the phone and not in her front room. "I came out here to show you this." He shoved a folded piece of paper in her face, but before she could read it he was walking in circles around her. "It's a secret message from headquarters. I got to deliver it to Ballerina Girl—that's Emma's superhero name—during camp."

"You did?" she asked, her heart melting. Today marked the first day he'd come home from camp happy. Maybe Ford was right and all he needed was time.

"Yup. She had to give rocks to get it. That was the rules. And she did it. In front of everyone. Then she showed me some cool moves."

Paxton did some kind of disco move, and Liv bit back her smile.

"That is cool. But what is 'rocks'?" Liv asked, knowing she was going to owe Harris big-time. She didn't know what he'd said to Emma, but she'd never seen Paxton so excited about playing with a kid. Not even Tommy, the little boy who sometimes came over to trade comic books.

"Like this." Paxton punched the air like he was some kind of ninja. "Now bump my fist when I say so." He looked at her. "Rocks . . . That means go, Mommy."

"Oh, okay. Rocks." Liv bumped fists, and Paxton fell back on the grass as if the explosion was too much to be contained. Kind of like the joy pumping through her chest.

"Then everyone was like, 'Cool, do it again,' so we did. Like a hundred times again, and then Captain Jason called us in for a power chat." He jumped up, fist-pumped the air, and held the pose before continuing. "And he tolded us our Super Assignment. And guess what it is? Guess—you won't guess it right."

Liv gave her best perplexed look. "You all have to make your own superhero pose?"

Paxton rolled his eyes. "Poses are for babies. Us big kids get to come up with a secret handshake for the last day of camp. Captain Jason said it should show our superpowers, so we all have to have one, but no one can have the same one. And no one will have mine."

Liv agreed. Her kid had more superpowers than DC and Marvel put together. He might be shy and slow to warm up, but he had more heart than anyone she knew.

"What does yours look like?" Liv asked, heading Paxton up the stairs and inside the house.

"It's a secret," Paxton said in the same *God, Mom* tone he'd used when she'd asked who was stronger, Superman or Batman. "But me and Superdog are going to practice it a million times. It will be even cooler than *rocks*."

"I bet it will." Liv set the pizza on the counter and poured Paxton a glass of juice. He crawled up onto a stool and took a big gulp. "So every kid teaches it to the whole camp?"

"Yup." He wiped his mouth with the back of his hand. "Just like me and Bullseye did today."

Liv froze. "Bullseye was at camp?"

"Yup, I was waiting for Grandma, and he found me. I thought he wanted Superdog to chew on, but then Ford told me they had to get a secret message to Ballerina Girl, and he needed me to deliver it. But first I had to learn the secret handshake and then do it with him in front of the whole camp. And look." Paxton yanked at the cape, flipping it around to the front and pointing to the huge patch safety-pinned to the center.

"Super Star," Liv read, her heart rolling over.

"Every day one kid gets to be the Super Star, and today it was me, so I get to wear this until tomorrow, and then somebody else gets to be Super Star."

Liv had been wrong. Her son didn't need to be around people. He needed to be around the right people. And today that person had been Ford.

Let today be enough, Liv told herself. It didn't matter that Ford was kind and thoughtful and made her legs turn to mush. When the season ended, so would his time in Sequoia Lake, and he'd be gone, off helping another family.

Carolyn walked into the kitchen with a stern brow raised in Paxton's direction. "Which is why we should take the cape off and hang it up."

Paxton shut down faster than a ski lift in a blizzard. And the kitchen turned equally as frosty.

"I don't see why you can't wear it," Liv said encouragingly, but Paxton was sipping his juice. Well, the glass was to his lips, but he was just breathing into the cup and watching the glass fog up.

"At least take it off at the table so you don't get food on it," Carolyn said, walking to the cupboard to get three plates, then setting them around the table.

"Sweetie, why don't you grab a slice of pizza and take it the front room while Grandma and I talk."

Paxton didn't wait for Carolyn to weigh in on the decision, just grabbed a slice and ran as fast as his blinking shoes could carry him.

"He's never going to talk if you don't encourage family dinners," Carolyn said, moving the pizza box to the table.

"He was just talking." Like a happy, normal kid who'd had a great day at camp.

"Well, he hasn't spoken a word to me," Carolyn said primly, taking a seat at the table and spreading her napkin across her lap. Great. Apparently they were going to sit for this discussion.

"He just has to get used to you." Liv sat down. "The more you're around, the more he'll open up."

"I've been here for three weeks, and he's said more to that stuffed dog than he has me."

"He doesn't feel judged or anxious when he talks to his toys," Liv explained.

Her mouth tightened. "Are you saying it's my fault?"

"No," Liv said, resting a hand on Carolyn's, and she realized the older woman was trembling. "This is nobody's fault—it just is. But the more time you spend together, the more comfortable he'll feel around you, the more relaxed he'll become, and then he'll start talking."

Reason number one why Liv had asked her in-laws not to move across the country. She'd moved here so Paxton could have a stable group of people in his world, but Carolyn needed space from the loss. And Liv got that, but space created distance, and distance didn't allow for the relationship to bloom.

"I can't even count the times I've offered to bring him to Palm Beach to spend the holidays or the summer with me," Carolyn said, placing a slice on each of their plates. "It's like you don't want me to get to know him."

Liv closed her eyes and counted to ten. When that didn't help, she got up and poured herself a glass of wine. After a fortifying sip, she grabbed another glass—and the bottle—and brought the bottle to the table.

"I want you to know him, more than anything," Liv said, pouring her mother-in-law a glass of wine, because they were both going to need it to get through this conversation. She waited for Carolyn to take a sip before adding, "But you need to want to get to know him for who he is right now, with all of his quirks and uniqueness, and that means meeting him on his terms. And with you coming here for a few weeks at a time, it might take a while."

"You make it sound as if I'm not trying," Carolyn said dramatically. "If Sam were here, he would be horrified by these terms."

It was like an arrow sliced through her chest, creating a wound that would never quite heal. One more to add to the collection.

Liv set her glass down and focused on keeping it together. Yelling wouldn't help, and she was past crying. Sadly, she was just tired. The kind of soul-deep tired people got when they'd taken so many beatings they couldn't remember where the last one ended and the new one began.

"Sam isn't here," Liv said steadily. "And these terms aren't here to hurt you—they are here to help Paxton overcome his loss, adapt to his new reality. And I know we have all had to adapt to a world without Sam, but when it comes to Paxton, his journey had to come first."

Carolyn's face puckered as if she'd eaten a lemon, but Liv knew the taste in her mouth wasn't bitter—it was pain. And Liv wished she knew how to make the melding of this family easier, but she meant what she said. Paxton came first.

Always.

Carolyn carefully folded her napkin and placed it on the table, taking the time to smooth over the seams. "Maybe if you had put Paxton first, Sam wouldn't have come home alone that Christmas." Carolyn looked up, tears pooling in her eyes. "And maybe we wouldn't all be in this situation."

CHAPTER 13

"How is this my fault?" Ford asked, because there was no way his friend could be serious.

"You asked for volunteers who had the interest and the time," Harris said with a shit-eating grin. "So I found you volunteers who have all the time and interest you could hope for."

"But can they walk without a cane?" Ford grumbled.

"I don't know, let's ask. Ladies," Harris said, addressing the group of ten, who came in all shapes and sizes. The only thing they had in common, besides dogs, was a senior discount card for the Bunny Slope Supermarket. "How many of you can walk without canes?"

Every hand went up, except Mavis, who had no dog, but she did have a wheelchair that could do zero to speed-of-light in point four seconds.

"See." Harris clapped Ford on the back. "Now, get to teaching, Officer Doolittle. I approved that permit, so you have two weeks to train four of these teams so they can handle some basic crowd control."

Harris disappeared back inside the station, leaving Ford in the back lot, standing in front of his first volunteer search-and-rescue training class, which consisted of a handful of Sequoia Lake citizens on his personal top-ten list of Most Likely to Get Lost While Shopping.

He spotted Dorothy Pines in the front of the class with Bubbles. Dorothy was holding a leash so bright it almost distracted from the sports bra she was trying to pass off as a top, and Bubbles was dressed in an orange construction vest. Right beside them were Patty and LuLu Moberly, dressed in matching jogging gear.

Kill him now.

Leading Bullseye to the front of the group, Ford began. "Why don't we start by sharing a little about ourselves. My name is Officer Jamison. This is my partner, Bullseye, and he is a scenting dog, which means he can detect and follow human scents. We've been partners for six years, and I've been a part of search and rescue for eight years."

Bullseye, knowing the drill, sat tall and proud as if he were waiting for someone to pin a silver star on his chest.

"Ms. Pines, you want to go?"

"My name is Dorothy Pines, and this is Bubbles. She lives a vegan lifestyle, believes in pet equality, and likes long walks on the beach. Oh, and she is working hard to overcome her fear of small, enclosed places. Like air vents." She shot a glare at Patty. "And we signed up as a way to give back to the community that has given us so much, and because when we heard that the personal-statement part of Wagon Days Darling was canceled, we thought we could up our tricks for the talent section."

Ford gripped the back of his neck. "Ms. Moberly, are you here to increase LuLu's chances for being the Wagon Days Darling?"

"Heavens no." Patty clutched her chest as if horrified by the idea. "LuLu and I are here because we heard Dorothy was trying to get face time with the judge. So we put on our best hiking gear and signed right on up."

"It's called being a responsible citizen," Dorothy argued.

"It's called being a brownnoser."

"All right," Ford said, loudly enough to silence the crowd. "Is anyone here for something unrelated to Wagon Days Darling?"

One hand went up, and Bullseye let out a whine and lay on the ground. Ford was ready to call it a day as well. "Mavis?"

"I'm here because I'm in the market for my own partner, and I heard you were some kind of whisperer."

Okay, not what today was about, but at least she'd come with the idea of dog training as the focus. "You mean a dog whisperer?"

Mavis grinned. "No, son. I heard you were a panty whisperer." Patty started snickering.

And so went his first day of search-and-rescue training.

He instructed them on how to walk a dog on a lead, and he lost two candidates when he explained that dog strollers weren't allowed in searches. They'd covered the different types of search dogs and gear, and they quickly moved on to the basics of sit and stay—which to his surprise most of the dogs already knew.

In fact, the dogs were well socialized and trained. It was the owners who needed some training. So when Ford spoke about the importance of leash rules and Patty announced that Dorothy was leash-aggressive and should be disqualified, Ford put them in a time-out.

It wasn't until Ford addressed their main job for Wagon Days—wandering kids and crowd flow—that something clicked.

"I don't know, that sounds a lot like my house when the grandboys come over," Prudence Tuttman, a retired mill worker turned senior pro bass fisherman, said. "Which is why I installed a trampoline in the yard. First sign of trouble and, pow, I put them in the trampoline and let them jump it out."

"Last Christmas, we got the grandkids one of those bounce houses," Patty said. "It's like our own personal MMA fighting cage. Thirty minutes in there and they're too tired to argue."

"I live in the over-fifty-five community, so we don't have yards," another said. "My girls get fussy and I get them busy—baking cakes for the church raffle."

Several of the ladies voiced their agreement, and Ford felt himself start to smile.

Maybe he'd been looking at this all wrong. He didn't need terrain-ready volunteers. What he needed was added presence for a family-friendly event. Crowd control sounded intense, but in reality it could be as simple as directing people to the medic booth or blocking off streets. Harris had deputies assigned to specific places on Lake Street to beef up their presence and help with traffic flow.

There wasn't a person in town who would take on these biddies. In fact, doggy-toting grandmas in orange vests would be as approachable as the Easter Bunny, even for the most timid of lost kids. And they'd be as strict as prison wardens when needed, to keep any potential trouble-makers in line. Ford looked at his team and did the math—between them there was at least two hundred years of town history. He'd bet there wasn't a resident they didn't know—or hadn't pointed one of their bony fingers at.

"You came here to teach your dog tricks, up your scores for the Wagon Days Darling. I came here to train a volunteer team," Ford said, gaining everyone's attention. "So here's my offer. I'll teach you guys some tricks that will wow the panel, but that means I have to recuse myself from judging the talent portion."

A roar of grumbles came from the crowd.

"Hold on, I'm not done. I will still do the final judging, just not the talent portion, but we can have our own helicopter-flying hero, Officer Donovan, step in."

"He may not have this one's backside, but those arms of his are nice to look at," Mavis offered.

"It is two for the price of one," Prudence added.

Not sure how to respond to that, Ford went on. "In return, you become my volunteer team, helping the department the day of the event. You won't handle disputes—you'd just be there to keep things moving smoothly, assist people with questions. And every one of your dogs would be singled out for their service."

It was like watching a time-out at a football game. Without warning, the ladies huddled in a circle, and an intense conversation comprised of tuts, bickering, and a few inappropriate hand gestures took place. After a few moments of deliberation, Mavis popped her head out. "Do we get to carry?"

"Your dogs?" he asked, hoping to God they weren't talking about a weapon.

"No, a gun."

Ford was shaking his head even before she finished asking. "No. Absolutely not."

"You won't have to provide it—we can bring our own," Mavis said. "And Prudence here's one of the best shots in the county."

"In case you're on the fence, I can take out a pea at a hundred yards, open scope," Prudence added.

Ford was so far from the fence he couldn't even see the posts. With a scope. But he needed to give them something. "No guns. But each dog will get an official-looking patch that you can sew on their vests."

"An official patch would look great on Bubbles's vest," Dorothy said.

"Official *looking,*" he clarified, but no one was listening. They were already debating the color scheme of the patch and where it should be sewn for uniformity. "And it will count as community service toward the Wagon Days Darling."

The ladies resumed their positions in two straight lines, and Mavis said, "Deal."

Ford had to laugh. "Great. Next class we'll cover leash control and how to work a crowd with your dog."

Mavis's hand went in the air. "Can I be the test subject when you go over leash techniques?"

He shot her a stern look—not that it helped. Patty was back to snickering. "See you Saturday."

Someone mentioned that there was still time to catch a matinee at the theatre—which was a dollar cheaper than the senior price—and since Brad Pitt had a shower scene, the place cleared out pretty quick.

After giving Bullseye some water, Ford headed out to the side parking lot where his truck was parked.

In the end the class had turned out okay. Not that he'd admit that to Harris, but he couldn't wait to see the look on his good friend's face when he learned he was a new judge.

His smile was back. If he pulled this off, his debt to the department would be settled. So would his promise to Sam.

And Liv.

Ah, Liv. He hadn't seen her since the bar. After his talk with Harris, then his run-in with Paxton, he wasn't even sure what he'd say when he did. So he hadn't said anything, and now another two days had passed and the window to call had slammed shut. And she probably thought he was a complete ass.

Not all that surprising. Nearly every serious relationship Ford had attempted ended in the same fiery death. The whole man-in-uniform thing only lasted so long, because Ford could only last in one place for so long.

"Too busy saving lives to commit to just one," his last girlfriend had said, when in reality, commitment wasn't the issue, it was finding *the one.*

He wasn't saying Liv was the one, but when he was with her he wasn't thinking about the last job or the next job. In fact, he wasn't thinking about the job at all. And that was as much the appeal as the problem, Ford admitted as he crossed the lot.

He turned the corner and saw Harris standing by his vehicle. He was completely suited up, which meant he was headed out on a search.

"If you're here about the pee on your tires, it wasn't me. The dogs got confused and thought your Jeep was a tree."

Harris didn't laugh. "We just got a call, and I need you."

"If it's about a missing dog or Mr. Gordon, my shift ended with my class." Ford walked past him, and Bullseye gave Harris the stink eye.

"Father and two sons, fifteen and eleven, went hiking at Canyon Ridge," Harris said. "One of them called his mom twenty minutes ago to say the father was teaching them how to anchor a rope, when he slipped. The oldest stayed to try to get his dad, and the youngest hiked down to where he could get a signal."

Ford immediately kicked into crisis mode. No one climbed down Canyon Ridge—it was too steep. The only way down was to rappel or fall. "Did he make it to the bottom?"

"Nope, he got halfway down and landed on an outcropping of rocks."

"So we've got a boy and his dad stuck on the side of a cliff?" Ford asked, unlocking the metal storage box bolted to the bed of his truck.

"And an eleven-year-old somewhere in the woods with a dying cell," Harris said. "Ty's working at the lodge today, I have a team working a missing kid over by the high school, and I don't have time to call them back here."

Which meant Ford was officially off desk duty.

"Sixty seconds to gear up, and Bullseye and I will meet you at the chopper."

◆ ◆ ◆

It was past sunset by the time Ford walked through his front door. Exhausted and covered in blood, he dropped his cap on the table, a six-pack in the fridge, and his dirty clothes in the hamper. He should have taken a hot shower and called it a day, but he was too wired to sit still.

Needing to clear his head, Ford slipped on his wetsuit and headed out to the lake, grabbing his board on the way. Usually standing on a board in the middle of a current helped Ford find balance, but tonight the control he needed to stay afloat was a struggle.

Seeing the look on the kid's face when they'd handed off his still-unconscious dad to the EMTs had unearthed things better buried. But no matter how hard he paddled or how far he went, he couldn't rid himself of this feeling that he wasn't finished.

He'd rappelled down to secure the father, getting him on a back-board and into the chopper headed toward Mercy General. He'd even doubled back out and helped locate the missing eleven-year-old and got him safely to the hospital.

Ford had done his job. Logically he knew this, but the feeling that it still wasn't finished settled like lead in his chest, making every breath that much harder. The farther out he paddled, the heavier the paddle got, until it felt as if he were moving through tar.

He could have stayed at the hospital until the kids' mom had arrived. Or maybe waited until they heard the status of the father. Though, technically, he wasn't privy to that kind of information. Nope, Ford's job was to locate and rescue. Period. Whatever happened after that—with the subject, the family—was out of his hands.

Ford paddled faster to get it out of his head. This case was over. Soon there'd be another. And if he had any plans to be there when the next family needed him, then he needed to start focusing on his certi-fication and not shortcomings.

His or the job's.

Arms exhausted and breathing heavily, Ford paddled back to shore, going under the water, welcoming the jolt to his body as he sank beneath the cold ice-cap runoff. Unzipping his wetsuit and freeing his arms, he grabbed his board and walked up the beach to his house.

The moon was high, reflecting off the lake and illuminating the beach and the surrounding area. The shoreline was lit with a million twinkle lights, which hung off the back of nearly every deck lining the shore.

Including Liv's.

Which was how he noticed her small shadow sitting on the bottom step, a few houses down. Wrapped in an oversize sweater, feet in the sand, with Bullseye's head in her lap.

Not trusting himself to be around her right now, Ford considered heading straight inside the house and letting Bullseye enjoy a sleepover at the pretty neighbor's house. Only that would leave Ford alone. And alone was the last thing he could stomach right then.

Not when she was sitting there, those fathomless eyes locked on him, looking like a safe shelter in the storm.

He walked down to the sand and headed toward her house. He was a few feet away when she spoke.

"I was cleaning up Paxton's room and found a stowaway," Liv said, standing and making him wonder if she had anything on under that sweater. It was baggy and hung to midthigh, leaving nothing but silky, bare skin and pink-tipped toes. "I saw you go out on your board, so I let him stay for dinner."

"I hope it wasn't pizza."

"Nope." She walked toward him, her feet sliding in the sand, her hair swaying beneath the breeze, not stopping until he was standing close enough to touch. Close enough to smell—and she smelled like redemption. "Chinese, but I offered the delivery guy a special gift if he picked up a bag of dog kibble at the market on the way."

Ford let his gaze slide slowly over her body, which was a complete showstopper. "What kind of gift are we talking?"

"A cupcake," Liv said, taking in his bare chest, a teasing glint in her eyes when she finally met his. "But don't look so sad—I brought you one too."

To prove it, she held up a plastic bag and offered it to him.

"You made me cupcakes?" He weighed the bag and looked at her. "Or a bag of flour to make my own?"

"They're store-bought cupcakes, but the Chinese food in there is freshly made."

"Are you buttering me up?"

"No," she said, but he didn't believe her.

Opening the bag, he took in the to-go boxes and crooked an amused brow.

"What? I said freshly made, not homemade. But if you need your gutters cleaned, I'm your girl."

Three words that in a different scenario he'd take her up on in a hot minute. But things weren't different, and she couldn't be his. At least not for the long term.

But Ford wasn't thinking about the long term right then. He was just thinking about making it through the night.

"What if I need something else?"

CHAPTER 14

Liv's bones turned to mush. "What?"

"Not that, cupcake," Ford said on a groan. "Although, *that* I want more than you could possibly know. But Paxton is home, and I'm not feeling gentle tonight."

He sure felt gentle, the tender way he cupped her hip, pulling her closer until she was dizzy with his scent. Yet it wasn't the desire lacing his eyes that had her taking his hand and leading him to his deck. Although there was enough heat to melt her panties, there was something much more than chemistry humming between them. Something raw and vulnerable.

Something desperate.

"Whatever you need," she said quietly as they walked up the steps.

Ford stood at the deck's edge. "Clark White was brought into Mercy General today. He was unconscious, suffering from a punctured lung, and probably has some internal bleeding."

Liv linked their fingers. "Is he a friend of yours?"

"No," Ford said, looking out at the lake. Wetsuit clinging to his hips, water still dripping from his body, the blue light of the moon casting shadows on his face. He looked invincible and fragile at the same time. "He and his sons were rescued from Canyon Ridge this afternoon."

Liv had been working the ER when the father was airlifted in. She remembered hearing about a father-son team that had kept Dr. Bristol, one of the best trauma surgeons in the area, in the OR for most of the afternoon. "Were you on the team?"

"I helped lift Clark out." His tone said it was just another day at the office, but the hard lines bracketing his mouth told a different story. "On your next shift, can you just check in on him and see how he's doing?" Ford faced her. "I'm not asking you to do anything that could get you in trouble, so no details needed. Just let me know if he made it."

Her heart pinched over this big, capable man's struggle with the need for answers and the need to protect.

"And if he didn't?"

The pain that filled his eyes winded her. Ford had said it was the not knowing that stuck with him, but Liv wondered if it went deeper than that. Wondered what he'd lived through, experienced, that made reaching out so difficult.

Wanting to explore and heal all of his scars, but knowing that there might only be the time for them to explore this one, Liv pulled her phone from her shorts pocket and dialed the hospital.

"You don't have to do that," Ford said, reaching for her phone.

"I know." She cupped his cheek. "I want to. Let me do this for you." When he still didn't let go of her phone, she explained, "It's just a call, Ford."

He studied her for a long moment, and then with a nod, he disappeared into the house. Liv waited until she saw the kitchen light flicker on and then hit "Send."

It took less than five minutes to get the information she needed, and then she thanked the attending nurse and hung up.

Letting herself in through the back door, Liv found the kitchen. It was painted a warm yellow with antique cooking utensils framed on the walls and a long table in the middle. Complete with six place mats, diner salt-and-pepper shakers, and a pot filled with lavender-and-green peonies, the kitchen was family ready and made to be lived in.

Only Ford stood at the sink window, chest still bare, hair still wet. Gone was the wetsuit, and in its place was a pair of soft-looking button-flies and bare feet. His dinner was spread out on the counter, which, based on how untouched everything appeared, was where he'd eaten his meals since moving in.

He didn't move, just braced himself against the counter with his palms and stared blankly out the window.

Even from a distance she could feel the emotions churning inside him. He looked spooked, his body braced as if ready to run. She wanted to tell him that running didn't solve anything. It was as destructive as shutting down. Without steady, consistent motion, the pain lay dormant, waiting for the next time to come to the surface, and the healing was intensified and prolonged.

Beneath that easygoing charm and flirting, Ford was fighting a battle of his own. His personal relationship with loss and guilt clearly kept him from what he desperately needed: genuine connection.

A peaceful place to rest his head.

"I talked to Mr. White's attending nurse," she began, and when Ford didn't move a muscle, she knew he'd been aware of her the entire time. "He got out of surgery a few hours ago and is in recovery. They repaired his lung, and there was minimal internal bleeding. He's going to be there for a few weeks, but he'll make a full recovery."

It was as if all the air was knocked out of Ford with a single whoosh. His shoulders slumped forward, his body curved in, and he hung his head. "Thank you."

Liv placed a gentle hand on his back, offering comfort and connection, surprised to find him shivering. "Are you cold?"

"Just the adrenaline crash," he said, his head still hanging. "It'll pass."

She stepped up behind him and wrapped her arms around his middle, resting her cheek on the middle of his back. His stomach muscles bunched under her fingers.

Liv knew what "bad days" in their line of work could look like. Knew how hard it was to come down from the intensity and chaos of it all. Just like she knew that what Ford really needed right then was human connection.

So she tightened her arms and held on. Neither of them spoke—they didn't need to. She just wrapped herself around him and waited until his breathing normalized and his heart rate slowed enough to match hers. Even then she closed her eyes and held tight.

When the shivers stilled and his skin had warmed some, Liv realized that the energy between them had shifted. She felt his chest fill and slowly empty with an edge of finality that made her want to hold tighter.

"You should go," he said.

"I know." Neither of them moved.

"Paxton is probably wondering where you are."

"He's watching a movie with his grandma. *The Lone Ranger*." Ford tipped his head to the side so he could look at her over his shoulder. "He wears a mask and fights crime. She's trying."

Which made Liv happy. Sleepless nights and spiraling guilt aside, something positive had come out of their conversation. And she'd take the win.

He straightened, causing her to drop her arms. "And I'm trying to do the right thing here, Liv."

"And why do you think being alone is the right thing?" she asked quietly.

"Because having you here like this, touching you . . ." Leaning against the counter, he reached out and cupped her hip and slowly drew her toward him. He parted his legs to make room for her and—just like that—she wanted to be had.

Like this and by him.

More than anything she wanted to remember what it was like to be touched. Not just touched, but moved in a way that rerouted her emotions and left a mark. A mark that would last all summer and maybe for longer.

"It makes me forget why I'm here."

"Maybe it's not the forgetting that's the problem," she said. "What if it's all about the remembering?"

Fire flickered in his eyes, telling her that he was remembering every detail of their kisses. "Have dinner with me, Ford."

He looked at her hands on his pecs. "You keep saying dinner, but all I can think about is what happens after."

"Dessert," she said with a smile.

"Damn, I do love a good cupcake," Ford said, and lowered his head, taking her mouth without warning. It wasn't the gentle teasing they'd shared in the past. No, this was Ford—raw and unfiltered.

Reminding her why he was going to be so hard to give up.

Dessert doesn't necessarily mean getting naked, Ford told himself again.

It was the same thing that had been on repeat since she'd walked into that kitchen and wrapped her arms around him. Soft and sweet, Liv, with her big heart and caring ways. The right thing to do would be pull back, clarify, and go in a new direction if necessary.

One that wouldn't lead them into dangerous territory.

But then her hands were on the move, sliding down his chest—shy and hesitant but defiantly headed for uncharted waters and, *thank you, Jesus,* he was pretty sure dessert meant step four.

Then her body moved against his in this little swivel-hip move that had his eyes rolling to the back of his head, and he discovered her cupcakes were sans a bra, and knew that while dessert might not mean sex, step four sure as hell did.

And Liv was telling him she was ready for both. Please, God, tell him he wasn't misreading the signals. Because while he knew how to read women, he didn't know jack shit about reading *this* woman.

Normally this would be an open-and-close case, one that would start on the counter and finish with breakfast in bed. But Liv wouldn't be here come breakfast, and Ford wasn't even sleeping in his own bed. His bed was two hours away, in another state, and rarely slept in.

A part of him wondered how often he'd travel if he knew a woman like her was keeping his bed warm, but the other part knew better—he wasn't that guy.

But he also refused to be that other guy with her. The one who was too busy checking to see if his earlier hypothesis about her cupcakes was correct—which a gentle slide up her back confirmed that he was—to clarify that this was an intentional turn in direction and not some spur-of-the-moment road trip.

He wasn't ready to pull the emergency brake, but he wanted to tap them long enough to see where she was at.

"What are you doing?" she asked, her eyes fully dilated to sex kitten.

"Checking to make sure you're okay with this."

"I thought you were checking to see if I'm wearing a bra." She bit her lip and shook her head.

It took everything he had to keep his eyes on her face. "I'm just looking out for you."

"How about tonight we look out for each other?"

And with that, she pulled her sweater up and over her head and . . .

No.

Fucking.

Bra.

Just a pair of cutoffs, silky skin, and a set of perfect tens that had his mouth watering and his unnavigated waters going as wild as the rapids.

And in case *that* wasn't crystal fucking clear enough, she grabbed the band of his jeans and whispered, "When you're done looking after me, I want to look after you."

Question answered.

Always a team player, Ford did his part of the heavy lifting, undoing the first two buttons on her shorts. Lucky guy that he was, Liv wrapped her arms around his neck and went up on her toes, giving him all the room he needed to slip the shorts off her hips and down to the floor. Leaving her in nothing but a tiny pink thong.

"My turn?" she asked against his lips.

"I haven't even looked yet," he said, skimming his hands down her sides to cup her cheeks and then lifting her onto the counter. Where he looked and tasted his fill. Kissing her mouth, her neck, her breasts, showing her just how insanely beautiful she was.

"Perfect," he whispered against the curve of her breast. Opening wide, he hummed with pleasure as he covered her, then drew his teeth over the delicate flesh until he reached the nipple. He carefully bit down, searching for her reaction.

The sexy gasp that ebbed from her throat flushed his veins with heat. He released her, soothing the sting with his tongue. "You like that?"

"I think so," she said, and Ford looked up to find her curiously surprised, the earlier confidence taking on a shyer tone.

"You think so as in *you're not sure* or *you don't like it?*"

"I liked it, I just wasn't sure that I would," she admitted quietly.

He straightened, moving between her legs and running his hands over her thighs. "Well then, let's go slow so we can see what you are and aren't sure about," he said, and she nodded. "Now, I know you're sure about this."

Ford took her mouth in a gentle kiss that told her she had all the time she needed. He wasn't going to rush her. He couldn't give her forever, but he could give her the perfect entry into living after loss. Show her what she deserved in a man and how treasured she should feel.

He was going to set the bar so fucking high that she'd never settle.

The kiss picked up heat until Liv was panting against his lips, reminding him of exactly why he couldn't stop thinking about her. Her ankles were locked behind his back, and she was wiggling against him to create friction. Nothing between them but his jeans and a scrap of silk so thin he could feel how wet she was.

"I'm sure," she moaned when he slowly raised his hand up to cup her breasts. When he replaced it with his mouth, she dropped her head back against the cabinet. "So sure."

And when he was sure she was lost in the haze, he nipped her again, not hard, just enough to feel her legs tighten around him. "Yes, sure. I didn't think I'd be sure, but God, I'm so sure."

He smiled against her skin as he did it again and then decided to head south, see if she was open to a little assistance below the equator. His lips skimmed across her belly, down to the little patch of skin that peeked out above her panties and, *hallelujah*, look at that! Her legs parted on their own.

He kissed her inner thigh, then the other, teasing every inch along her panties until she was panting. She moved her hips, trying to show him where she wanted him, so he moved back down to her inner thigh.

"Higher," she begged. "I'm already sure about all of those places."

"I'm a thorough guy," he said, and to prove it, he licked her right up the center, and she cried out. So he did it again, only this time he moved the strip of silk aside.

"Oh God, I am so sure," she panted. "More than sure. Positive!"

Ford did his best to drive her positively over the edge. Licking and sucking, even using his teeth until he could feel her tighten, feel her thighs wrap around his shoulders. Then he added a finger to the mix, just one at first, then two when she begged, and then he gave a flick-swirl combo, and she came apart in his hands.

So beautiful, he thought as the moonlight came through the window and reflected off her wet lips and bedroom eyes.

"Lift up," he coaxed as he gently slid her panties off and onto the floor.

"Is it my turn to do the looking?" she asked, sounding very relaxed, her hands fumbling with his button fly.

She managed to get two undone by the time he'd reached for the condom in his back pocket. Because even though he'd promised to keep his hands off her, he knew the second she'd followed him inside he wouldn't be able to.

Ford was tearing open the condom when her delicate fingers slid into his pants to wrap around him.

"Are you sure?" she asked, this sexy little purr to her voice, then slowly stroked him from base to tip and back down, tightening as she went.

"I'm sure that if you keep that up, we won't get to dessert."

"You already had my cupcakes." And they were incredible, but her hands were even better. Soft and sure, giving him an eyes-rolling-to-the-back-of-the-head squeeze that nearly caused him to drop the condom.

"We said look not touch, and we said we were looking after each other." He put her hand on his shoulder, quickly sheathing himself and stepping into her. "So the next time either of us comes, it will be together. Agreed?"

Liv gave him a sexy smile. "If you're sure."

"Oh, I'm sure," he said, and wrapping her legs around him, he entered her in one slow thrust that had both of them moaning in pleasure.

He might have moaned a second time, because she felt that good. That right. So right he knew that once he had her in his bed, he'd never want to leave.

And then in a move that knocked him out at the knees, she leaned forward and whispered, "I'm sure about you, Ford."

And then she kissed him sweetly, softly, until he felt his entire world spin back to right. Her mouth was like sunshine, and her hands rolled over his body as if molding his image.

Then she wrapped her arms around him and buried her face in his neck, and he was pretty sure he'd found peace. But then she started moving, up and down, their bodies getting slick in the evening air, and Ford changed his mind.

It wasn't peace he was feeling—it was coming home. He didn't want to run, didn't feel the need to search. He felt as if he'd been lost, searching for his way home, and Liv had rescued him.

"Ford," she said, and he realized she was watching him, concern in her eyes.

"I'm sure," he said, moving inside her with strong, healing strokes. Trying to get as deep inside her as he could, wanting to fall right into her and never come up.

Eyes never leaving his, she tightened around him, her body pressed so tightly against his, they were moving as one unit. She hid nothing from him, locked on, opened and honest.

"Ready?" he asked as he slid under her, lifting her off the counter so he could go deeper. Using her arms, she rose and nodded.

She lowered herself back down right as he thrust up. He felt something inside of him start to crumble, felt the first tremor of her release, and when he did it again, he felt her shatter around him, squeezing so erotically tight that it was too much and not enough all at the same time.

All the guilt, the frustration, the past coiled into a tight ball in the center of his chest, and then it too shattered. So hard his knees gave out and they slid to the floor.

Resting his head back against the lower cabinets, Ford fought for breath as Liv curled around him. Heart still hammering, he gathered her close and pressed his face into her hair, breathing her in. And damn if he wasn't wrong.

She didn't smell like cupcakes—she smelled like home.

◆ ◆ ◆

Liv lay there, her arms tight around Ford, listening to his chest rise and fall, and waited. Waited for the reality of what had just happened to slam into her. For the guilt and the second thoughts to kick in and press down.

Only as she lay there, waiting, the only thing she felt was elation. A lightening of her chest, a clarity in her heart, and all kinds of wonderful zings floating through her body.

God, she'd missed this.

The intimacy, the connection, the weightlessness that came from opening up to someone else in such a basic, elemental way.

She'd mistakenly thought that this part of her life was securely wrapped up in Sam, so when he died she'd let it go with him. But she'd been wrong. And tonight she was reclaiming it for herself.

This jubilation and freedom was hers. It had always been hers, and now she was allowing herself to share that experience with someone else.

She'd been wrong to think that one relationship could diminish another. It only made her realize how amazingly different two men could be. And how far she'd come in her journey.

Liv opened her eyes, surprised to find Ford watching her. He looked so serious she wanted to laugh. She also wanted to cry, but since that would probably freak him out even more, she kissed him.

"I'm still sure," she whispered and kissed him again. "And in case you're still worried, I was sure twice in fifteen minutes. That's a record for me."

That time he smiled. "It could have been three, but you started getting handsy and sped things up."

"I'm a nurse. We excel with our hands."

"I noticed." He gave her another brush of the lips and then lifted her off him and placed her on her feet. Her legs were almost as wobbly as her heart.

Because this hadn't been a precursor to step four. It *was* step four. They weren't dating, and they didn't have a title, but they did share a relationship. However tenuous it was, it would forever shape her life.

"Don't move." Ford stood, walking all six-plus glorious feet of him down the hallway like naked was his thing, and Liv got her first chance to really look at him. And *sweet baby Jesus*, the man was big. Everywhere.

A gentle giant, she thought, picking up her sweater and slipping it on. She grabbed her shorts and was looking for her underwear when a scrap of pink silk came into view, dangling from a manly finger.

"Need help?" he asked, and she snatched it back.

Stuffing it in her shorts pocket, she slipped them on and went to button them, when Ford pushed her hands aside. He'd tugged on his jeans but was still missing the shirt, so when he stepped closer, she had a yummy overload.

He took his time buttoning her shorts, then linking his thumbs into her belt loops, he tugged her close to kiss. "Now, why were you buttering me up earlier?"

Liv laughed, and it felt good. "It doesn't matter. We can talk about it tomorrow."

When she couldn't still taste him on her lips.

"I don't like it." He lowered his mouth and kissed her until she forgot how to argue. With a satisfied grin, he grabbed the chopsticks off the counter and handed her a set. Then he grabbed Liv by the waist and set her on the counter.

Stepping between her legs, he opened one of the to-go boxes, Mongolian beef, and offered her the first bite. "Now, why did you stop by?"

Liv speared a piece of broccoli. "To be clear. This." She waved the chopsticks between them. "Wasn't part of the buttering."

"This," he said wickedly, "is too sweet to be anything but frosting."

Liv didn't know why that made her heart pitter-pat, but it did. "I need a favor."

He chuckled. "Last time you asked for a favor, I spent my day being ogled by a bunch of old ladies."

"You also got cupcakes."

"Point taken." He popped a bite in his mouth. "What's the favor?"

"I want to rent your dog."

She looked around, realizing that she hadn't a clue as to where Bullseye had gone.

"He's a gentleman—he's in his room. And why do you want to rent my dog?"

Liv pulled out the note she'd stuck in her pocket and handed it to him. She'd read it a dozen times since seeing it, and it still made her tear up.

Ballerina Girl~

Superboy is one of us. He has shown you the secret handshake. Show him our secret dance moves.

~Bullseye

"I found him standing by the road, alone," he said. "Actually, Bullseye found him. I was going to call you, but I decided I'd try to get him to go back on his own terms."

"I'm glad you didn't," she said, running a hand down his arm. "It ended up being his best day of camp. Probably his best day of the summer."

He shrugged self-consciously, and Liv found it odd that for such a confident man, Ford had a hard time accepting a genuine compliment.

"The handshake went off so well that Paxton was nominated Camp Super Star, and the counselors asked everyone to come up with their own handshake for the parade. Which is why I need to borrow Bullseye. I think it will help Paxton relax in front of his peers, and maybe even open the door to making some friends." She pulled out another folded paper, this one an article she'd printed out. "I found this shelter in

Denver that helps shy or anxious kids overcome their fears of public speaking with kitten therapy."

"Kitten therapy?"

"They bring kids who have a hard time reading in front of class into a room full of kittens and have them read to the kittens," she explained. "It helps socialize the kittens for adoption, but researchers found that the kids' stress levels dropped significantly because they could practice reading aloud without being judged."

"It's another reason we bring nonthreatening dogs like Bullseye on searches for kids. Most of the trailing K-9s can track a week-old scent, but kids are more likely to respond to the calls of the officers if they see a goofy dog by their side rather than a German shepherd or a Doberman. It also calms the kids and creates an immediate conversation starter," he said. "Sometimes we only have a few seconds to gain their trust, and an animal can help with that."

Liv wasn't so sure about his theory. There was a gentleness and sincerity about Ford that made him easy to like. Easy to really like, she thought, staring at his lips. "So can I rent your dog?"

"You can borrow him, on one condition," he said, and she met his gaze, steady and warm. "Have dinner with me? A real dinner?"

"Unless it comes in a box or off a menu, I'll burn it."

Ford cupped her cheek. "I didn't ask you to cook for me—I asked you to come to dinner with me."

When he looked at her like that, Liv was afraid she'd go anywhere with him.

CHAPTER 15

"How many more sheriffs' badges do we have left to paint?" Grace asked, wiping gold glitter off her fingers onto her apron. "I'm starting to see doubles of everything."

Liv was having a hard time seeing anything past her upcoming date with Ford. It had been three days since their impromptu dinner turned dessert, and her body was still tingling. In fact, her whole world felt all tingly. Which accounted for the goofy grin she wore.

"At least you're on paint duty. I've stabbed every finger twice." Avery sucked on her pointer finger. "There is no safety in these pins."

"There's only one more box, and then we're done," Liv said, looking at the rows of drying sheriffs' badges lining her kitchen counter. "The Stroller Patrol is taking care of the spurs for their feet, and Mr. Burns got us a deal on pink cowgirl hats for the girls."

A few weeks ago, Liv hadn't known even half of those people except in passing. Now she was making connections, building relationships, and spreading her wings.

And the stretch felt good.

She'd always been afraid that spreading her wings would require her to lose her footing. But the higher she flew, the more grounded she became.

She enjoyed working with the other mothers. Enjoyed being someone other people came to with questions. And she especially enjoyed how full her life was starting to feel. Not full to where it was hard to breathe like before. This kind of full had a lightness to it.

All she'd had to do was let go of some of the weight.

"What are those?" Grace asked.

"Eye masks for kids who want to be outlaws," Liv said, finishing up the stitching on the eye mask and cutting the thread.

"Cute idea," Avery said.

"It was all Paxton." She held the mask up to her face. "He watched *The Lone Ranger* with his grandma and said kids should be able to pick between being a sheriff and an outlaw."

"I still can't believe Carolyn blamed you for Sam's death," Grace said.

"She didn't blame me," Liv said, trying to ignore the hollow ache in her chest. She'd been trying to ignore it since her last conversation with Carolyn, without much luck. "She knew Sam and I were having problems. I mean, who shows up to their parents' on Christmas Eve with their son and no wife?"

"People whose wives are nurses and drew the short straw to work Christmas Eve," Avery said.

"I could have found someone to work my shift if I had wanted." But she'd been more interested in making a point.

Sam had been working so many hours at the hospital that he was rarely home. He'd worked on Thanksgiving and was booked to work New Year's, so when he agreed to assist in a surgery in Las Vegas on Christmas Eve, Liv drew the line. Told him something needed to change. That she missed him, missed their marriage.

And Paxton missed his dad.

He'd promised to put the family first and make a valid effort to be home for family dinners and important dates—and Liv believed him. Then the surgery was moved to Christmas Day, and he wanted Liv to change her schedule to go with him to see his parents on Christmas Eve.

She'd put her foot down. Told him to take Paxton to Sequoia Lake to celebrate with his parents, and they could do a quick present opening Christmas morning as a family before he flew down to Vegas. But when he got home, they would need to have to have a serious talk.

"Do you think that's why she always rents a cottage instead of staying here?" Grace asked.

"I think she sold the house because it reminded her too much of Sam, and now it hurts for her to see how much the house has changed," Liv said. "I just don't know how to make her understand that by moving to Palm Beach, she's missing out on the biggest part of Sam."

"It's sad, but that's her choice," Grace said, setting the paintbrush down.

"Her choice or not, Paxton is missing out too," Liv said, thinking about how awkward and uncomfortable it was when the three of them were in the room together. "He won't even talk to me if he thinks she's in the house, and she's too busy judging my parenting skills to see how far he's come. It's this horrible cycle that's only getting worse. I don't know how to fix it."

"Then stop trying to fix it," Avery said, as if it were that easy.

"And what? Let Paxton miss out on how amazing it could be having a grandparent? No way. I know what it's like to grow up with just a mom, and I remember what it was like when I lost her. I don't want that for Paxton."

"But this isn't amazing," Avery said gently. "And before you give me that look, hear me out. You're a nurturer—that's what you do. You want to make sure everyone is taken care of, and taken care of right." Even though Avery made her sound a little like a control freak, Liv decided to take that as a compliment. "But if you're always smoothing things over, it will never get hard enough for him to push through the fear."

"Exactly—Paxton's had enough hard in his life."

"So has Carolyn, and they've both pushed through. I bet if you remove yourself from the middle, they'd be forced to work this out too. At some point, Carolyn will have to see that she can't force Paxton to be someone he's not ready to be. And Paxton will get tired of eating tuna casserole because he's too scared to say her casseroles are toxic."

Liv's brain said it was a logical solution, one worth experimenting with. But fear reminded her just how easy it was for Paxton to close back up. School started in just a few weeks, and she didn't want to risk losing what they'd worked so hard to gain.

"Are you saying I should agree to let her take him to Florida for a few days?" Liv asked, her mouth going dry.

"At some point, but how about starting with a sleepover. A normal grandmother-grandson thing to do," Avery suggested. "She's right down the lake—let her take him for the night. What's the worst that could happen? They don't talk and things remain the same, or something changes in the situation and they have to address it."

Panic soured her stomach just thinking about it. "And what if he's having an awful time or he gets sick? It's not like he'll tell her, and she won't call me."

"She shouldn't. It's his first sleepover at his grandma's—it's supposed to be awful for both of them." Grace laughed. "By design, trips to the grandparents' include things such as watching morning talk shows, eating casseroles, and sleeping in a bedroom that smells like mothballs. But they also include learning cool games to impress your friends, like poker and blackjack, sneaking into the candy jar to find leftover mints from restaurants, and getting to understand a different generation."

"And getting to know more about his father."

Grace placed her finger to her nose. "Bingo."

It was often difficult for her to see the difference between Paxton being uncomfortable because of his disorder and being uncomfortable like every other six-year-old. Maybe this was a simple rite of passage.

Letting him spread his wings, like she had hers.

"Look at you," Avery said, giving her shoulders a shimmy. "You had your first sleepover and came home early, but I didn't hear you complaining."

Her face heated at the reminder. "It wasn't a sleepover. It was a friendly dinner."

"I need more friends like that," Grace said dreamily. "I should try ordering from your Chinese place. All I ever get is fortune cookies telling me, 'Your future is around the next corner.' Did you know if you keep looking around corners you'll end up in the same place you started?"

All three women looked up at what sounded like a mini Running of the Bulls stampeding through her front door. The skidding and stomping drew to a close, and Paxton slid into the kitchen.

"Mommy," he said, vibrating with excitement, "guess what Bullseye and I just . . ."

Paxton's face went slack, and his eyes swung from Liv to Avery to Grace, and back to Liv, his little mouth hanging open with the word still right there on his tongue. The joy slid down his face, caving in and bringing his confidence with it.

It was as if he'd been doused in ice-cold water. Grace put an encouraging smile on her face, and Avery said, "Hey, Pax."

But Paxton didn't talk back. His lips closed and his gaze slowly began to sink toward the ground, and Liv wanted to wrap him up in her arms and tell him it was okay. But he hated it when she babied him, so she deflected the attention off him. "We're working on the cool eye masks."

"They are cool," a smooth and sexy voice said. "But not as cool as this trick Paxton just taught Bullseye."

Behind Paxton, looking larger than life, stood Ford with Bullseye at his side. He was wearing flip-flops, board shorts, and a T-shirt that clung to him. His nose was pink as if he'd been on the water, and his hair was damp, finger-combed at best, and just looking at him made her mouth go dry.

Which was the exact opposite of what was going on beneath the table. "The trick?"

"A general's salute," Ford said coolly, his eyes on Liv. "I came out of the lake and found Pax and Bullseye playing. And I asked him what they were playing, and Paxton said the Lone Ranger, so we came up with a cool trick so Bullseye could feel more a part of the game. And Paxton helped him out. Watch.

"Bullseye, come." Ford pointed to the ground, and Bullseye sat in the exact spot.

"Is that how he talks during these friendly dinners?" Grace whispered.

Liv didn't answer. She was too busy watching Ford control his world in a way that allowed for others to find their freedom. "Now, Paxton, he's going to need you to give him the order."

Paxton looked up at Ford, and his face fell because he was afraid that if he didn't talk, this fun day would be over. But if he tried and couldn't, it would be even worse. So when Paxton took on that far-off stare that always made Liv nervous, she wanted to ask if maybe Ford could show them.

But Ford knelt down in front of Paxton, a mountain of calm confidence and gentle understanding, and something inside Liv told her to hold back.

"He wants to do the trick," Ford said right to Paxton. "But he needs you to tell him what to do."

There was no question mark at the end, but he wasn't ordering Paxton either. Ford was simply stating what needed to happen, then assuming Paxton could handle the task.

Paxton looked at Bullseye, and when he was about to look back at Liv and the guests, Ford did the most amazing thing. He moved with Paxton, staying in his line of sight and retaining his attention. "Do you need anything from me first?"

Heart in her throat, Liv watched in silence as Paxton shook his head.

"All right, then just have him sit, and you know the rest."

Paxton turned to face Bullseye, who was on his side on the floor. As soon as Paxton made eye contact, the dog stood up. Paxton stood taller, and taking a big breath, he said, "Sit." And the dog sat. "Good boy. Salute."

Paxton stuck his hand on his forehead in example, and Bullseye saluted. The table erupted in applause, and when Paxton turned around, he didn't look scared. He looked proud.

Happy.

Liv hopped up to give him a big hug, but Ford slid her a gentle look. "Good job, Bullseye. Look at all the pretty ladies who want to hug you." Then he turned to Paxton and lifted his hand. "That was awesome."

"Awesome," Paxton said, smacking Ford a high five.

And Liv understood. For Paxton the reward wasn't the praise—it was being treated like any normal kid who'd taught a dog a trick.

"Amazing," Liv said to Paxton, her gaze locking with Ford.

With a toothy grin, Paxton grabbed Bullseye's leash and ran back out the front door, joyous laughter rising in his wake.

Ford stood on the threshold silently looking at Liv, which worked for her because she couldn't stop looking at him. Her friends, she noticed, were looking at what was happening, so Liv excused herself and walked Ford into the other room.

"I feel like I keep saying thank you, but thank you."

"He's a strong kid, Liv. And you've done a great job," he said, brushing his knuckles against her fingers. "I'd better go grab Bullseye. He stole one of your masks."

"That one's all his," Liv said, wondering what it would take to make the man in front of her all hers. "I have five hundred more if you want one too?"

His lips twitched. "You into outlaws, cupcake?"

Her entire body reacted. But Liv knew better. He might flirt like an outlaw and even go from town to town looking for trouble like an outlaw, but Ford didn't have the heart of an outlaw, because while he appeared to be a lone gun, Ford craved deep connections.

Otherwise he wouldn't make a point to keep checking in on his friends. Ford was on the outside of all his relationships looking in, just waiting for an invitation.

"I'm into you," she said, pressing her hands to his chest, and he groaned.

"A statement I'd love to explore." Ford grabbed the loops on her pants and tugged her close, her nipples perking up for a nice hello. "In a place that doesn't have so many ears listening."

Liv turned to find both Avery and Grace craning their necks to peek. "How about that dinner you promised? I have Saturday night off. I just need to see if Carolyn is free to take Paxton home after camp."

"You're going to ask Carolyn to sit while you go out on a date?"

"No, I'm going to ask Carolyn if she wants to spend some time with her grandson. Celebrate his big day." Spread her wings.

"I work until four," he said—to her mouth.

"Does that mean you'll be showing up in uniform?"

"Only if you agree to play assisting nurse," he said, and with that he walked out the door.

◆ ◆ ◆

Saturday, Ford had finished his second dog-training class, surprised to find that his students had shown up prepared, eager—and all in matching WAG AND WADDLE PATROL shirts and vests. The dogs in vests, the ladies in shirts, and everyone in neon pink—Dorothy had overseen the design.

They'd focused on dog cues and managed to get though leash techniques with only three inappropriate comments from Mavis. When it was over, the ladies presented him with a shirt of his own.

Which was how he found himself driving to Liv's house in a pink muscle shirt that read LEASH MASTER.

Liv.

He'd spent most of his week on the phone, burning through his network of search-and-rescue guys trying to find a few willing to work the ropes course—for free. And the rest of it fantasizing about his dinner with Liv.

The one they'd shared and the one that was yet to come.

He hadn't heard confirmation yet—she'd said she was going to talk with Carolyn—but that had been three days ago. Oh, they'd shared a few sexts and some pretty steamy calls, even bumped into each other at the market—her basket was full of cupcakes, string cheese, and macaroni and cheese. Boxed. He didn't have a basket. Just a toothbrush and a box of condoms.

She gave him one of her cupcakes. He gave her a kiss that had her vowing to talk to Carolyn.

Ford was considering asking one of his Wag and Waddlers to sit, but after spending the morning with them, he was looking forward to a quiet afternoon at home.

A hot shower followed by a cold beer and a game on the jumbo flatscreen. Old Man Keller might be old, but the man knew his electronics.

But as he came up on his own driveway and saw a bunch of kids sitting on his lawn, Ford pulled over. Then he swore. These weren't just any kids. They were giggling, frolicking, female kids dressed in tutus and tiaras.

Then he saw a big blow-up castle in his driveway with Emma bouncing for her life, and Ford got a bad feeling in his chest. He threw his car into park and opened his door.

The moment his foot hit concrete, Emma raced over, squealing, "You're here! Did Daddy tell you we get to play dress-up? Real dress-up, with makeup and boas and plastic princess heels."

"Where is Daddy?" he asked, letting Bullseye out of the truck.

"He saw you drive up and went in the house," Emma explained with a toothy grin. "Can Bullseye play dress-up too? We want him to be our prince."

"Go on, Bullseye." Bullseye glanced at the herd of princesses and looked up at Ford as if he'd rather play with a litter of kittens. "You cuddle with a pink lamb—now go."

With a huff, Bullseye went with Emma. And Ford went to find Harris.

He didn't have to look long. The fucker was sprawled out on the couch, cold beer in hand, feet on the coffee table—making himself right at home.

Even worse, Ty was in the recliner, the only piece of furniture Ford used in the house besides the bed.

"Nice shirt," Harris said when Ford approached. "I think Emma has a headband that would match it. You should ask her about it."

"That better not be my beer." Neither of them responded. He took in the empty pizza boxes, the cooler filled with soda cans and juice boxes, and pointed to the purple whoops-I-squeezed-too-hard stain on the rug. "What's that?"

"That, my friend, is me cashing in on the favor you owe me."

"I said I'd babysit Emma—not her whole dance class."

"Actually," Harris said, lifting a piece of pizza to his lips, "you said anything."

"Food stays in the kitchen," Ford said, snatching the pizza away and taking a bite. "And how do you know I don't already have plans?"

The assholes busted up laughing, but it was Ty who spoke. "You handed your leash over to the pretty neighbor, who is busy working on Wagon Days shit with Ty's wife. So, I'd say your night is open."

"I didn't hand over my leash." Ford said. "And maybe I was going to watch the game and throw back a few beers?"

Ford snatched the fresh beer from Ty's hand. Twisting off the cap, he sat on the couch and decided there were worse ways to spend the afternoon. It had been a while since he'd hung with his buddies and watched a game.

"No can do," Harris said. "Chaperones can't drink. Parenting Party Rule Number Two."

Ty took the beer back, then put his lips all over it. "And this is the last craft brew. Sorry, bro," he said, not sorry at all.

Ford leaned back on the couch and stared up at the ceiling and wondered if, as a temporary tenant, he could change the locks.

"Whoops . . . Parenting Party Rule Number Three states that a chaperone must be within line of sight at all times," Harris said. "So you can finish my pizza outside on the porch. The good news is the party only lasts three hours."

Ford looked at the mess that started by the front door and blasted all the way down the hall to the bathroom. "How long have they been here?"

"Party started at the same time as the game. Four," Ty said.

"They've only been here fifteen minutes?" he asked, and Harris grinned. "What the hell am I supposed to do with a bunch of girls for two hours and forty-five minutes?"

"You can always cut the cake early and sugar-load them," Ty suggested.

"That's Parenting Party Rule Number One," Harris said. "The Holy Grail of all rules. Never mix sugar, carbonated beverages, and a bounce house."

"Well, that's your problem, because while I owe you, I already have plans."

"What? Practicing your outlaw moves?" Ty joked.

"My moves are just fine," Ford said, giving Ty the *Shut it* look, but he was too busy trying to be funny to notice.

"Cooking for the first date?" Ty gave a low whistle. "Pretty smooth."

Harris looked at Ford. "Date?"

Ford cut Ty a glare. "I invited her over for dinner tonight."

Harris studied him for a long moment, and then his face went slack with understanding. "You really have to work hard to be this stupid. You know that, right?"

He did, but if this was what stupid felt like, then label him and stamp it on his forehead. He couldn't seem to stop.

"Oh, and there's the look," Ty said, pointing to Ford's face. He smacked his hand away.

"If I have any look, it's because I came home to find a dozen little girls in makeup and plastic heels in my yard, my house destroyed, and two assholes drinking my beer."

"No, the other look you get when you think about Liv. Yup. That one," Ty said, going at him with the finger again. "Like she's beer, bacon, and boobs all in one. You've got it bad, bro."

"And the more time you guys spend together, the more likely it is for something to happen . . ." Harris faded off when Ford paced to the window. "Something already happened."

Ford's silence was enough.

"Did you at least tell her about Sam?"

Ford felt the air in his lungs expand until they were too pissed to breathe. "No. And if she ever finds out, she'll hate me."

"What about Sam?" Ty asked, trying to follow the conversation. Which would lead to a deeper conversation Ford would rather avoid right then.

"None of your business," Ford said.

But at the same time, Harris said, "Ford was the officer who was with Sam when he died." And then because his friend seemed to forget he wasn't a part of the recovery, he went on to tell the story as if he'd been right there in that cave with Ford.

Ty let out a long whistle. "Something like that is not 'if'—it's a 'when.' This is a small town, and Liv is a smart woman. She might not know what you're hiding, but she knows you're hiding something."

"You didn't know Avery was hiding something."

Harris snorted. "He's a man—he sees boobs and gets tunnel vision. Women aren't like that. They don't have the Y chromosome, so they think with the right head. Eventually she'll sniff out your secret and ask you about it, most likely when you're naked and snuggling, and you won't have the state of mind to deal with it right, because it won't just be boobs, it will be naked boobs. And you'll only see two choices. Tell her the truth while she's at her most vulnerable or lie."

Liv deserved more than the disappointment either of those choices would bring. She deserved more than Ford could give her. She deserved more, period.

His intent had never been to bring up Sam. Then again, he'd never intended on getting this deep with Liv. Which left a third option.

"Or I just move on after my certification is over and no one gets hurt," Ford said, turning around.

Ty set his beer on the table and leaned forward. "I don't know where Liv is at, but I do get that when it comes to a woman like her, there is no moving on for guys like us. Believe me, I tried."

Last year before Ty married Avery, he discovered that she'd been keeping a life-threatening secret from him. He broke things off and walked—until he realized he couldn't live without her and asked her to marry him.

Ford didn't see marriage for himself, but he also couldn't see himself walking out of Liv's life and never seeing her again.

"Did you forgive her?" Ford asked.

"Wholeheartedly," Ty said without hesitation. "I was a lucky son of a bitch that she chose to forgive me. Because while she might have kept something from me, I walked when it got complicated, took the easy way out. I'm not saying that it won't be hard, or that she won't push your dumb ass out the door. But she deserves to hear the truth from you."

Something that Ford could no longer argue.

"Maybe before you sleep with her again," Harris jabbed.

"Hard to do with a houseful of uninvited guests."

"Christ, you're acting like this is a sleepover. We'll be out of here by seven," Harris said.

Before Ford could say he'd better take his mess with him, shrieks sounded in the distance. The front door burst open and Emma came racing in, her baby blues wide, her face flushed.

"Brianna dared Hadley to do ten aerials in a row," she said, breathing heavy. "So she did it even though I tolds her not 'cuz she ate three whole slices of pizza and a bag of goldfish. She gots to four and said her tummy hurt, but Brianna said a dare is a dare and Hadley started crying and Brianna called her a baby. But she's not a baby, her brother is, so she kept going and when she finished the last, she said, 'Your turn, Brianna, or are you a baby?' And then she threw up all over the bounce house."

Harris tipped his bottle toward Ford. "I think I saw some extra towels in the garage."

"And when I run out," Ford said, heading toward the front door, "I'll use that sleeping bag in the back of your Jeep."

CHAPTER 16

"How about your pillow?" Liv asked as Paxton dragged his back-pack down the hallway with one hand, his jacket with the other, his Superman slippers scuffing the floor with each step.

"Grandma didn't put it on the list," Paxton said, shrugging into his jacket. "She said I only had to bring what was on the list. And a pillow wasn't on the list."

"Then no pillow needed," Liv assured him, kneeling down and zipping him up tight. "But if you decide you need yours, all you have to do is call and I'll bring it over. You're right across the lake. I can be there in a few minutes."

"I know," he said. "You showed me her house."

"That's right," Liv said, pulling Paxton's backpack out of his closet. She'd spent most of yesterday preparing Paxton for the idea of a sleepover at Grandma's, then all of today wondering if she should just cancel. "Now is there anything else you think you might need?"

"I got my cape and my mask." He patted his bag. "And I packed an extra one in case Grandma wants to wear one. Do you think Bullseye would want to do the sleepover with me?"

Liv took a deep breath and cupped her son's cheek. They'd been over this a dozen times. "Bullseye has to sleep at his own house, but Grandma said that her neighbors have a cat named Miss Peepers who likes to sit on her porch at night and be petted."

"I like Miss Peepers, but I like my own bed more." Paxton exhaled a shaky breath and toed at the floor.

Last week when Paxton saw Miss Peepers, he had been ready to give up his bed and all of his toys if he could keep her, but Liv didn't bother to point that out.

In fact, the mother in her wanted to call the whole thing off too, postpone it for another year or three. But the warrior in her, who knew that her son was about to have his first sleepover in a safe and loving environment, said, "Your own bed will be right here when you get back, and when you come home we can snuggle up in it and you can tell me what a good time you had."

"If the good doesn't come?" he asked softly. "Do I have to lie?"

"Nope, you are free to have whatever kind of time you want." And to show her confidence in the situation and in Paxton, she added, "In fact, I wouldn't be surprised if you had an awesome time. I hear Miss Peepers likes to chase toilet-paper rolls, and she will give purrs for treats."

"But she can't fly like Superdog can. So if something goes bad, who's going to come down and save me?" he said, and Liv felt a bead of familiar panic start to grow. He hadn't told that story of Superdog in more than a year. A story that he'd clung to after the accident.

Sam had given Paxton the stuffed dog as an early Christmas present. And he'd been holding it when they'd skidded off the road. Her son had clung to that dog the entire time they'd been out in that storm, the doctor had told her, so it was natural he'd find comfort in it.

Most parents would just tell him that nothing would happen, but she wasn't about to promise him something she couldn't guarantee. Lying would only give him a false sense of security.

"If something feels weird in here"—she pointed to his belly—"all you have to do is tell Grandma what you need to feel better—that way she can hold your worry for you so you can enjoy your big-boy sleepover."

"What if she makes those smelly fish noodles?" he asked, so serious Liv had to bite back a smile.

"Sometimes grandmas make smelly fish noodles." When Paxton looked as if that was the worst answer ever, she added, "If it's that bad, then tell her. And if it takes you a while to find your words, that's okay too—just show her what you want."

"How?" he asked, his voice heartbreakingly quiet.

Liv had thought about this too, wanting to give him all the tools he could need to have this be a positive experience. "If you need a snuggle, you don't ask me—you just snuggle in. Grandmas love to snuggle. And they love to laugh and read books to their grandkids. So if you want her to read you a bedtime comic, then crawl up in her lap, and I bet you a cupcake for breakfast that she'll start reading."

"I packed three comic books," Paxton said proudly.

"See, you're a natural at this." And then taking a page from Ford's handbook, she asked, "What do you need to have an awesome time?"

Paxton thought about that for a minute, then stuck his hands on his hips in a pose that was all Sam. "A dog of my own that I can bring with me to sleepovers. Cuz if I'm big enough to do big-boy sleepovers, then it means I'm big enough to have a pet."

Liv's first reaction was to tell him that after he got settled in at school, they'd talk about it. Then she realized that school was just a few short weeks off and he was going to be fine. "You're right. You are growing up. So why don't we talk to Ford about what kind of dog we should consider."

"Yes!" He punched his hands in the air, and Liv wondered if she'd just been played.

"Is there anything else you need?"

"My book," he said, but instead of racing down the hall to grab a book from his room, he walked into the family room and reached up high on the bookshelf, stretching to get to the third shelf, and pulled a journal down. Cradling it to him, he said, "So I can see you before I go to bed."

Liv's chest shrank when she saw the book. It was a journal, really, a memory journal Avery had made for him for his birthday. She'd taken photos and news articles and ticket stubs from Liv and Sam's first date and created a beautiful scrapbook for Paxton so as he grew older he'd never forget his parents' story.

Not all of the story, but the best parts. Liv pulled it out every time he asked about Sam, but Paxton usually got bored after a few pages. This was the first time he'd initiated the interest. "Did you want to look at that while we wait for Grandma?"

Paxton climbed on the couch and put the book in his lap. Overcome with emotion, Liv sat beside him, opening the book so that it rested on both of their laps. Clearly focused on a specific destination in this walk down memory lane, Paxton flipped past the first few pages, and that's when Liv knew what he was turning to.

"What's his name?" He pointed to a photo of Sam when he'd been in high school, down at the lake with his dog.

"I think that was Shadow," Liv said. He was a black Lab and loved to dive off the dock.

"Could he fly?"

"It sure looks like it in this photo," she said with a smile. Shadow was front leg forward, hind legs straight back, in midair hovering over the water with the dock behind him.

"Where's his other dog?" Paxton asked right as a soft knock sounded.

Moments later, Carolyn opened the door and peeked in. "Are you all packed up?" she asked, cautious hope lacing her words.

Paxton looked up at Liv and whispered, "My belly feels funny."

"Some of that is nerves, because it's normal to be nervous about doing something new. But some of that is also excitement, because you're going on an adventure." Liv stuck her hand out. "Try to find the nerves and put that in my hand for me to hold, so all of the flutters left are excitement."

Paxton closed his eyes, a look of concentration causing his tongue to peek out. Then her brave little guy placed his hand over Liv's and dropped the fear in her hand. And when he opened his eyes, he didn't look confident, but he also didn't look as scared.

"All right." She stood and grabbed his backpack. "Let's get you guys on the road."

Walking to the door, not looking back to see if he was coming, Liv handed the backpack to Carolyn.

"Thank you for this," Carolyn said quietly. "After what I said the other day, I wouldn't have been so forgiving."

"You were right when you said Sam wouldn't have liked that his son didn't get to spend time with you," Liv said. "And I don't like the distance his death has brought between us, Carolyn."

"I don't either," the older woman said.

"Then let's fix that," Liv said, and Carolyn nodded, looking as if she were one blink from waterworks.

Right there with you.

"Now you two have fun, and I'll see you in the morning at Shelia's so we can all grab a family breakfast."

"Sounds good," Carolyn said, taking his mini-size backpack. "Ready, Paxton?"

Paxton looked up at Liv, and she pulled him in for one final hug before he set off. And before she let go, she said, "You got this."

Paxton didn't look as if he completely believed her, and she couldn't be certain there weren't going to be some tears and rough patches over the next twelve hours. But she knew that they'd be okay. Because Paxton didn't answer his grandma, but he walked out the door instead of running back to Liv, and he took his grandma's hand.

Telling her what he needed. And wouldn't you know it, it seemed that was what Carolyn needed too, because she looked up at Liv with glassy eyes and mouthed, *Thank you.*

Liv watched them go. She watched as he climbed into Carolyn's car and didn't stop watching until the brake lights disappeared around the corner.

◆ ◆ ◆

Normally, when Ford invited a woman over to his place to talk, the majority of the lip action took place in the bedroom. Yet there he was, three feet from a beautiful woman in a blue strapless number that was designed to be slowly peeled down her body—with his teeth—and the only thing he was peeling was carrots.

He didn't even like carrots. But since steak and salad took five minutes to prepare, leaving him with idle hands and memories of exactly how creative they could get on this counter, Ford had gone for a five-component meal—including boneless pork chops, apple chutney, white cheddar potatoes, endive slaw, and candied carrots. Not that there was enough to keep him distracted all night.

At some point, he'd have to come clean. Which would lead to the reason why he was here . . . in Sequoia Lake. As soon as he did, no amount of reasoning would make her understand why he hadn't told her about Sam.

"Are you sure I can't help?" she asked, leaning against the island. "I might not be Martha Stewart, but I can be trusted with a peeler." Ford looked pointedly at her fingers, most of them tipped with Band-Aids. "Sewing machines should really come with an emergency brake." She reached for the endive and a knife. "At least let me help with the salad."

"It's not salad. It's slaw." Ford lifted the knife from her hand and set it on the counter. Then he lifted Liv by the hips and set her stubborn ass on a bar stool, and damn if she didn't feel like sex wrapped in silk. "And you can help by sitting your stubborn ass right here and relaxing."

He handed her a glass of wine, and not waiting for an answer or the right moment to do the wrong thing, Ford went back to his plan—keeping his hands to himself.

"Cooking is actually relaxing for me," she said, sweeping her long dark hair off her shoulders so that it spilled down her back.

"The delivery guys all know you by name," Ford pointed out. From what he'd seen, her house was like a revolving door for takeout.

"By the time I get off work and get home, Paxton only has a little over an hour before bedtime. I can spend that in the kitchen cooking or hearing about his day. Takeout lets me do both."

Ford knew that becoming a single mom had reshaped a lot of the ways Liv approached the world. But he'd never stopped to wonder about the daily struggles and sacrifices she'd been forced to make—like something as simple as making her son a home-cooked meal.

Guilt tightened in his chest at the thought of whatever else she'd been forced to choose between.

"Plus, with takeout I know dinner won't turn into a three-hour standoff over why he won't eat his broccoli," she said with a smile.

"I'm in my twenty-eighth year of my standoff with broccoli," Ford said, and Liv laughed.

"In my house, the topic has caused a filibuster. One time he talked me into submission, claiming that broccoli was Superboy's Kryptonite, then went on to list every reason why broccoli was the worst vegetable on the planet, including that they fed it to the guinea pig, Buttons, at school and Buttons pooped green pellets. So he refused to eat his greens on the argument of pooping green pellets."

"My mom used to say it would put hair on my chest," Ford said, dropping the carrots in the pot. "The fear of broccoli among boys is real."

"And so is the punishment for not eating your vegetables," Liv said, channeling her mother-knows-best tone. "Straight to bed with no dessert."

Ford glanced over at Liv, who had one lean leg crossed over the other, her mouthwatering cupcakes on display, her fingers fiddling with the hem of her dress, and he decided that was a punishment he'd take.

What he couldn't take was how uncomfortable she was with not participating in the preparation.

"Are you sure I can't help?" she asked.

"Almost done. I just need to chop the endive."

She jumped to her feet. "I can do that."

"Or," he said when she was about to take the knife from his hands, "you can take your wine out on the deck. I'll just grab a beer and meet you out there in a minute."

With a sassy grin, she grabbed him a beer from the fridge and popped the top, before heading through the kitchen and out onto the deck. Her hips swishing the whole way. His hands twitching to touch her until she disappeared.

And it was only when she was out of sight that he was able to fully breathe. He wanted her to relax, but he also needed air that didn't smell like sheer temptation and questionable decisions.

Ford finished with the slaw, checked the chops, and after counting to ten, with each number imagining the unsexiest thing possible, grabbed the wine bottle and walked out onto the porch, coming to a full and complete stop.

He could have counted to a hundred in a cow pasture for all it mattered. Liv sat on the chaise lounge, her bare feet curled up beneath her, the moon casting a gentle glow on her face and bare shoulders.

She was resting against the back of the chair and looking every bit the peaceful, calm oasis Ford had been craving.

"All I had to do was get you away from the knives for you to relax," he said, walking over to fill up her glass.

She moved her feet so he could sit next to her, then gave a shy smile. "It's been a long time since a man has offered to cook me dinner, so I didn't know what to do with my hands."

Ford knew exactly what she could do with her hands, but since that wasn't on the menu, he sat on the coffee table—a good two feet from touching her. "What did you do when your husband cooked for you?"

She thought about that for a moment and then took a sip of wine. "He didn't really cook all that often. Between his patient load at the hospital and paperwork, he rarely made it home in time for dinner. And when he did, he usually had work to catch up on."

That surprised Ford. He'd always assumed Sam was the kind of guy who managed to do it all, and do it all well: family, patients, career. A real Dr. McDreamy meets Husband of the Year. "Balancing what we want to do and what we need to do can be hard."

"I know. Sam had a big heart and even bigger dreams. I loved the way he cared about everything so deeply, but over time he'd commit himself in too many directions to come through for everyone. Something had to give," she said casually, as if it were no big deal. But the sadness in her eyes told him a different story. A story that Ford had a hard time reconciling with the one he'd conjured about a man whose undying love for his wife kept him going for twelve hours in a blizzard.

"And you think he gave up on you?" Ford asked quietly.

"Sam didn't give up on anything. Ever. Especially love, and he did love me. And I loved him. So much." She shook her head, a nostalgic smile touching her lips. "Which is why I knew he'd drive himself ragged trying to be everything to everyone, so I made sure home didn't feel like another obligation. Which made it hard to be mad when he forgot special days or worked weekends."

It also made it harder for him to tell her about his connection to Sam. Something he had to do before she confided more details about the marriage. "About Sam—"

"I blew it, didn't I?" she asked, covering her mouth and looking horrified. "I don't know what to say. I followed all seven signs, exactly, so I could come over here with a fresh page to add to my story, but somehow I flipped back a few chapters to my marriage."

"Seven signs?" Ford asked, setting down his beer.

"Yes. Primping, touching my hair, direct eye contact—I even bought new underwear." She flapped her hands. "There's more, and I did them, but then Sam came up and I kept talking about him and . . ." She took a breath. "Please don't let that sign confuse you."

Ford couldn't help it—he smiled. "I love your primping. I've been staring at your primping all night. I want to touch your hair every time you do." To prove it, he ran his fingers through the long, wavy strands, then lifted her chin. "And I would expect nothing less than direct from you, cupcake."

"I like direct," she whispered. "I like to see what's coming."

So did Ford. But right then all he could focus on was that blank page of hers. And how much he wanted to be a part of it. Be a part of her.

"Then I'll be direct. I've been confused since that first morning when you ordered me to press your spot. I'm not sure what to say, where the line is."

This time she smiled, and damn it was beautiful. "There are no lines—that's the sign I meant to give."

"So why don't you explain what each of the signs means so I know how to respond to each and every one of them."

"That's easy. They all mean the same thing," she said, and he knew that nothing about this was going to be easy. But walking away from her at this point would be impossible.

"What?"

"That I want you to kiss me."

"I've already kissed you," he said quietly.

"In many different places," she said, and damn if his eyes didn't slowly roll over her body. "This kiss would be different. It would last all the way through breakfast," she said, as if breakfast included the two of them pretzeled around each other in tangled sheets.

"What about Paxton?" he said.

"He's at his grandma's." She paused for an entire beat that had Ford's lungs shutting down. "All night."

"All night? That's a big step." He swallowed, reminding himself that the right thing would be to proceed with caution. But he was tired of being cautious. He was ready to trust his gut again, and his gut was telling him that everything about this woman was right for him.

"For both of us," she said, and with a smile that was 100 percent trouble, she moved to the end of the chair until their knees were brushing, and then she leaned even closer. Which—*hello?*—brought her breasts right into his line of sight. All he had to do was look down and *Can you say, Dessert before dinner?* "And I'm yours all night. If you want."

And if that didn't clarify things, then her taking his mouth without warning did. Liv making the first move was hot, but her delivery left no room for talk.

That kiss packed more force than pulling the chute after free-falling from thirty thousand feet up. It was one of those hands-in-the-hair, zero-to-let's-get-naked, new-panties-worthy kind of kisses that told Ford that Liv wasn't looking for a walk down memory lane. She was looking to pen a little Nicholas Sparks and a little *Fifty Shades* action into her new chapter.

Damn if he wasn't ready for a fresh page in his own life. Where he got to write the ending. And if he had his way, it would last a hell of a lot longer than all night.

◆ ◆ ◆

"Oh, I want," Ford moaned against Liv's mouth, sending a kaleidoscope of tingles over her body. He kissed her like a man who knew what he wanted and would stop at nothing to get it. Always big on encouragement, Liv wrapped her arms around his neck and held tight as he kissed her like she was his dessert.

He pulled back, resting his forehead to hers, breathing heavy. "Are you sure this is what you want?"

"Check my panties," she said, and he groaned.

Forehead to hers still, his eyes lowered to her legs and then back up. "The new panties?"

"The first seven signs were to tell you I wanted to be kissed, so I decided I needed a sign to tell you I wanted to do a sleepover. And since showing up with my pillow seemed pushy . . ."

"You bought new panties," he said in a low voice, but she saw other, deliciously big, signs that he was as excited over her panty choice as she was.

"Red ones."

"God, I love red." He placed his hands on her calves and skimmed them up to the backs of her knees.

"I do too, but I felt like I was trying to be too bold. So I went with pink."

"Pink, huh?" Ford leaned in and kissed the corner of her mouth. "Pink is sweet and sexy. Just like you."

"The problem was, I wasn't feeling very sweet."

"Right now, I'm not either, cupcake," he said, tugging her forward to the very edge of the seat. "So what did you pick?"

"Something that was honest and bold and left no question about what I wanted." She looked up at him through her lashes. "Why don't you check and tell me if I did a good job?"

Pulling her to stand between his parted legs, Ford slid his hands up the back of her thighs, not stopping until he got to her very bare, very bold ass. And groaned. "No clarification needed."

His eyes were intense, and locked on hers, as he leaned up and nipped at her neck, then her shoulder, pressing a kiss right above her belly button in a move that was so gentle it stole her breath—and left no room for misunderstanding.

Yup, they were on the same page, thank God, because for a moment there Liv was afraid he'd want to talk all night. Not that she wasn't into talking, but tonight she wanted to feel. And Ford made her feel things she'd long given up hope on feeling.

Running her hand in his hair, Liv held him to her as he ran kisses across her ribcage and down her belly, sending a flood of feeling pooling between her legs. His hands were like a heat-seeking missile. They were under her dress and going from question to confidence as they cupped her bottom, his callused thumbs working their way forward, lightly grazing along the edge of her inner thighs until she thought her knees were going to buckle.

"Come here," he whispered, guiding her onto his lap.

Not only did she go, she cupped his face and brought his mouth to hers for a series of languid, drugging kisses that had her melting against him until the soft denim of his jeans pressed against her sensitive skin.

Ford was the most excellent kisser. In fact, he should have been given a gold medal in the kissing department. And his fingers should be considered one of the seven wonders of the world. Soft but purposeful, patient and demanding. Sneaky as well.

One minute they were close to her hot zone, driving her insane, and the next the top of her dress was sliding down. But she had a trick up her sleeve too—or should she say, under her dress, and she knew the second Ford found it.

His hands stumbled, and fire lit his eyes. "The bra matches the panties."

She lifted a shoulder. "Big step all around tonight."

Ford's face softened, and a tenderness filled his eyes. "Big, small, I'm right here keeping pace."

Liv's heart waved its white flag and fully surrendered. "I think I'm ready to run."

"Then let's get you warmed up," he said, and placed a hot open-mouthed kiss right on her nipple.

Liv's heart raced as if she were in the final stretch of a marathon. He cupped her in his hands, slowly attending to one and then the other, taking his time as if the warm-up was as important as the finish. And Ford would finish, of that she had no doubt.

She let out a breath and shivered from head to toe, it felt so good.

"Are you cold?" he whispered. Before she could say no, her body was in overload, and he was standing with her in his arms, then leaning down to rest her back against the lounger. Her dress hit the floor moments before his big, warm body was covering hers. "Better?"

"Getting there," she teased.

"Let me show you what getting there feels like." His gaze swept down her body in a hungry manner that brought on another wave of tremors. "And how much more fun it is with two."

Unable to speak, Liv watched as he kissed his way down her body, getting closer and closer to her hot zone. With agonizing slowness, he licked and nipped, his breath dancing over her skin, until every nerve ending was screaming out that he needed to get *there*, and get there quick.

As he got closer, she was afraid to move, afraid to breathe—she couldn't even form the words to tell him what spot needed his attention. Just like she couldn't look away when he winked at her right before he ran his tongue in one long, thorough swipe straight up her center.

"Closer?" he said against her.

"Please, get closer," she begged.

"One?" He ran the pad of his thumb over her good spot, and she arched into him. Then he placed his mouth there. "Or two?"

"Two," she cried.

"Just two?" His clever mouth ascended until she could hardly stand it. Bringing her right there, hovering on the edge, but not enough to send her over.

"Both," she amended, although it came out sounding a lot like begging. "One and two."

"Because two is always better than one, cupcake." And to prove it, Ford found her perfect spot with his talented finger and pressed in the perfect way, while his mouth continued to nuzzle and tease. And her body began to coil and climb until she was racing so fast she broke through the finish line and collapsed against the lounger.

Her heart was beating too fast to breathe, and her body was still shaking from the burst of energy when Ford stretched out over her, his own body naked and hard—everywhere.

In one fluid motion he was covered and filling her. Without slowing down he was moving, and Liv's body was begging to go the distance.

"I think this is your perfect spot," he said. "Right here."

Using slow withdrawals and even slower thrusts, Ford showed her. And the man sure had an amazing sense of direction, because he was able to show her over and over again until she was panting his name.

Not just show her, guide her so she could get to the place with him, open and vulnerable. No longer afraid to run or afraid to fall. Because she knew that when she fell, he'd be right there next to her.

He'd proved that to her a hundred different ways over the past few weeks. Small little things he did that spoke to his character.

His kindness.

Small little things that made taking that last step easier.

"Ford," she whispered, cupping his face so she could see his eyes. Wanting to see if he took the step with her.

"I'm right here," he said, lacing his fingers with hers and holding her hand to his chest, his other arm straining under the pressure of trying to hold back.

A gentle breeze blew over her hot skin as the water gently lapped against the shoreline, and Ford moved—deep within her until all she felt was him. Them. Moving together toward something healing.

The thrusts became harder and shorter, their breaths mixing in the evening air, but his gaze held her captive the whole time. Not releasing her even as her body started to tighten around him. And even when she was a moment from losing her sanity, she couldn't look away.

And Ford didn't let her down. One more of those masterful thrusts and she was there. By the second, he was gritting his teeth. And with a final move that had Liv straining to hold on, Ford made good on his word.

He took them both home.

It was a long few seconds before Liv could open her eyes, but when she went to move, he brushed his mouth over hers in a gentle kiss that felt like home.

"Don't move," he said. "I'll be right back." And he disappeared into the house.

He needn't have worried. Liv was in the same position when he returned two minutes later with a fuzzy blanket. He slid in behind her and pulled her close, then wrapped them both in the blanket. Holding her as if he'd never let go.

And Liv allowed herself to admit that if this was what being part of a twosome felt like, she never wanted to stand alone again.

CHAPTER 17

Liv didn't know how long they lay there, watching the stars and listening to each other breathe, but when she heard a ding come from inside the house, she looked up. "The pork?"

He traced her lower lip with his finger. "Sorry, cupcake. It was already burned when I went back inside, so I ordered pizza."

Liv leaned up and kissed his chin. "I love pizza."

"Good." He stood, not concerned that he was on his back deck in all of his glory. "I'll go get it."

"You might want to get dressed before you answer the door," she said, tossing his jeans at him—which he caught midair.

If the man got dressed, he waited until he was back in the house to do it, gifting her with an amazing view. Liv lay back and looked up at the sky, wondering when the stars had become so bright.

Right around the time she'd opened her eyes. And her heart.

This wasn't just a relationship starting to bloom. This was love. At least the beginning stages of it.

Liv had loved before. Knew what the real thing felt like. And this thing between Ford and her had the potential to become the most real connection she'd ever had.

She was thinking about that when she heard her phone. She glanced at the screen and saw it was Carolyn. Telling herself that her mother-in-law had absolutely no clue that she was naked, she answered. "Hey, there, how's Paxton?"

"He's fine. We watched *The Lone Ranger*, and then he showed me his favorite Superman cartoon," her mother-in-law said, but she didn't sound fine.

"Did he talk to you?"

"No, but he did let me tuck him in. He wanted me to read him one of his comic books, and while there aren't a whole lot of words in those things, he seemed to enjoy it."

Liv bit back a smile. A story with few words for a boy of few words, read by a grandma without a shortage of words. "Sounds like a fun night."

Carolyn paused again, so long that Liv's stomach started to knot. Clutching the blanket to her chest, she sat up and cradled the phone closer. "Is everything okay?"

Liv heard a door open and close through the phone, then the sounds of Carolyn pacing. She was on her front porch. "Paxton brought that scrapbook of yours."

Her heart took a stumble. She hadn't considered that, for Carolyn, a living memory book of her deceased son might not bring the same kind of connection it brought to Liv and Paxton. "I am so sorry. If it upset you, that wasn't my intent. Paxton was asking about Sam's childhood pets, and I mentioned that you knew all about his dad when he was a boy. I think he was excited to show you his picture book."

"It didn't upset me," Carolyn said, and Liv could hear the emotion thick in her voice. "It actually gave us something to talk about. Well, he didn't talk, but he'd point to a picture and I'd tell him about it. It gave me a chance to share Sam with Paxton, and it didn't feel like he was completely gone." And the loving mother-in-law Liv remembered didn't sound so far away either. "Thank you for giving me that."

Hugging her knees, Liv rested her cheek on top of them and fought back happy tears. "I'm so happy, for you both."

Liv looked out at the lake, a rippling dark mass with only the reflection of the moon visible, and opened herself up to every emotion she was feeling. Hope. Joy. Peace.

Lots of peace.

It washed through her, filling every empty space and swelling until her skin felt too tight to contain it all.

"After we watched *Superman*, I asked him about camp. He was so excited that he showed me some handshake he made up. I guess it means I'm in the club or something."

Liv's heart couldn't get any fuller. "He showed it to you? Carolyn, that is huge." She paused. "Why don't you sound like that was huge?"

"Because he also showed me a picture of the dog who he is doing it with."

"Bullseye?" Unable to remember if she'd seen him earlier, Liv looked behind her through the sliding glass door to see if she could find him. Paxton's backpack wasn't big enough to smuggle a sixty-pound dog, but Liv wouldn't put it past her son to sneak a furry friend into his sleepover. "Please tell me he isn't there?"

"No, but . . ." Liv could practically hear Carolyn choosing her words. And the longer she took, the higher Liv's heart rate rose. "He's in the scrapbook."

"I don't understand."

"He's in the scrapbook, Liv," Carolyn said gently. "In the article about Paxton's rescue."

Liv set her feet on the ground. "There's an article about the accident in there?"

Avery had asked if she could include some newspaper clippings, but Liv had assumed it would be their wedding announcement and the article on Sam when he'd been hired on as chief surgeon in Sacramento. But the accident? Liv hadn't even read those.

"In a pocket on the back page." Liv had never looked that far, only flipping to the pages that Paxton found interest in. "And the article talks about a search-and-rescue K-9 team who sat with Sam and Paxton until the storm had cleared."

Liv already knew this story. The police had told her what had transpired when they'd shown up on her doorstep that Christmas morning. But hearing about it again, while naked and completely exposed on another man's porch, brought on a strange sense of shame.

Liv grabbed her dress and tugged it over her head, covering herself.

"There are a lot of K-9 teams." So then why did it hurt to breathe?

"Teams that fly down out of the sky to rescue Paxton?" Carolyn said with soft steel. "Why do you think he's obsessed with a superdog who flies and saves people?"

Liv thought about how Bullseye had sought out Paxton, how easy Paxton was around Ford, and how Ford had come to Sequoia Lake for his certification. Then she told herself it was just a coincidence. Because the alternative was too painful to comprehend.

"What does the dog look like?"

Above the sound of her thrashing heart, Liv listened to Carolyn describe the dog, heard herself say that there must be a simple explanation—that didn't include Ford misleading her. But nothing about what she was feeling was simple. It was heavy and complicated and at odds with the peace she'd fought hard for.

Carolyn finished reading the article, and Liv didn't remember standing up or walking back to her house. But when the back door slammed shut on its hinges and the sound of the house settling around her became defeating, she remembered the suffocating feeling of isolation that rained down.

She remembered how loud the silence could be. And the longer she stood there, staring at the wall lined with memories, the more she remembered. Until the silence grew to a point that she was afraid it would never stop.

◆ ◆ ◆

Ford didn't even bother with shoes. He took off across the beach at a swift pace.

He'd come back out on his deck, pizza in hand, stupid-ass grin on his face, to find Liv gone. At first he thought she'd gone to the restroom, but after a good twenty minutes had passed, he went to check—only to find it empty.

Like the rest of his house.

He'd called her five times, left five messages, with no response. He'd considered the idea that Paxton had changed his mind and wanted to come home—not a far stretch since a sleepover with Carolyn sounded about as fun as a tea party with the Queen of Hearts—but then he spotted Liv's car parked in her driveway.

He also saw a soft glow flickering from one of the bedrooms. Meaning she was the one who'd changed her mind about the sleepover. And for the life of him, Ford couldn't figure out why.

Harris had warned him that kissing a single mom got women thinking. Ford wondered what kissing Liv naked on his porch had meant to her. He thought about all the options, and the first inkling of doubt began to creep in.

"Liv?" he called as he tapped on her back door. When she didn't answer, he let himself in and quickly scanned the dining room and kitchen. There wasn't a single light turned on in the entire house, but he could see a glow coming from down the hallway in Paxton's room.

Maybe she'd already picked him up and come back.

He rapped a knuckle softly against the door frame. "Liv, you guys in there?"

The only confirmation he got was a small sob coming from inside the darkened bedroom. Ford opened the door and stepped inside, his heart dropping into crisis mode.

Liv sat on the child-size bed, her body curled tightly in the corner, a tissue in her hand and a laptop in her lap. The light glow from the screen showed enough tear tracks to know that she'd been crying for quite some time.

Alone.

No Paxton, no emergency, just Liv with those sad fucking eyes and heartbreaking sorrow.

Ford had just experienced the single most life-altering moment of his adult life, and while he'd been grinning like an idiot over it, she'd been wading through the fallout.

"Liv," he said softly, entering the room.

She looked up at him and recoiled, making him stop dead in his tracks. So did his heart. Because she hadn't just been crying—she'd been mourning. Ford had been around enough survivors to recognize the difference.

She stood and rubbed at her eyes with the back of her hand. It did nothing to erase the red rims and wet cheeks. Or the bad feeling burning in his chest.

"Is everything okay—"

Liv flipped the laptop around, and any uncertainty he had over the cause of her pain died fast and hard. Every question left his head, and he couldn't speak past the article staring him down.

He recognized the photo of Bullseye in his rappelling gear, recognized the terrified boy huddled next to him, but the one thing he didn't recognize was the look of utter betrayal on Liv's face.

"I was going to tell you."

She choked out a mirthless laugh. "Over breakfast in bed, or after you'd left town for good? Because you still had another week to string me along."

"I was waiting for the right moment," he said, but knew it was a lie.

"The right moment would have been when you ran into me that first day," she said, swiping angrily at her tears, and he could tell that her hands were shaking. "Or maybe when I brought Bullseye over to your house. That way, instead of worrying myself sick over my son swearing that a dog really flew down from the sky to rescue him, I would have thought, 'Hey, maybe he just saw Ford's dog come down from the chopper that airlifted him out.'"

Her chin started quivering in an attempt to hold it together, and it nearly did him in. "But even if those times weren't perfect enough for you, then how about when I sat in your office, told you that if anything was awkward between us, then you could bail. No harm done."

"I'm so sorry," he said, but he knew there weren't enough words in the world to make up for the ones he'd so selfishly withheld. "When I came back to Sequoia Lake, I had no intentions of making a connection more than to see how you were doing."

"I was doing just fine." She smacked her chest so hard he felt the thud in his own. "Paxton was doing fine. So why come back and dredge it all up?"

"I had to see it with my own eyes," he said, and the truth had never sounded so callous. "I knew what you'd gone through, and I couldn't let go. So when you asked me for help, I thought that this could be one last thing I did to help you move forward."

"One last thing?" she said on a shaky breath, tossing the laptop on the bed. "What do you mean *one last thing*?"

She shook her head and took a step back, her hand slowly gripping her heart. "Oh my God." She took another step back—away from him. "The gifts, the flowers, Paxton's summer camp. That was all you? Two years of boxes on my doorstep, of wondering who was sending them, two years of lies? Is this some sick game you play—sweet-talk a lonely widow into bed and give her one last good time?"

"God, no." He took a step forward, but she held up a shaky hand.

"Sweet-talk her into thinking she's going to be fine?" She wrapped her arms around her stomach. "That she's worthy of finding love again? Of being loved?"

"You are so damn worthy it hurts." But he could tell by the look in her eyes that she didn't believe him. Didn't believe that she was lovable.

"Do you know why I came here that first time?" he said, because even though he knew it would sever any hope he had for winning back Liv, he knew that she needed to hear it. "I sat next to a dying man and listened to him talk about his wife for twelve hours. About how beautiful and amazing she was, and how she'd filled his life with warmth and love. About how his biggest regret was that he wouldn't be able to spend the rest of eternity caring for her the way she deserved to be cared for."

Ford took a step closer and took her hand in his. "His love for you was so raw and deep I couldn't help but promise to deliver his Christmas gift to you." Liv reached down and touched the platinum-and-diamond necklace Ford had rescued from the trunk of Sam's car and delivered to the hospital.

He'd watched as the sheriff handed her the box, explaining that it had been recovered, then left her alone in an empty hospital room with the last thing she'd ever receive from her husband. Only, she hadn't opened it—she'd clutched it to her chest as if it would fill the empty gap if she pressed hard enough.

Ford had stood in the shadows waiting for her to cry, because he knew that it would be the first sign of letting go, but she never cried. She finally opened the box and gave herself a minute with the necklace—he'd timed it—before she slid it around her neck and went to check on Paxton.

Ford couldn't pinpoint the exact moment when he'd decided to continue sending her gifts from Sam, only that her unwavering determination was the cause.

"He loved you, Liv," Ford said.

"You think I don't know that?" she said. "I've always known that. What I didn't understand was how love could be solitary. I've spent my entire life trying to be a part of a team, but never finding someone who's willing to put the relationship first. They're too busy making all 'the right' decisions that they never take into consideration what's right for me. For my son who's going to mourn the loss of yet another person in his life when you disappear."

"I don't have to disappear," he pleaded, taking her hand. "Reno is only an hour away."

"And what, you come into our lives a few days at a time? And then when you're finally able to let go of this tragic case, you move on to the next case? Once again, you're not thinking about what I need and want."

"What do you need?" he asked, his head pounding with desperation.

"I need honesty, openness, a choice in the things that affect my happiness." She took her hands back. "You can't give me those things."

"Yes. I can. All I ever wanted was to see you happy," he said, his voice shaking now too.

"And just like Sam, you decided what I needed to be happy. Instead of letting me find my own path to happiness, you swept me off my feet, let me believe that I was starting a new chapter. Only you want to know how the new one is reading?"

No. He didn't. Not right then. Not when her eyes were filled with a defeat and anguish that made his chest hollow out. Because for the first time since that day in the hospital, Ford saw a flash of the woman who knew that gaping hole was never going to go away.

"A lot like the last one. And the one before that," she cried, a fresh pool of betrayal lining her lashes. "Only this time, it's even worse. I can't say that the last man I made love to actually loved me back. Or that loving someone would never be something I could ever regret. Because *this*"—she pointed between them—"I can't ever trust whatever *this* was."

"It doesn't matter how we met or how we got here. What matters is how we feel. In here." He pounded his chest. "I love you, and you have to trust me, Liv. We can make this work."

He reached out to cup her cheek, but she turned her face. "That's the problem. I can't trust you. It took me two years to get to this place, to open myself up for a future that wasn't bound by my past. And with one secret you ruined it all. Including my ability to trust myself."

Ford's chest tightened to the point of pain. He would have given anything to go back to that day in the hospital and deliver Sam's gift himself. Because watching her shut down and curl back into herself was killing him.

"Sam wasn't your responsibility, and neither am I," Liv said, and the words cut through him, leaving a hole he was certain was visible. "You don't have that kind of power, Ford. You never did."

CHAPTER 18

"Sit still," Emma said a few days later, waving a metallic-pink hair-chalk pen in Ford's direction. "One more color and then I'll put it back to normal."

And because normal sounded like something Ford could get behind, and his heels were killing his feet, he shifted his leopard-print tutu and took a seat. His butt squeezed into the tot-size barber chair, Ford looked in the mirror at his metallic-purple-and-pink-streaked tips and cringed. "Are you sure this will wash out?"

"Uh-huh. And it turns the bathwater sparkly pink," Emma said, as if that was an added bonus to letting a six-year-old color your hair.

"All right, just don't get it in my eyes this time."

"I won't!" Emma said, giving not one but three more strokes of the hair chalk. "Daddy, Ford's almost ready for his family picture with Bullseye. He just needs his lips glossed."

Bullseye had gotten off light, as far as Ford was concerned. Dressed in a pink tutu with a matching bow behind his ear, he was sound asleep by the couch.

"I've got my camera ready to go," Harris said, grinning at Ford from the safety of the couch. He lifted a beer, then gave a two-fingered salute, just in case Ford wasn't aware of just who was the village idiot.

Ford had a salute of his own, but since it only required one finger and there were kids present, he said, "One photo makes it around the office and I will tell everyone about the time you thought Bullseye was the barfly from the night before."

"What's a barfly, Daddy?"

"Kind of like a horsefly, only harder to get rid of," Harris said, shooting Ford a look. Ford just smiled. "Hey, pumpkin, why don't you go and get that red lipstick upstairs."

Emma's eyes went owl-like. "The one that comed with my Barbie and you said I can't use in the house?"

"That's the one." This time Harris grinned. "I think it would go great with Ford's hair color."

With a squeal of delight, Emma took off, her feet sounding like a stampede as she raced up the stairs.

"You're an asshole," Ford said when she was out of range.

"Says the guy who's trying to dump his responsibilities on me." Harris leaned back into the couch, taking way too much pleasure in Ford's current situation.

It had been four days since Liv had escorted him out of her house, and still no word. She hadn't returned his calls, his texts, and was even a no-show for a meeting about Wagon Days.

"I'm not dumping. I'm just trying to make this easier for everyone involved," Ford said. "I'm still doing all the work—I just won't be here for the event."

It had taken Ford a whole ten minutes to realize that staying in town would only make it harder on Liv. Even less time to figure out he'd blown any shot he'd had at a relationship with her. He'd known that the second he saw the anguish on her face. So he'd called his boss and asked if he could move the certification up a few weeks and return to Reno early.

"Because you'll be licking your wounds in the mountains while Liv is down here facing everything head-on," Harris said.

Yeah, that too. He'd hurt her. Badly. She'd finally opened herself up to the idea of more, and Ford had given her more of the same.

"Or you could stay, help her," Harris offered.

Ford had shown up at Harris's house to talk to him about the early transfer back to Reno. He was surprised Harris hadn't grilled him about his reasons for leaving. Or his situation with Liv. He'd just said that if Ford played dress-up with Emma, then he'd sign off on the transfer. Ford figured either Liv hadn't told anyone what had gone down, or Harris finally wanted him gone. Only Harris loved to ride Ford's ass—especially when he'd screwed the pooch. So when Harris sat forward, his expression dialed to Dirty Harry, Ford knew he'd just been waiting.

"Last time I helped her she ended up slamming the door in my face and crying herself to sleep." He shrugged, but even that hurt. "Plus, I live in Reno. She lives here."

"Thanks for that nice geography lesson. With logic like that, you couldn't think yourself out of a fucking paper bag," Harris said.

"She asked me to leave. I'm leaving. End of story." Ford rubbed his hand over his chest, trying to ease the raw ache that had been gnawing at him. It didn't help.

"And when exactly did she ask you to leave? Before you told her you loved her or after?" Harris snapped his fingers. "Oh, wait, I remember. It was when you decided to ignore the single-mom code and sweet-talk your way into her panties instead of straight-talk your way into her circle of trust."

"Again, these pep talks are always a highlight," Ford said in a tone that would have a smart man shutting up.

Harris was not a smart man. In fact, he was as stupid as they came, because he leaned forward, resting his elbows on his knees, and said, "Well then, let me be the one to point out the big fucking fact that you seem to be missing. You don't want it to be the end."

"It doesn't matter what I want!" Ford stood. Arguing while sitting in a tiny chair with pink tips felt as ridiculous as the idea of Liv settling for weekends and rotating holidays. She'd done that before, and he didn't want to put her through that again. "She deserves more."

"Okay, then be more," Harris said, as if the solution were that easy. "How?"

"Stay," Harris said, and he let the one word settle.

Ford shook his head. "Not an option. By coming here, I made everything worse for her."

"And you think leaving will make it all better?" Harris said it as if Ford were dim-witted. "Because I can tell you it won't. You're never going to find whatever it is you're looking for by chasing disasters. The only thing that will make this better is to stay here and face it."

Ford looked his friend in the eye. "Since when did you become a fan of me going after Liv?"

"When I realized that you love her and you could make her happy," Harris said. "And she can make you happy too, if you'd let her."

"Let her? She hates me."

"She'll get over it—I have." Harris smiled. "But trust me, you'll never get over losing out on love."

The last word fluttered around his chest and then landed like lead. He told himself it would be better for all if he just walked away before it went too far. But the truth was, he was already gone.

"Fuck." He sat down, the weight of what he'd had and then lost too staggering to remain upright.

"Yeah, that's what I thought." Harris handed him a beer. "Now you might want to figure this out before Saturday, because while single moms don't like being blindsided, they go ballistic when some dick with a charming smile leaves a mess in her sandbox."

◆ ◆ ◆

The sun was high, and a gentle breeze blew off the lake. Liv stared blindly as it glided through the pine trees, stirring the white canvas of the canopy tents and the big WELCOME TO WAGON DAYS ~ THE WILDEST ADVENTURE IN THE WEST sign that hung over the main strip of town.

The vendors were already set up, Lake Street was lined with the fairgoers, and the Wild West Roundup was assembled and ready to go. The seventy-fifth annual Wagon Days parade was about to kick off the festivities to the largest crowd on record, and Liv felt like she was going to be sick.

To be honest, the gnawing ache in her stomach had started when she'd told him to leave, expanded to her chest when she'd ignored his first call, and hit critical mass when she'd heard that Ford had cashed in his ticket for home. A single stopover at Canyon Ridge—no return fare. And she didn't think the ache was going away anytime soon.

She'd always thought that if she'd had one last chance to talk to Sam, to see where things went wrong, the loss wouldn't have cut so deeply. But she'd asked Ford his reasons, heard his explanation, and still couldn't reconcile how things had gone so incredibly wrong.

She couldn't, because even though the pain was so intense at times it hurt to breathe, there wasn't a single moment over the past few weeks that she'd change.

Even now, knowing how it would end with Ford and with Sam. The ache would eventually fade, she promised herself, but changing one bit would mean changing it all. And that would be far more devastating than never experiencing it to begin with.

Liv swallowed past the lump in her throat to watch Paxton, keeping a constant vigil at the front of the alley next to Sips and Splatters, where all the floats were lined up, waiting as if Superdog were going to swoop down and be his sidekick.

"You want to practice it one more time?" Liv asked, smoothing out a nonexistent crease in Paxton's new and improved cape. Liv had stayed up three nights in a row trying to create a costume that was so super it didn't require a crime-fighting partner.

"Nope," he said, bouncing on his tiptoes to look over the ready-to-go floats and down to Lake Street. "I have to practice it with Bullseye."

Heart in her throat, Liv cupped her son's cheek. They'd been over this a dozen times already that morning. "I don't think he's coming, but either way you're going to be awesome. Plus, you've got Supermom by your side."

Liv put her hands on her hips and puffed out her SUPERMOM-clad chest, in her best superhero pose.

Paxton took in her black combat boots, shiny red spandex, and floor-length cape, and then those big blue pools looked up at her—panicked. "None of the other kids brought their mommies."

Liv looked at the dozen or so pint-size superheroes already on the float—not one of them had an adult with them. They'd either paired up with another camp friend or had a sibling.

With a smile that was so fragile it was destined to break, Liv reached into her purse and pulled out her backup. "Well then, it's a good thing I brought Superdog Stan."

Paxton wasn't the only one who'd received a costume update. Liv had stayed up until the wee hours of the morning sewing him a matching costume.

"Cool," Paxton said, taking his furry standby, but his expression said it wasn't as cool as a living, breathing superdog. "Thanks, Mom."

Paxton exhaled a shaky breath and leaned into Liv, wrapping his arms around her.

The protector in Liv wanted to tell him he didn't have to get on that float, and then take him to get ice cream, but the warrior in her knew that Paxton needed to see this through.

"We got this, Pax," she whispered.

He nodded his head but didn't let go. Liv scooped him up and held him close, breathing in his little-boy scent and slowly exhaling while holding him tighter.

It didn't matter if it was just the two of them—her little family had enough love to go the distance. All that Liv needed to be happy was right there in that hug, and as long as she remembered that, she and Paxton could handle anything life threw at them.

"Will you walk next to the float so I can see you?" he asked so heartbreakingly soft Liv had a hard time speaking.

Liv was supposed to be selling tickets to the Wild West Roundup booth during the parade, which meant she was expected to work the booth at the end of the parade trail. It would have to wait. Right now, it was all about getting Paxton through his debut performance.

"Every step of the way," she promised, tugging on Paxton's cape.

He looked up at her with panicked eyes. "What if the other kids see you?"

"That's why I brought my invisibility cape." She pulled the lapel of her cape over her face, covering everything but her eyes, and Paxton laughed. "I'll walk in the crowd so only you can see me. Okay?"

"Okay," he said, and for the first time that morning, he sounded as if he'd be okay.

"Now let's get you on that float before it leaves without you." She double-tugged the bottom of his shirt and stood.

Paxton froze. He stared at the packed float, the ever-growing crowd, and then the ground. Liv's stomach knotted, and her palms began to sweat. Her baby had come so far, but he was getting ready to crawl back inside himself. Getting on that float was important, but having an anxiety attack in front of the whole town wouldn't do anyone any good.

"Pax? You okay? You need a sip of water?" she asked, because sometimes ice-cold water was enough to snap him out of it. But he didn't answer, just continued to stare at the ground, his breathing nonexistent, his eyes dilated and clouded over.

And just when Liv thought he was going into complete shutdown mode, he took a deep breath and slid his tiny hand into hers. "I got this."

"Yes, you do," she said, surprised that her voice came out so strong. Inside she was a nervous wreck, but for her son she would be Supermom.

Capes flapping in the breeze, Superboy and Supermom walked side by side down the alley and onto the float. It was the first float, at the corner of Lake Street, visible by the thousands of people already looking their way.

Liv stationed him at the front of the float and attached the safety harness to his belt. "I'm going to be right there, walking through the crowd." She pointed to the back part of the sidewalk, behind the crowd, and Paxton shook his head. Hard. He was also shaking in his combat boots. "You want me to walk right next to the float, Pax?"

Paxton was considering this, considering what his friends would say if his mommy walked next to the float, when what sounded like a windstorm echoed in the near distance.

The wind picked up, scattering fallen pine needles and sending a rainbow of capes soaring. People shielded their eyes and looked to the sky in delight as the *whomp whomp whomp* drew closer, became louder. And Paxton's smile grew bigger and brighter.

"It's him!" he said, loud enough for everyone on the float and surrounding area to hear. But her son didn't seem to notice. He was too busy focusing on the showstopping red-and-yellow helicopter cutting down Lake Street and right toward their float. With Superdog, complete with a bright red cape, blue booties, a hoodie with ear holes, and goggles—flying through the air.

But what had Liv's heart doing some stopping of its own was the real-life superhero hanging off the side of the chopper. Dressed in his uniform of black pants with a million and one pockets, a bright orange shirt, and a ball cap that said LOOKING TO BE RESCUED was her own personal hero coming to save the day.

He isn't yours, she reminded herself. But even though he wore mirrored aviators, Liv could feel his intense gaze, locked on target and zeroing in on her.

And her alone.

The crowd sucked in an excited breath as the chopper came to a halt, hovering right above the first float. Paxton's float. And just when the crowd thought that the show was over, Ford gave a hand signal to someone on the chopper that was as confident as it was sexy, and without warning, Ford and Bullseye slowly made their descent down onto Lake Street.

His boots hit the asphalt, and the crowd erupted in cheers. And a warm ball of hope erupted in Liv's chest.

"Mommy," Paxton called out over the thundering sound of the blades, "you don't need to walk beside the float. And the name's not Paxton," he said, hitting his super-secret superhero pose, "I'm Superboy!"

"Yes, you are," she yelled back. And even though Ford was going to disappear back to Reno on Monday, he'd come to give Paxton the send-off her son desperately needed.

"Bullseye," Paxton said loudly, holding his hand out and then pointing to the ground. "Come."

Bullseye's legs were moving even before Ford set him on the ground, and then those toothpicks tore across the street and leaped up onto the float, not stopping until he was sitting in front of Paxton. Head back, ears straight up, tongue lolling, Bullseye waited for the next signal. And when Paxton gave it, Bullseye stuck one paw out in front, his hind leg back, and held it.

And *be still my heart*, with the wind from the chopper, the dog looked like he was actually flying through the air. And her son, her beautiful, strong son, held his pose—proud, bold, and something to behold.

The crowd erupted into cheers as the helicopter lifted off and disappeared over the quaint skyline and behind the mountain range. The air stilled, and the town grew silent, until Liv could only hear the tattoo of boots on the pavement.

Six-plus feet of built, badass swagger carrying a duffel bag and double-barreled dimples was on course and coming right for her. Liv couldn't have moved if her life depended on it. Then he took off his sunglasses, and Liv wasn't sure if she wanted to.

"If you're mouth-to-mouth certified, I'm looking to be rescued, Officer Best Buns," Mavis said from the sidewalk. Sitting in her wheelchair that had flashing red-and-blue lights on the back, and sporting a pink WAG & WADDLE PATROL shirt, she was leading her team of volunteer officers toward the head of the parade.

"Actually, I'm the one who's in need of a rescue," he said, making his way forward, his eyes never leaving Liv's.

"Well, this crew only works locally," Mavis said with a tut.

"That's all right. I'm not going anywhere." Ford dropped his duffel bag at Liv's feet and tangled his fingers with hers. "I've spent my whole life looking for families to save, which is why I came to Sequoia Lake, to save one more. Instead, I found this sexy, strong woman who amazed me at every turn, and instead of saving her, I think she saved me. Only I blew it." He brought her hand to his lips and kissed it. "I was so busy trying to play the hero, I didn't realize that she didn't need saving."

"All Mommy needs is cupcakes and hugs," Paxton said from the float. "Tell him, Mommy."

"Yeah," Ford whispered, resting his hands on Liv's hips, nudging her closer. He was dusty, rumpled, and looked as if he'd been living in a cave. Which, if the rumors were true and he'd taken his certification exam, he probably had. "Tell me what you need, because I'm listening."

"A partner," she whispered, her heart pounding against her ribcage until she was sure it would burst free. "Someone who wants to find the same pace with me. Someone to hold my hand and who isn't afraid to let me hold his. Someone I can count on and who respects the relationship enough to count on me. Someone who knows life is too short not to eat the cupcake first."

"I do love cupcakes, cupcake." His voice dropped low when he spoke, and his hands dropped lower the closer she got. Then he wrapped those strong arms around her waist and gave her a slow, easy smile. "And I love you."

"Love is the easy part, Ford." She crossed her arms over her chest in hopes of keeping it intact, because it was pounding so hard she was afraid it would shatter even further. "It's the rest of it that worries me."

"No, love is the foundation, and when it's pure, it means putting the other person first."

"But this foundation was built on a lie," she whispered.

"No, it was built on friendship and understanding, things that are real and matter. And yes, I lied. I lied because I thought I was protecting you," he admitted. "By the time I realized that love doesn't require protection, it was too late, Liv. Which is why I will never make that mistake again."

Ford stepped closer, so she couldn't look anywhere but at him, because he was right there in front of her, completely unfiltered with his heart in his eyes.

"I need a favor, Liv," he asked intently, and Liv knew she was about to lose it. "And I need it to be one of those all-in, no-questions-asked kind of favors."

Ford had never asked her for anything. He was always strong and stoic and the first one to lend a hand even if he already had his hands full. But right then, he looked uncertain and tired. The kind of tired that came from pushing through when all the signs said to stop. And for that reason, she said, "Okay."

"I need you to give us a fair shot."

"I did."

"No, baby," he said, holding her gaze. "You've been looking for a reason to shut me out since the first day we met."

"Because I knew you were leaving." And then she'd be alone. Again. Left to pick up the pieces and find a new path. One that wouldn't be as shiny or fun—or as magical.

Not that it mattered. He'd wiggled his way in, and she'd lost him all the same.

"That's not the same as leaving you, Liv," he said quietly, and Liv's throat tightened with the truth. "Because there's something you need to understand. I'm an all-in kind of guy. It's how I operate, and the second you let me in, I went all the way in. There's no leaving that."

With a tender look that was so achingly familiar, he pulled an envelope out of his pocket and handed it to her. It had "Reno Sheriff's Department" as the return address.

"Is that your certification?" she asked, afraid to touch it for fear that today was just a brief stopover.

"No. It's me listening and putting you first," he said, pulling out the letter and holding it up. And Liv's heart swelled in her chest until she was afraid that she would run out of room. Because at the top of the letter, right under his Type 1 certification ranking, were two words that had hope bubbling up until it overflowed.

"Transfer approved," she said, trying to read the details, but all of the words began to blur. "You're transferring?"

"I'm the head of the new K-9 search-and-rescue division for Sequoia Elite Mountain Rescue." He pulled her even closer, their hips and thighs brushing.

"For how long?"

"I was thinking until Paxton heads off to college, and then you can pick a place on the map you've always wanted to visit and we'll go exploring. Together."

Compromise, she thought. Ford was offering her everything she needed, while keeping an eye on his own dreams. That was what a relationship was about. It wasn't give or take—it was finding the right combination every single day.

"I love you, Olivia Preston." He cupped her cheeks and tilted her face up, and what she saw staring back made her breath catch. Ford was looking down at her with so much intensity and love and heat that some of her doubts that stemmed from their past began to fade and give way to a few hopes for their future. "You're my home base. You and Paxton."

"You're the biggest adventure I've ever had," Liv said, wrapping her arms around his waist and holding tight, all of the excitement and joy bubbling up until she could feel it settling on her lashes. "You're also my perfect fit. So I'll be your home base, as long as you promise to be ours."

"Always," Ford vowed, caressing her cheek. His thumb catching the first loose tear. "I came here searching for answers and found meaning." He looked into her eyes. "I found you, Liv."

"With you, I found myself." She lifted her arms and twined them around his neck, pressing so close she could hear the steady beat of his heart. "I thought I'd lost her, but it turns out she was just hiding," she said. The emotion, too much to hold back any longer, spilled down her cheeks. "You reminded me how freeing love could be." She pressed her lips gently to his. "I love you, Ford."

"God, I love you." Ford covered her mouth with his in a kiss that was open and honest and everything a kiss should be. And Liv knew that even though her little family of two would be just fine, a family with Ford would be magical.

And she needed a little magic in her life.

"Does this mean I get to sleep with Bullseye?" Paxton asked, and Liv pulled back to look down on her son and his cape-wearing partner, both staring up at her with giddy excitement.

"I don't see why not," Liv said, and Paxton and Bullseye gave each other high fives. Liv turned back to her partner for life and whispered, "Will you sleep in my bed?"

"Every night until forever comes," he said, and Liv decided that forever sounded like her kind of adventure.

ABOUT THE AUTHOR

Photo © 2012 Tosh Tanaka

Marina Adair is the bestselling author of beloved romances such as The Eastons series; the Heroes of St. Helena series; and the Sequoia Lake books, *It Started with a Kiss* and *Every Little Kiss*. Her St. Helena Vineyard series was the inspiration behind the Hallmark Channel original movie *Autumn in the Vineyard*.

Marina enjoys writing contemporary romance novels in which the towns are small, the personalities are large, and the romance is explosive. She holds a master of fine arts in creative writing and lives with her husband, daughter, and two neurotic cats in Northern California. She loves interacting with her readers. You can follow her on Twitter @MarinaEAdair and sign up for her newsletter on her website at www.MarinaAdair.com/newsletter.